The Munchkins

Candice Zee

Disclaimer: This is a work of fiction. All characters, locations, and businesses are purely products of the author's imagination and are entirely fictitious. Any resemblance to actual people, living or dead, or to businesses, places, or events is completely coincidental.

Cover design by Jeff Brown Graphics
Interior design by Lorna Reid

First Edition
Published in Cleveland, OH

ISBN: 978-1-7372339-0-9 (paperback)
ISNB: 978-1-7372339-1-6 (ebook)

Library of Congress Control Number: 2021912554

www.munchkinsbooks.com
readthemunchkinsbooks@gmail.com

Prologue

Why did this happen to us? We were all so happy. We had the best life. And now…it's gone. Everything's gone.

It's been months since we've been here, and the sheer shock and horror of what has happened seems to be just now sinking in. I've been numb for a long time.

I had a family once. A wonderful family. Now all who's here with me is my sister Kitty, who lays in this cage as I write this, desperately trying, fitfully, to sleep without the nightmarish memories coming to haunt her. But they don't disappear when we're awake. Memories so horrific are impossible to forget.

We exist here. Not live. Just exist. Our happy lives were viciously stolen from us. Snuffed out by a sadistic monster. But I'm getting ahead of myself. I guess I should start from the beginning.

I'm determined to get this all down because I want everyone to know what's happened to us. I want everyone to know about the absolute cruelty inflicted on a bunch of innocent kids. I want him to pay for what he did.

Big Boss is going to come in here soon so I must hurry and get as much down as I can. Kitty and I stay here, wasting away in this prison, hoping, praying for someone to find us, to finally come and save us. I'm terrified to let myself think that we will remain trapped here in this hell for the rest of our lives. I *can't* think that. That thought is just too horrible to endure.

I know in part I'm writing this as a frantic attempt to simply hold on to my sanity. Every day I feel it slipping away. And I need to hold onto it because even though escape in the form of insanity is rather tempting, I need to stay sane for Kitty. I cannot leave her alone here.

Not with that sick, demented, malevolent psychopath.

Chapter 1

My name is Capricorn. Some people think: That's not a name, that's a Zodiac sign. Trust me, I've heard it before. But that's the name I was given.

I want to tell you first and foremost about my family. I have the most unusual family that has ever lived. By the time I'm done explaining why you'll have no choice but to agree with me.

First, I have twelve brothers and sisters, so there are thirteen kids in our family. However, we're not biologically related to each other, except for Breezy and Hazy, who are twin sisters. We were all adopted, but we were as close as any biological family would be, perhaps even closer. We have one parent, our father Casey Munch, the man who adopted us all. We hardly ever called him Dad though; instead, we called him CC. It's a nickname we came up with a while back and the name stuck.

You're probably not going to believe what I say next, and I don't blame you. I wouldn't believe me either if I didn't know otherwise, but I swear every word is true.

Alright here it goes…my brothers, sisters, and I have special powers.

Some people would even call it magic.

I know, I'm full of it, but it's true. I can't explain why either which I'm sure doesn't help my credibility. All I know is around the time my sister Ashley reached the age of ten (she was the oldest, so the first to turn 10), she started developing these unusual powers.

She made CC jump ten feet in the air the day she came running into the room to first show her new powers off. "CC! CC! Watch this!" she squealed excitedly, as she raised her hand and with no more effort than it takes to wave, produced a beam of light, making the cereal box sitting on the table lift smoothly into the air, float across the room, circle around, then land gracefully in the same spot on the table.

CC gaped at her. I was afraid his eyes would pop out of his head. "H-h-how did you do that?" he stammered.

Ashley gave him a mischievous grin. "I don't know, but I can. And wait till you see what else I can do."

It didn't take long before we found out what that was as Ashley started showing more of her powers. CC didn't know what to make of it, and honestly, I think it frightened him, but somehow he instinctively knew to keep it a secret. But what really astounded CC was as the rest of my siblings and I reached the same age, we acquired the same powers. Pretty soon every one of us was walking around using magic like it was the most natural thing in the world.

We could do things far more powerful than levitating cereal boxes too. This was discovered the day our brother Ryan hit the curb at full speed while riding his bike, and went flying headfirst over the handlebars, busting his head open on the sidewalk. He laid sobbing and screaming in pain, his leg bent at an abnormal angle, while the rest of us surrounded him, looking on in horrified shock.

"Oh my God!" CC screamed as he dialed 911. "An ambulance is on the way! Just hold on, Ryan!" He was so distraught he didn't see our sister Breezy step out from the crowd and approach Ryan, gently resting her hand on his head to comfort him. "It's okay. Everything is going to be okay," she soothed, lightly caressing his forehead. Suddenly a warm, yellow light appeared from under Breezy's hand and burned brighter and brighter with full intensity. Just as it reached maximum brilliance, it promptly died out, and Breezy lifted her hand, revealing unbroken, healed skin on Ryan's forehead. Breezy quickly moved to Ryan's leg, and the beam of light once again radiated from her fingers, sputtering out more rapidly this time, but when she moved her hand away Ryan's leg was no longer twisted, and he was able to move it as easily as before. By the time the paramedics arrived, the only thing they found was the circle of us standing in open-mouthed astonishment, gaping at the little girl who stood beaming in the center, appearing to glow with the warm light that had emanated from her just moments ago.

We have different theories on how we happened to possess these powers, but they are only guesses. We've never been able to verify a single one. You're still with me, which means I haven't lost credibility yet, so I hesitate to add this last point but I have to. When we developed these powers at the age of 10, that was the last year we aged - physically and psychologically. We think something in the energetic makeup of the powers crossed with our natural biological makeup to cause a chemical reaction that permanently stunted our growth. Therefore, we could never grow up. We lived our lives as eternal children. I deliberately chose the word eternal because due to our healing powers, which could mend any sickness or injury, death and serious illness became something we could easily avoid.

When CC finally came to terms with the powers we had and everything that meant, he sat us down for a family meeting. He directed us not to tell anybody, under any circumstances, about the magic. He warned us that power in the wrong hands is dangerous, and if anybody found a way to get ahold of that power, it could have disastrous consequences. We didn't think this was a problem because who would ever believe us anyway? Then CC set some major ground rules regarding the use of the powers.

"You're going to have to learn how to use these powers responsibly. Use them only for good and to help and heal. Don't use powers just for fun or treat them like they're toys. Power like this is very serious, so take it very seriously," he stressed.

Now you understand why we are unlike any other family on Earth. I even came up with a name that perfectly fits us.

"Hey, I thought of the best name for us," I said to everyone one day during dinner. "Want to hear it? Munchkins. Think about it: Our last name is Munch, plus because of the whole not growing up thing, we stay small. Like munchkins. It's perfect."

Twisty wrinkled her nose. "Eh, I'm not sure I like it, Capricorn. It sounds a little insulting."

"I think it's cool, Cap," Allie smiled. "You're right, especially with our last name being Munch, how could we not use that?"

"I agree," Breezy added. "There's something else too, Capricorn, that makes it even more fitting. The word 'kin' means family. So "munchkins" is perfect because we're the Munch family."

"I like that," CC smiled. "Munchkins it is."

Chapter 2

It occurs to me people probably have a million questions. One of the biggest ones I'm sure is CC. I could almost hear you saying, "Why would anyone in their right mind ever adopt thirteen kids at one time?" Right? Fair enough. I'll tell you the story we've heard numerous times from CC about how he came to adopt us.

CC was an activist who always felt a calling to make the world a better place. CC inherited his house and a large fortune from his father, who was a real estate tycoon. CC and his wife, Erin, used to travel the world doing social justice work. He used part of his inheritance to create a nonprofit called Shelter for All to have houses and properties built for people in need all over the world. The free housing is all funded by the organization. CC fought injustice in the world and cared deeply about all life, both humans and animals. He and Erin talked about adopting children one day, but then sadly, Erin became severely ill. Knowing she was dying, Erin left CC. CC was heartbroken but he still went on continuing his work. Then one day, he decided to move forward with adopting children and having a family. This is what drew him to visit the children's home where we resided.

"Mr. Munch, it's a pleasure to meet you. I've been a long admirer of the great work you do," said Mr. Frank, the director of the children's home, when CC met him. He also introduced him to the co-director, Ms. Terrance.

Mr. Frank and Ms. Terrance showed CC some files of the different children available for adoption. While CC was looking, he said he could see Ms. Terrance whisper something to Mr. Frank. All he heard was, "Show him the file."

Mr. Frank and Ms. Terrance approached CC with a special red file, the file about us. "Mr. Munch, can I show you something?" Mr. Frank said. "Now what I'm about to say is going to sound very strange…" Mr. Frank paused a moment and glanced nervously at Ms. Terrance before continuing. "About six months ago," Mr. Frank began, "a group of children suddenly showed up on our doorstep. Thirteen children to be exact."

"Thirteen?" CC asked.

"Yes, thirteen." Mr. Frank repeated. "These children, they didn't have any records with them, no one was with them, and we had no idea where they came from. We tried to track down any parents or relatives and have been unsuccessful. We have been unable to find any records on them whatsoever. We couldn't find any birth certificates, no recorded history, no files, there is nothing on them. No one has any idea who they are. Oddest thing...like they appeared out of thin air…."

Mr. Frank's voice trailed off and CC cleared his throat.

"Is this the file on the children then?" CC asked, taking the file. "Is that why it's so thin because you have no records?"

"Yes," Ms. Terrance responded. "All we have are names, ages, and photos. We have not been able to trace the children's identities."

"Craziest thing about it is..." Mr. Frank said, hesitant to

continue, "The kids have no idea where they came from either."

"What? How?" CC questioned.

"*They don't know.* They have no memories of their past. They don't remember any parents, any relatives, they didn't even know how they got here. They didn't even know what they were doing yesterday! All they knew were their first names and how old they were. That's it!" Mr. Frank explained.

"All thirteen of them?" CC asked in amazement.

"*All thirteen,*" Mr. Frank emphasized.

"So are these children related? Are they all brothers and sisters?" CC asked.

"We did some tests," Ms. Terrance replied. "All we've been able to find is that these two," she said, pointing to Breezy and Hazy in the file, "are likely twins. The others appear not to be related."

"That's the strangest thing I've ever heard!" CC exclaimed.

"Yes, I'll say!" Mr. Frank cried. "Twenty years I've worked for this institution and I've never seen anything like it. I'm telling you, Mr. Munch, It's like something out of a science fiction movie. There's something very strange about those kids. It's almost otherworldly, almost paranormal…."

Ms. Terrance kicked Mr. Frank under the table. "But they're wonderful children!" Ms. Terrance said quickly. "They are very sweet and extremely bright and clever! You'll just love them!"

"Oh, you're saying I should adopt one of these children?" CC asked.

Mr. Frank and Ms. Terrance looked at each other, trying to decide how to proceed.

"Um…Mr. Munch, this is going to sound a little crazy, but heck, no crazier than this whole situation, uh...how would you feel about adopting all thirteen of these children?" Mr. Frank asked skittishly.

CC laughed loudly. "I'm sorry, you're kidding right?"

"Well, why not?" Mr. Frank answered. "After all, these children need a home and you seem like you would be the perfect father for them. I know you can afford it and I'm sure you have a nice big house."

"I do," CC answered. "Still, that's not the point. How am I supposed to take care of thirteen children on my own? My wife has been dead for years. I'm by myself."

"I'm very sorry to hear that, Mr. Munch," Ms. Terrance responded politely. "My condolences. Still, I think you can find a way to make this work. I'm not saying it will be easy, but you seem like the best match for these children."

"What do you mean the best match? You just met me!" CC said, stunned this was even happening. "I haven't even met these children yet. You expect me to adopt all thirteen of them?"

Mr. Frank and Ms. Terrance exchanged another nervous look. CC finally picked up on what they were feeling.

"Are you...are you *afraid* of these children? Are you trying to get rid of them?" CC gasped.

"Oh no! No, that's not it at all!" Ms. Terrance rushed to reply way too fast, indicating that was exactly it.

"No, no, don't be silly. Of course not!" Mr. Frank echoed. "Why would we be afraid of children? There's no reason to be frightened of such...strange children…."

Ms. Terrance kicked Mr. Frank hard under the table again.

Mr. Frank straightened up and looked CC in the eye. "Look. Mr. Munch, do you believe in fate?"

"Yes," CC answered. "I believe in a higher power."

"Okay," he said. "That's what I thought. And here's what I believe. I believe it was fate that brought you here today. I believe it was no coincidence that you came here, looking for a family, and you are exactly the kind of man who would be able to care for these children and give them a good home. Things like that don't happen by random chance. What do you believe?"

When CC's told us this story before, he says at that moment he felt something he believed to be divine providence. That the universe meant for him to be there and fate brought us together.

"I have to say," CC responded, "I suddenly feel that way too. But still and all, thirteen kids is a lot." He paused. "What if I were to adopt some of the kids, but not all thirteen? I'm sure you could find homes for the others."

"Well," Ms. Terrance answered, "The thing is, these children have become very attached. Since the time they've been here together, and possibly before that, they have become very close. It would seem almost cruel to break them up."

"There's something else I think you should know, Mr. Munch," Mr. Frank continued. He looked at Ms. Terrance, and she nodded him on. "I hesitate to say this, but, last week we got a call from the National Institute of Health, and they were very interested in these children."

"The NIH?" CC said, surprised. "What does the government want with a group of unknown orphans?"

"I think it's the 'unknown' part they're interested in," Mr. Frank responded. "They asked lots of questions about who we think these kids are and where they came from. They expressed a desire to run tests on the children to find out more."

"Tests? The government wants to do experiments on a bunch of children?" CC cried.

"I'm afraid so, Mr. Munch," Ms. Terrance replied. "We feel a lot of pressure to get these children out of here before the government comes knocking on our door. Since they are wards of the state, we, unfortunately, don't have much power to stop it. The government could easily take them into custody. If they're adopted though, they have legal protections. The government won't have any standing to take them." Ms. Terrance gave CC a hopeful expression. "I'm not going to lie, Mr. Munch. There's something about this whole situation that scares me, but at this point, I'm more afraid *for* the children. No child should have to live in a government laboratory, Mr. Munch."

"No, no child absolutely shouldn't. The very idea is sickening," CC agreed, incensed at just the thought. He picked up our file and looked through it again. "They do look like really sweet kids."

Ms. Terrance nodded eagerly, wringing her hands. "Oh yes, they're delightful. Such amazing children."

CC sighed. "Okay. Let me meet the kids."

CC fell in love with us immediately. In no time at all, he was filling out the adoption paperwork, with Mr. Frank and Ms. Terrance happily speeding him through the process. That's how we became the Munch family, or to use my word, the Munchkins. Now I'll tell the rest of our story.

Chapter 3

I will never forget the first day we met Big Boss. The day began like any other day. Allie bounded down the stairs for breakfast, grinning from ear to ear, the freckles on her light-toned skin that became visible only when she smiled glowing like specks of sunshine. But since Allie was always smiling, her freckles were a regular sight for us.

I sat next to Breezy and Hazy, and Allie took a seat on the other side of them. "The Four Musketeers" CC called us. The four of us were always together. Not just sisters, but best friends.

"Eat up," CC said, putting a plate of fresh pancakes on the table in front of us.

"Yeah, before I eat them all," laughed Chase across the table.

"Well if you do, I'll just replicate them and make some more," Allie said, grabbing the plate of pancakes.

"Allie," CC warned, "How many times do I have to say no magic at the breakfast table?"

"You said dinner table, CC," Allie challenged.

"It's the same table, Allie. And you know that. Don't make me say it again."

"Okay, CC, got it. No magic at the breakfast-slash-lunch-slash-dinner-slash-dessert-slash-any-other-meal-that-we-may-possibly-eat table. Got it." Allie flashed CC one of her huge charismatic grins.

CC sighed. "Allie, you just got up 10 minutes ago and you're already starting."

Our sister Becky entered the room listening to music through a pair of bright pink earbuds.

"Hey, those are my headphones," Allie said, pointing to Becky's ears.

"Oh yeah," Becky mumbled. "I was borrowing them."

"Interesting. You think borrow means taking something without asking," Allie responded.

Becky huffed. "I couldn't find mine and yours were sitting there. I'll give them back later."

"Oh, how kind of you," Allie smirked. "You're so considerate to return the headphones you stole from me."

CC interjected. "No headphones at the table either. Becky, give them back to your sister."

It was a bright Saturday in May, the kind of day where you want to spend every moment outside, just to be able to breathe the sweet air, admire the brightness of the flowers, and take in the sunshine. That's just what we had in mind as all of us headed to our backyard that day after breakfast. Actually, it was more like CC sent us outside to play because he "needed some peace and quiet so he could hear himself think." Breezy, Hazy, Allie, and I huddled together by the big oak tree in our yard, talking together before the rest of our siblings joined us.

"I don't think Becky meant to steal your headphones, Al," Breezy said. "I think she sometimes does things without thinking."

"That's obvious," Allie laughed.

Breezy and Hazy stood close together, having a silent conversation with their eyes only they could hear. Allie looked at me with a widening smile and a knowing expression. "Hey Cap! The Bopsy twins are talking to each other in their minds again!"

Allie was only half kidding. Everyone knew Hazy and Breezy were so close they seemed psychically connected. It was rare to see one without the other. The two seemed to complement each other perfectly. Anyone could tell they were twins, almost identical, except Breezy had piercing, soulful blue eyes and Hazy had sweet, innocent brown eyes. Both of them had golden-brown skin, where Breezy's complexion was slightly lighter than Hazy's. Even though none of us knew where we came from, it seemed pretty safe to say they had Hispanic descent. Hazy was also about an inch shorter than Breezy, which given neither of them was that tall, gave Hazy this precious doll-like quality. The only one in the family who was smaller than Hazy was Carlie, who around 4 feet tall was often mistaken for a 5-year-old.

There were other ways Breezy and Hazy went together like ying and yang and peanut butter and jelly. You may have noticed their unique names. Whoever Breezy and Hazy's biological mother was, she gave them the perfect names to go with their matching personalities. Then there were their voices. Breezy's voice did have a breezy quality to it. Soft-spoken and gentle, her voice was airy, with a register that carried just enough wind to be heard but would often finish in a whisper. I loved listening to her talk because it felt as if your ears were being mildly caressed, although when Breezy had something important to say, she'd make sure she made herself heard. Hazy, on the other hand, had the kind of voice that made it sound like her nose was all stuffed up and she had a permanent cold. It was fun to hear her talk as well, for the way she would pronounce certain words and vowels, like "thoat" for "thought" and "scoo" for "school," I found adorable.

Allie grabbed Breezy's attention by cocking her head to look directly into Breezy's face with her characteristic winsome smirk. Something unsaid passed between the two that made them both burst into laughter.

"We're going to play a game," Ashley said, approaching us. The rest of our siblings gathered at the tree.

"How about we play tag?" said Justin.

"No," said Carlie. "I don't like tag."

"What are you talking about, Carlie? " Ashley said. "You love tag."

"Well I don't want to play it today," Carlie scowled.

"You're so stubborn," Ashley frowned. Ashley, being technically the oldest (she was nine when adopted), felt it was partly her responsibility to keep the rest of her siblings in check, especially Carlie, the youngest of us (she was five when adopted).

"How about Simon Says then?" Justin said, quickly making another suggestion before an argument surfaced between Carlie and Ashley. Justin, kind and sensible, hated conflict and strived to find compromises that would make everyone happy.

"That sounds good but I want to be Simon," said Becky. Everyone groaned in unison. Becky seemed to thrive on telling her siblings what to do. Simon Says was the perfect game for her.

"How about we play Simon Says *only* if Becky doesn't get to be Simon," said Allie.

"Agreed!" shouted out half the group, their hands in the air.

Becky gave Allie a contemptuous look. Her sandy blonde hair cast a sheen in the sunlight. "Oh, be quiet, Allie. Nobody asked you."

"Oh, see that's funny because I don't recall anyone asking you to be Simon either," said Allie.

"Okay," said Breezy, with her hands raised, stepping into the middle of the group. "We're only going to play a game together if we can all agree on it. Does anyone have any other suggestions?" Justin gave Breezy a grateful smile for her quick mediation, which Breezy returned with a nod.

"How about we play baseball?" I said.

"Hey, great idea, Cap!" Allie cried.

All around various cheers in favor of baseball arose. We divided amongst ourselves to form two teams, and Kevin agreed to serve as umpire. But there was one problem.

"We need a bat and ball," said Ashley. "Someone took them in the house."

"Let's go in and look for them," Justin suggested.

"Nah," Kevin said. "That could take all day. We'll just whip some up. No biggie."

"You mean use our powers?" Ashley asked. "Should we?"

Breezy clenched her face and shook her head. One of CC's rules was our power should be used only when necessary and with good reason. Frivolous use of magic was a serious no-no. I had a feeling for manifesting a bat and ball, CC wouldn't consider "we didn't feel like going in the house to look for our old ones" a good reason.

Just as I expected, Breezy objected. "I don't think this counts as a necessary use of our powers. CC wouldn't approve of this."

"Well, CC's not here right now, is he?" Twisty declared defiantly, spinning rapidly on her heels and running off with her braids bouncing behind her. Twisty (a nickname for Theresa, but she hated that name and didn't allow it to be used in her presence), had always been a bit of a troublemaker and had a real rebellious streak. Just the thought of doing something that was against CC's rules excited her greatly.

Breezy turned to Hazy, Allie, and me looking for support. Allie signaled her sympathy for Breezy's position by rolling her eyes in Twisty's direction and gave a hapless shrug. Hazy's apprehension mirrored Breezy's. I mumbled feebly, "Well, it's only a bat and ball." Breezy shook her head and repeated, "CC would not approve of this."

My siblings didn't always see it, but there's a good reason for this rule. There are limitations to our powers. There are certain things we're not able to do at all (such as make ourselves disappear and reappear, make ourselves invisible, magically teleport ourselves from one place to another, the list goes on) but more importantly, the powers we do have aren't inexhaustible. Using a power takes a lot of energy, and once that energy is used, it takes a while before you have enough energy to use a power again. Think of it as a battery. If you run something on a battery that uses a lot of power, you'll drain your battery quickly and have to recharge. Recharging means you have to wait for your energy levels to restore themselves before you can use them again. The time required to recharge depends on what type of power you are using and the task. A telekinetic power like moving an object in the air is one of the lowest energy uses and takes about 10-20 minutes before you're good to go again, but of course, it depends on the size and distance of the object. Healing a wound or injury, depending on how severe the injury is, can take over an hour or two. Replicating an object, disappearing objects, or putting up a protective shield will put you back a few hours. Manifesting an object into being? That's huge and will cost you a whole day's worth of power at least.

Knowing that bit of information turns a seemingly

stringent mandate into an important safety measure. If using power means you're prevented from using power again for a certain length of time, you better make sure you're not squandering it. Fortunately, there are thirteen of us, so if someone is out of energy, chances are someone else will have enough. Still, Breezy was right. CC would have put a stop to this in an instant.

"Alright," Kevin said. "Who's got the juice?"

"I haven't used any powers since Wednesday. I'll do it," Becky volunteered.

"Great, do it then. Presto changeo abracadabra and all that jazz," Kevin said.

The group gathered around and watched Becky as she put her hand out and a yellow drop of light emerged from it that gradually grew bigger and bigger until it became a ball. The light grew more intense and in a flash, burnt out and died, leaving a brand-new baseball falling to the ground.

"Yay!" Carlie cried, clapping her hands. "Now we need a bat."

Twisty's hand shot up. "I can do it!"

Twisty repeated the same movements as Becky, only this time the light-shaped object that appeared was in elongated form instead of a sphere. In no time we had a wooden bat to go with our baseball.

"Our team will take the field, you guys are first at-bat," shouted Chase, running off to take first base. That meant the team Breezy, Hazy, Allie, and I were on were first up. Breezy hesitated, looking at the ground.

"You guys are still playing, right?" Ashley asked the four of us. "Because if you're not, that means our team is down by 4 teammates."

Allie turned to Breezy and gave her a questioning look.

"Are we doing this? Or are you going to stand witness as conscientious objector?"

I thought for sure Breezy would refuse to play. But she surprised me. "Well, I guess the damage is already done," she sighed and ran off to line up to bat. Hazy smiled and tailed off behind her. Allie gave me a shocked expression and mouthed the word "wow," then followed them.

"Well, Ashley, it looks like we're playing," I said, as I ran to join them.

Ryan was first to bat. The other team decided on Kitty as their pitcher. Kitty swung her arm back and threw the ball to Ryan, and he hit it easily, running off to first base. Our team cheered, and Allie was next at-bat. She stepped up to the batter plate and gave Kitty a big, warm smile. "Okay, Kit-Cat! Give me your best shot!"

Kit-Cat, short for kitty cat, of course, was Allie's nickname for Kitty. Allie tended to give cute nicknames to almost all her siblings, one of the ways Allie showed her affection for her family. For instance, she called me "Cap." Since "Cap" is easier to say than "Capricorn," others called me "Cap" sometimes too, but to Allie, it might as well have been my full name.

Kitty, her blonde hair hanging loosely against the sides of her face, grinned at Allie and tossed the ball towards her. Allie saw it was too low to the ground and didn't move the bat.

"Ball one!" Kevin cried, throwing the ball back to Kitty.

Kitty tried to throw a curveball but it curved too much in the air and moved out of bounds of the batter plate.

"Ball two!" Kevin shouted.

Allie gave Kitty another kind smile. "Throw them a little higher, Kit-Cat! You're a little too low!"

Kitty nodded appreciation and threw the ball higher this time, but still not high enough to make contact with the bat.

"Ball three!" Kevin yelled.

"We want a pitcher, not a belly itcher!" Twisty chanted in a taunting, singsong manner from the outfield. Becky laughed and joined in with her.

Kitty, the shyest of all our siblings, turned red and hung her head down, looking like she wanted to sink into the ground.

Allie dropped the bat to the ground and glowered at Twisty and Becky. She cupped her hands over her mouth to amplify her voice and yelled straight out in their direction. "If you think you can do so much better of a job pitching, Twisty, then, by all means, you come over here and pitch! But I don't think that would be in your team's best interest!"

Twisty balled her hands into fists and shouted right back at Allie. "I bet I can pitch better than you, Allie! And I *know* I can pitch better than Kitty!"

Allie rolled her eyes with incredible exasperation. "No, you can't!" Allie shot back. "Kit-Cat is doing just fine, leave her alone! She's doing a lot better than you ever could! I've seen you throw a ball before, Twisty, and trust me, you're doing your team a favor by staying right where you are!"

Rolling laughter erupted from everywhere in the backyard. Twisty stomped her foot and muttered something under her breath. From the pitcher's mound, Kitty beamed at Allie with pure gratitude. Allie shot her a quick thumbs-up and picked up the bat again. "Ready, Kit-Cat? Remember, throw higher."

Kitty, who seemed to gain renewed confidence from Allie's defense of her pitching skills, pulled her hand back in the air and threw a quick curveball. This time it was high enough for Allie to hit, but she swung too late and missed it.

"Strike one!" Chase shouted out cheerfully from the field, met by a chorus of "yay" from his teammates. "That's more like it!"

"Great job, Kit-Cat!" Allie grinned. "That was perfect!

Now do it again."

"Hey, Allie!" Ryan called from first base. "Just whose team exactly are you on here, anyway?"

Allie gave Ryan a conspiratorial smile. "I don't know, Ry. Maybe I'm a double agent. I'm playing for both teams."

Ryan laughed. "Well, could you play for our team *only* for at least the next few minutes? I'd like to get off first base sometime today."

"Okay, Rye Bread," Allie sang back sweetly. Rye Bread was another one of Allie's nicknames, which even though I knew was a play on his name, I always found kind of funny because Ryan's dark skin was nowhere near the color of rye bread. Ryan liked to joke around, so it was no surprise he and Allie were good friends. "I'll see what I can do."

Kitty raised her arm back in the air and let another curveball fly. Allie barely saw the ball as it zoomed right past her ear and swung way too late.

"Strike two!" Chase cried out. "Just one more and you're out, Allie!"

"Wow!" Allie said. "That was a fantastic pitch!"

"Allie!" Ryan protested.

"Yes, yes, I know, you want off first base, I got it," Allie said, turning to Ryan again. "I'm trying Rye Bread, but Kit-Cat is too good for me. She's a great pitcher."

"Thanks, Allie," Kitty said modestly, blushing a little from the compliment.

"You're welcome. It's true," Allie replied. "And don't let *them*," she said, thrusting a finger towards Twisty and Becky, "tell you any different. They're just jealous."

Twisty heard her and couldn't resist firing back. "Oh please! Jealous! Did you ever think you're just a bad hitter, Allie?"

Allie gave another signature eye roll and blew her hair back from her face. "First Kit-Cat is a bad pitcher, now I'm a bad hitter? Sure, Twisty, keep going. At this rate, you can criticize everybody in the family before the game's over, and then succeed in your clear goal of alienating everyone so nobody wants to play baseball with you ever again!"

"Enough, Allie," Ashley said behind her. "Let's just keep playing." Then she chuckled and gave her a little wink through her glasses. "And try to hit the ball this time."

We resumed the game and Kitty flew the ball towards Allie. This time Allie was ready; she swung, and the bat cracked against the ball. Allie ran to first base, and Ryan made it safely to second before Justin caught the ball near third.

Allie waved to Ryan and pointed to the second base he was standing on. "Happy?" she asked, with her hands in the air questioningly.

"Yes," Ryan laughed. "Thanks."

"Sure thing," Allie replied. "Although I have to say, I'm a little surprised I made it here."

Ashley was next to bat. Everyone on our team exchanged grins and silent cheers. Ashley, the tallest, fastest, and most agile in our family, was one of the best players on either side of the field. Ashley picked up the bat with an expression of concentration on her face. Kitty, knowing she was pitching to an adept rival, closed her eyes and drew back the ball. It flew through the air and Ashley cracked it hard against the bat. The ball soared through our expansive backyard and kept on going till it cleared right over the straight line wooden fence surrounding the perimeter of our yard.

"Home run!" Kevin cried out.

Our team jumped up and down, cheering as Ashley, Ryan, and Allie cleared all the bases and ran back around to home plate, while the other team looked on sulkily.

"We just got three runs!" Ryan yelled out triumphantly. "That's 3 to 0! *In your face*!"

"Uh, yeah, I don't know what you're so excited about, because the game's over," Chase called back. "Ashley just hit the ball over the fence. No ball, no game."

The other team started coming in from the outfield at this realization, slightly irritated at the sudden end of the game. We gathered into a crowd together once more.

"Well, that was fun while it lasted," Kevin said. "What next?"

"No, let's keep playing baseball," Carlie cried. "That was fun."

"How are we going to play without a ball though, Car?" Twisty asked, glaring at Ashley.

"I'm sorry," Ashley said sheepishly. "I didn't mean to hit it that hard. I swear."

"You're apologizing for hitting a home run?" Allie questioned. "Yes, and I'm terribly sorry for scoring an A on the science test last week."

"Well…we could make another one," Justin suggested, avoiding Breezy's eyes.

Breezy immediately shut down that idea. "No, absolutely not. We're not doing it again. Anyway, the game was getting a little heated, so maybe it was time to quit."

"Yeah, I thought you two were going to come to blows or something," Chase agreed, pointing at Allie and Twisty.

"Oh, I wouldn't have hit her," Allie said. "Even if she did deserve it."

Twisty's eyes burned into Allie's. "Deserve it? Oh, no one deserves to get smacked more than you, Allie," she seethed. "And just what makes you think that you're the one who'd hit me?"

Allie took a step back from Twisty. "Why would you have hit me? It's not like I'm the one who started it."

"Hah!" Twisty scoffed. "Of course you started it. You said I couldn't throw a ball."

"Are you suffering from some temporary case of amnesia, Twisty?" Allie retorted. "Sure, that's what happened. You were just standing there on the field, minding your own business, when I said out of nowhere you couldn't throw a ball. That had nothing to do with the fact that you started picking on Kit-Cat for no reason!"

"Excuse me, brats!"

The voice came from out of nowhere and resonated like a thunderclap. We froze in mid-action, instantly silenced. The growing fight between Twisty and Allie, which seemed unavoidable just a moment ago, was immediately forgotten. Finally, we looked at each other and turned, nearly all at once, towards the source of the voice, which came from, amazingly to us, the opposite side of our wooden fence, in the next yard.

There, at the fence, stood a man. He was about 6 feet tall, like CC, light-skinned, and had a toned, but not overly muscular body. His hair was short, thin, and black, and his eyes were dark green. He stood with his left hand on the fence, leering at us, and held up in his right hand an object we right away recognized: our baseball.

We gawked at the man in astonishment, not sure exactly where he had come from.

"Is this your ball?" he asked us. He spoke in a low, smooth, icy tone. I felt the hairs on the back of my neck bristle at the sound of it. I decided at once I did not like this man.

Becky was the first to find her voice to speak. "Um, yes. We were-we were playing baseball. The ball...it went over the fence."

"Well, your ball came into my yard and broke my

window," he said glassily.

"Oh, I'm sorry, we didn't kn
Breezy apologized nervously. "W
We'll pay for any damages."

The man eyed Breezy and s
"Will you? Well, how nice of you.
upbringing."

Allie walked up next to Breezy with her arms crossed, glaring at the man. "And who, exactly, are you?"

The man narrowed his eyes at Allie. "I'm your next-door neighbor," he said in a resonant note. "Isn't that obvious?"

Ashley was next to regain her voice. "But we don't have any next-door neighbors. The house next door has been empty for years."

"Well I just moved in a few weeks ago," the man said evenly.

We looked at each other, not sure whether to believe this. After all, we hadn't seen any moving trucks, boxes, or any other signs that someone new was moving in.

"Okay. Well, welcome to the neighborhood then. Nice to meet you," Breezy said with a courteousness she didn't seem to feel.

The man flashed his eyes at Breezy again. "Are you always this polite?" he sneered.

"So are you ever going to introduce yourself? Tell us your name?" Allie questioned with obvious animosity. "Or are you just going to keep standing there staring at us?"

The man turned to Allie, looking at her with a mixture of coolness and amusement. "Oh, I have a name," he cooed. "But you may call me Big Boss."

"Big Boss?" Allie snickered. "That's cute. What are you? A 1920s street gangster?"

Big Boss met Allie's boldness with a caustic smile. "You're quite the saucy one, aren't you, brat?"

"And where do you get off calling us brats?" Allie demanded. "You don't even know us!"

Big Boss's cold smile grew wider. "Oh, but I do. I've been watching you, and trust me, that's what you are. A bunch of brats." He paused to let his next words hit us with the staggering effect he intended. "A bunch of real Munch brats."

We all stood gaping at him, stunned into silence. We all had the same question. Kevin finally brought voice to it. "How-how do you know our last name?"

Big Boss seemed pleased his statement had perturbed us so much. He didn't answer Kevin's question. "Stay away from my side of the yard, Munch brats. Or you'll be sorry."

"All right then. Nice to meet you too. And thanks for that just stellar example of neighborly kindness," Allie called back to him.

"Allie," Breezy breathed, daring to make her voice just audible enough so only we could hear her. "I don't think it's a good idea to antagonize this man."

Becky suddenly remembered something and yelled back towards the fence. "Hey wait! Mister, uh, Big Boss. Could you throw our ball back?"

Big Boss turned towards her and held the ball up, rocking it in his hand. "What, this?" he taunted. "Come over here and get it."

Becky glanced at us uncertainly, then crept up to the fence. When she got close enough, she held her hand out expectantly. All at once I got an ominous feeling and yelled out a warning to Becky, but it was too late. Big Boss lunged at Becky and grabbed her wrist with outright malice, squeezing it tightly. Becky's eyes widened in surprise, then she squealed in pain.

"Hey!" Ashley screamed. "Stop it! Let go of her! You're hurting her!"

We stood, suspended in shock, then we all started shrieking together in cries of protest.

"Stop it! What are you doing? Let go of her!"

Just as suddenly as he grabbed her, Big Boss harshly cast Becky's wrist forward, releasing her. Becky stumbled back, holding her wrist, with tears in her eyes, and immediately backed far away from the fence. She stared at Big Boss with an expression of terror.

"That," Big Boss said thickly, pointing to Becky, "Was for my window." He looked at our stunned faces with palpable contempt, and hurled the ball over the fence, driving it straight to the ground of our backyard. "Now we're even. No need to pay me for any damages." He gave a sudden hard laugh and imparted with another stony smile. "I'm sure I'll be seeing you around, brats."

We watched as he ambled back to his house, not daring to move or even breathe. When we were sure he could no longer hear us, we came to life again.

"Okay," Allie began, her eyes wide. "*What* just happened?"

"Man!" Kevin let out a long whistle. "What's wrong with that guy? I mean seriously! He didn't even *try* to be nice!"

"That's our new neighbor?" Allie said with bemused humor. "Wonderful. Lucky us. We must have him over for tea and cookies sometime."

We laughed at Allie's joke.

"And what kind of name is Big Boss, anyway?" Allie questioned.

"I know! And how did he know our last name?" I asked.

"Well one thing's for sure, that guy's a huge bully," Chase stated.

"Bully?" Becky walked up to the group of us, still nursing her wrist.

"Becky! I'm so sorry!" Breezy cried. "Are you all right?"

"Bully?" Becky repeated. "You think he's a bully? He's not a bully. Downright dangerous is more like it. Did you see what he did to my wrist?"

Becky took her hand off her wrist and revealed an awful red, swelling wound that circled all around the bottom of her hand. In the middle of her wrist was a small, square indentation, a cut that looked like someone pressed a shape into her skin, like cookie dough. We all drew in our breath at the sight of it.

"Wow!" Chase exclaimed. "He got you good!"

"What's this mark here?" Ashley asked, pointing to the indentation.

"I think it's his ring," Becky replied. "I think he pressed his ring into my wrist."

"But, Becky," Breezy said, "To do that, he would have had to turn his ring around the other way."

"Yeah," Becky said. She looked off past the fence again where Big Boss grabbed her just moments ago. She was visibly shaking. "I think he did it on purpose."

We looked at each other, allowing this disturbing thought to sink in.

"Well, I'll tell you one thing for sure," Becky said. "I'm not going near him ever again, and you shouldn't either. That man is dangerous. Keep him away from me!"

Becky turned to leave but Breezy stopped her. "Becky, you're not able to heal your wrist, are you?"

Breezy's question made us remember Becky was the one who used her power to make the baseball earlier, and as a result, had no energy left to do a healing power for herself. It turned out Breezy was right, and Becky's disobedient act came right back around with its almost inevitable consequences.

Becky looked down and shook her head, feeling ashamed.

"Give me your wrist," Breezy said gently. "I can heal it for you."

Becky hesitated a moment, afraid of Breezy's reprimands she thought she'd surely receive by offering her wrist. She was expecting a chorus of "Well, I hope you learned your lesson" and "I told you so," but Breezy was too kind for that. Instead, she gently took her wrist in hand and lightly touched her fingers to it tenderly, being careful not to disturb the painful wound. The beam of warm yellow light started shining underneath Breezy's fingertips, grew brighter, and then burnt out quickly. Breezy lifted her hand away and unveiled Becky's wrist: clean, unblemished, and fully mended.

"Thank you, Breezy," Becky said. "I-I'm sorry I didn't..."

Breezy shook her head, indicating Becky to stop. "It's okay. I know."

"Let's go back in the house," Hazy said in her muffled tone. "We'll need to tell CC about this."

Everyone shared looks that showed they were not looking forward to that experience but knew Hazy was right. We all headed back towards the house. I paused at the doorway before stepping in, looking out past the yard and towards the fence again, trying to ignore the dark feeling of foreboding passing through my head.

Chapter 4

In the living room, we told CC the whole story about what happened outside. He seemed a bit disquieted over Big Boss knowing our last name. Then Breezy revealed what Big Boss did to Becky.

"Wait a minute!" CC shouted. "Are you telling me this man put his hands on Becky?" he asked, his voice rising with emotion. "Becky, did this man hurt you?"

"Y-yes. He hurt-he hurt my wrist. He squeezed it really hard. And-and he pressed his ring into it," Becky stammered.

CC, seeing how upset Becky was, softened his voice and gestured Becky over to him. "Let me see your wrist. Or did you already heal it?"

"It's-it's healed," Becky replied quickly, shooting Breezy an anxious look, and holding out her arm as proof.

"Yes," CC said. "I wish you would have waited until I saw it, but I understand why you wanted to heal it right away if it was hurting you that badly."

Becky nodded. She realized she could get away with her unadmitted indiscretion in this story as long as the rest of us didn't say anything. "It was that bad."

"Well I'll have to take your word for it then," CC responded. "Being rude, impolite, and trying to scare you is one thing, but this man, Big Boss, has no right to hurt you, any of you," CC stated firmly.

CC said he was going to take care of this right now and marched over to Big Boss's house, but a few minutes later he came back with a scowl on his face. "I knocked and knocked but no one answered," CC reported. "There's something really strange about that guy though. It's a beautiful, sunny day, and he has all the shades on the windows down. Also, I don't think you need to feel bad about any broken windows, because I didn't see any. The next time any of you see him, I want you to immediately come and get me. I want to talk to him."

It didn't take long before Big Boss made his reappearance. It was a few days later, and again we were all playing in the backyard. Carlie started a game of tag with Twisty, and Twisty, Carlie's best friend, was quick to play along. They zig-zagged around the yard, giggling wildly, and suddenly, with a tag, made me part of their game. I dashed off after Carlie as she and Twisty split directions and announced the big oak tree we were approaching was base. Carlie ran towards the safety of the tree with her arms outstretched, as I reached it, seconds too late. Carlie jumped up and down victoriously. Instead of waiting for them to leave, I turned around and ran towards Allie, tagging her easily since it was so unexpected. Allie turned next to her and tagged Hazy, but Hazy tagged her right back. They repeatedly tagged each other, laughing deliriously, slapping each other's hands over and over.

"Let's play Chaos Tag! Everyone's it!" Hazy announced.

We all started screeching and running wildly around the backyard, chasing after each other, dodging each other's tags while also trying to tag the other at the same time. Chaos was a good word for it, but we were exultant, so lost in the fun of our game that we hadn't noticed Big Boss was once again standing at the fence, watching us. For the second time, the sound of his cold, smooth voice rudely disrupted our play.

"You brats sure are making quite a noisy racket. How is anyone supposed to get any peace and quiet around here, with the lot of you running around, screaming like banshees?"

"He's back," Ryan stated, from his position near the fence, pointing at Big Boss. "We were playing Tag, what's the big deal? And how long have you been standing there watching us, anyway?"

"Tag," Big Boss repeated the word with scorn. "I see. Another game. Don't you brats ever have anything better to do than run around playing silly games all day?"

"We're kids," Allie stated. "Sorry, but our long shift at the factory doesn't start again for another three hours. And what about you? Don't you have some moonshine or something to make, Big Boss? Oh, by the way, you got a call from Fat Tony. He wants you and Big Louie to meet him down at the docks tonight at 7."

Big Boss smirked. "You know, you sure do have a lot of spunk, Allie. I almost have to admire that."

Allie looked unnerved at this comment and a wave of uncertainty passed over all of us. It was seconds later before the reason why dawned on me: Big Boss said Allie's name.

Allie stalked towards Big Boss with a fixed glare. "How do you know my name? I want to know, right now, how do you know my name? Because I certainly didn't tell you and I know no one else did either!"

Again, Big Boss seemed pleased with himself. "Oh, don't worry, you didn't have to. I do my homework."

"Your homework?" Allie shouted. "What does that even mean? What, do you have notes on us that you study?"

Breezy came forward, putting a supportive hand on Allie's shoulder. She looked straight at Big Boss to address him. "Mr. Big Boss, our dad wants to talk to you. He's not happy with what you did to Becky the other day."

"Your dad?" Big Boss questioned, looking back at Breezy with an icy grin. "Oh, but don't you mean CC?"

A fresh wave of fury rippled through Allie the second our special nickname for our father crossed Big Boss's lips. "All right, that's it!" she yelled. "You tell us right now how you know all this stuff about us! Tell us right now!"

Big Boss threw his head back, bursting into loud, wicked laughter and I turned to ice. It was the first time we heard Big Boss laugh like that but unfortunately far from the last. It was the kind of evil, maniacal laughter that came from super-villains in cartoons and comic book movies, but when it's coming from a real person, there's suddenly nothing cartoonish about it. I felt something deep within me that at that point neither I nor any of my siblings were used to: cold, unadulterated fear.

When his laughter broke, he finally responded to Allie's demand. "Well, you know what they say, Allie, keep your friends close and your enemies closer."

"Enemies?" Allie cried out. "So even though it's only been a few days we've even known you existed, you've already decided we're your enemies? Okay, Big Boss, you want enemies, you got them now!"

All at once Ryan, Kevin, Chase, Ashley, and Twisty fell behind Allie, moving as if an army to back her up, ready for a fight. I turned around to look for Becky, curious where she was since, normally, she too would be part of this gutsy contingent. I wasn't surprised to find her way in the back of the yard, keeping a more than careful distance away from Big Boss. She was reflexively clasping and rubbing her wrist.

"I'm going to get CC," Breezy stated in an unequivocal tone. She ran to the house with attentive purpose.

The ragtag team of warriors made up of my most emboldened siblings rallied together, shouting their battle cries. Big Boss rested his elbow against the fence with his chin on his hand, watching them, entertained by this spectacle.

Breezy made her confident return through the yard, CC trailing right behind her. As Breezy came back to me and Hazy, CC wasted no time, marching up towards the fence. As he approached Allie and her feisty band mates, he held up his hand, signaling them to stop. At the sight of CC, they all stepped back and instantly grew silent. CC walked up to the fence and looked Big Boss right in the eye. Big Boss straightened up and smiled at CC with fake cordiality.

"I want to talk to you," CC asserted, without returning the smile. "My name's Casey Munch, but I think you already somehow knew that. And who are you? And don't give me any of this Big Boss nonsense. What's your name?"

Big Boss extended his hand to CC in mocked formality, and CC shook it quickly and curtly. "Pleased to meet you in person, Mr. Munch. My name's Robert Wheeler, but I don't go by that name. I go by Big Boss, so please address me as such."

"Fine then, Big Boss," CC practically spat. "I have a couple of questions for you. My first question is how did you know my last name's Munch?"

"Oh I make it my business to find out as much as I can about my neighbors before I move into a place," Big Boss responded. "It's no big secret, Casey. You have quite a following, you and your work. That kind of information can be easily obtained for anyone who wants it."

"Really?" CC said crisply. "Okay then. Second question. I see you've met my children," CC declared, sweeping his hand towards us.

"Yes," Big Boss confirmed, looking over us with a simmering smile. "Quite a colorful bunch."

"Yes, well, they tell me when you met them the other day you were extremely rude and nasty to them for no reason," CC stated severely. "Can you tell me why?"

"Oh really? For no reason," Big Boss replied, his tone growing hard. "Did they also tell you they broke my window with their baseball?"

"Yes, they did," CC answered. "And they said they apologized and offered to pay for the damages which you refused. And by the way, I stopped by your house right after this happened and didn't even see a broken window."

"Well, that's interesting," Big Boss stated icily. "There was a small crack. You obviously must not have looked hard enough. I'll still take that payment if you're offering."

"No. I am not offering because of what you did to my daughter Becky!" CC fired. "Which brings me to my third question: What exactly do you think gives you the right to put your hands on my daughter? What makes you think you can hurt one of my kids? Who on Earth do you think you are?"

"I'm sorry, I don't understand," Big Boss said in imitated confusion. "Your daughter Becky? Do you mean that little girl over there?" he asked, pointing out at Becky. "I did grab her wrist briefly, but I intended to teach her a lesson about respecting others' property. Honestly, I barely touched her. I didn't think I hurt her."

At this we erupted into loud wails of protest, calling Big Boss out on this outright lie.

CC held up his hands towards us. "Stop!" he roared.

A hush went up amongst us as we flashed the quiet signal. Silence descended across the yard once again.

CC turned back to face Big Boss. "Well, as you can see, my children strongly disagree with you. They've made it pretty clear they think you're a liar and I tend to agree. Admit it. You did intend to hurt Becky," CC hammered.

Big Boss remained unruffled. "Like I said, Casey, I didn't think I hurt her that badly. I'm sorry if I did. I guess I don't know my own strength."

Before we could sound another round of objections, CC put his hand up for us to remain calm. "You don't know your own strength? You squeezed the wrist of a 10-year-old hard enough to make an imprint of your ring in her skin. Do you think I was born yesterday?"

"Let me ask you a question now, Casey," Big Boss replied. "Did you actually see the mark on her wrist?"

My siblings traded more knowing looks. We all shared the same thought: Breezy healed Becky's wrist before CC could see it.

"No, I didn't, but I didn't have to. All thirteen of my kids are in solid agreement with what happened. And all of them saw the mark."

"Don't you think that would have been something you'd want to check out for yourself first before you stormed through here, accusing me of hurting your daughter?" Big Boss interrogated.

"I did check it out, but the mark was gone," CC said half-truthfully.

"So, wait a minute, exactly how long was it after my encounter with them that they reported this to you?" Big Boss asked.

"They came to me right after it happened," Casey replied

somewhat hesitantly, already seeing where Big Boss was going.

"I see," Big Boss said thickly. "So even though I supposedly hurt Becky badly enough to have left a terrible mark, this mark was not even visible to you just minutes later?"

CC drew in a breath and tipped back on his heels, studying Big Boss. He couldn't tell Big Boss the truth without giving away the secret of our powers, but he knew without volunteering that central piece of information he didn't have much of a case. Deciding the best thing to do was go on the defensive, CC narrowed his eyes at Big Boss and lowered his voice to take on a deep, menacing tone. "Are you calling my kids liars?"

"I'm not saying they're lying, Casey," Big Boss said. "I'm saying maybe they're just exaggerating the truth a bit. You know how overdramatic kids can be."

"My kids don't lie, and they don't embellish the truth," CC stated. "Not about something like this. If all thirteen of them agree on something that happened, that's a near virtual guarantee they're telling the truth."

"Where's the evidence then, Casey?" Big Boss scoffed. "Where's your proof that I did this? Where's the mark? Show me the mark. You can't because it wasn't even there when you saw it," he laughed.

CC, realizing that without giving away our family secret he didn't have a leg to stand on, decided not to belabor the point any further. "Fine. Let's just consider this matter closed then. But you listen to me, Robert, Big Boss, or whatever your name is, if you ever, *ever*, put your hands on one of my kids again, and I don't care what the reason is, you're going to be very sorry. Do you understand me?"

"I understand perfectly, Casey," Big Boss stated coldly. "Don't worry. I swear I won't touch them."

Breezy, realizing they were getting ready to part ways, ran up to CC at the fence and motioned him to come close so she can whisper something. CC bent down and put his ear up to Breezy's mouth. CC's eyes widened, then Breezy ran back to us, while CC stood up and turned again to face Big Boss.

"This is interesting," CC said pointedly. "My daughter Breezy says not only did you know my last name, but you also knew my daughter Allie's name and that their nickname for me is CC. Care to explain how you knew these things? That's not the kind of information you can look up online," CC stated, crossing his arms in a confrontational manner.

Big Boss waved his hand dismissively. "I must have overheard them say those names while they were talking. And by the way, Casey, I think you'd be very surprised by what you can find online."

"Mhm," CC intoned, indicating he was not impressed with this answer. "She also says you referred to my children as your enemies," CC challenged, his eyes flashing.

Big Boss put on a puzzled expression. "Enemies? Oh, it's because I said, 'Keep your friends close and your enemies closer', but it's just an expression. I didn't mean for them to take it literally. Although you have to admit, Casey, we didn't exactly start on the right foot, did we?"

CC was point-blank. "No. But that's your own fault."

The two stood at a face-off for a moment, measuring each other up. Finally, CC spoke up again. "You must really think I'm stupid, don't you? Do you actually think I'm buying any of the excuses you're shoveling me?"

"Believe what you want, Casey," Big Boss said. "It doesn't matter to me either way. It just seems to me there have been some major misunderstandings between me and your children here."

"No, on the contrary, I think they understand you quite well," CC denoted. He turned his attention fully to us. "Come on, kids, we're going inside."

"I'm sorry we're not parting on better terms," Big Boss expressed in a feigned manner of friendliness.

"Yes. I'm sure you are," CC said rigidly.

Big Boss shrugged half-contritely and went back to his house. CC waited at the fence until he was completely out of sight, and the rest of us were silent. It was at that moment I looked next to me and noticed Breezy and Hazy were in the middle of an intense conversation inside their heads. Their eyes were deep and intent, locked in, and thoroughly engrossed in each other's thoughts. I could tell in an instant that this was not their normal psychic exchange, and I didn't have to be an empath like Breezy to feel the heaviness between them.

Allie, who had just rejoined us by our sides, noticed Breezy and Hazy too and was watching them closely. I nudged Allie and whispered, "What do you think they're saying?" Allie shook her head. For once her response was serious.

"I don't know, but whatever it is, it's not good."

The yard was springing to life once again, everyone talking to CC at once.

"CC," Becky said, "He really did hurt me badly."

CC nodded at Becky. "I know. I believe you."

"He's such a liar, CC!" Carlie exclaimed.

"He really is a piece of work," CC agreed grimly.

"The only reason you couldn't catch him in his lie about Becky is because you didn't see the mark on her wrist before it was healed. I guess we should've waited until you saw it first," said Ashley, glancing over at Becky a little guiltily. Becky looked miserable.

CC put his arm around Becky and hugged her to his side.

Becky smiled lovingly up at CC. "It's okay. I understand why it had to be healed right away if it was that painful. I meant what I said. It doesn't matter if I saw it or not. You told me you saw it and that's good enough for me. Let's go in the house. We can talk more there if you want. Suddenly I don't want to be anywhere near this backyard right now."

We turned to shuffle into the house, and Allie, Breezy, Hazy, and I trailed behind at the end of the line. Allie gently elbowed Breezy to get her attention, asking the question she was waiting to ask. "Are you going to tell us what that was all about between you two back there, or are we going to have to take a class on mind-reading?" Breezy exchanged a solemn look with Hazy and Hazy's face fell flat. Allie put her arm out as a roadblock to force the three of us to stop in our tracks. "You two are killing me!" she cried. "What is it? Just say it. We're not taking another step further until you tell us!"

Breezy was grave. "We have a theory. We think Big Boss knew there was a good chance CC didn't see the mark on Becky's wrist. He knew there wasn't any visible evidence because we probably would've healed Becky's wrist right away before even talking to CC. And he knew CC would cover it up, so it looks like we either lied or greatly exaggerated the whole thing."

Breezy paused and looked up into our deeply confused faces.

"Don't you see what I'm saying?" she continued. "He set his argument up so that if this ever got to court, CC would easily lose, because there's no proof and CC would never explain the real reason why there's no proof. He was trying to play ignorant, but we think Big Boss knew exactly what he was doing."

Allie and I listened to Breezy with enraptured attention, trying to process everything she said. "You got *all that* from just looking into each other's eyes and reading each other's thoughts?" Allie exclaimed when she broke through her short-lived state of speechlessness. "Holy cow!" Then she frowned. "But wait, Breeze. That doesn't make any sense. For your theory to be true, that would mean Big Boss would have to have known we could heal Becky's wrist in the first place. And how could he have known that?"

Breezy's face turned sullen and she nodded slowly. The light bulb went off in my head as I finally reached the conclusion to Breezy and Hazy's theory, and my mouth snapped open at the shock of the realization. It couldn't be true.

It was then Hazy spoke up and confirmed that conclusion with direful finality. "That's just it," she said in the same solemn tone. "We think Big Boss knows about our magic."

The air gave birth to a sudden strong gust of wind that ripped through the place where we were standing and seemed to shake the very foundation of our bones. None of us spoke.

Chapter 5

The same horrific memories that always fill my head are once again consuming me. The high agonized screams. The desperate pleas for mercy. Grotesque, twisted images of violence my mind won't even let me fully remember.

The familiar sound of steady, hollow footsteps echoed down the hall. I sprang straight up from the concrete floor with a scream stuck in my throat, the nightmarish visions still hanging over me. Kitty was already awake at my side, staring out the bars, petrified at the dark corridor before us. I looked into Kitty's terror-stricken eyes as she began to tremble.

"He's coming," she breathed in a low whimper.

Big Boss emerged from the darkness and appeared in front of us with a cold expression. He stood with one hand wrapped around the bars of our cell, regarding us intently for a minute like we were exhibits in a museum.

"Dinner time!" he announced gleefully. He flung a can of cat food at our heads. "Eat up!"

I resisted the urge to hurl it right back at him. "We don't want your stupid cat food!"

Big Boss looked at me reproachfully. "I wasn't talking to

you, Capricorn. I was talking to Kitty." He beckoned Kitty with his finger tauntingly. "Here kitty, kitty, kitty, kitty. Time for dinner. Eat it all up like a good kitty, kitty."

Kitty suddenly grabbed the can of cat food and pulled the tab on the lid, tearing it open. I stared at her in surprise. She spoke, her voice barely above a whisper. "I'm starving," she said pitifully in explanation. "It's the only food he's given us in days." She slurped and sucked from the can.

"See? Kitty likes her din-din. That's a good kitty, kitty. Eat up all your din-din like a good kitty." Big Boss laughed viciously.

My hands balled into fists, seething with hatred for him.

"Aww, come on, Capricorn," he gloated. "It's only a joke."

"A *joke*?" I yelled. "You think starving us and forcing us to eat cat food is a *joke*?"

Big Boss set me with a cruel smile, enjoying his game. "Well, the food wasn't for you; it was for Kitty. Although I'm sure if you wanted some, kitty-kitty will share."

I couldn't hold my fury in any longer. "You're a horrible excuse for a human being, Big Boss! I doubt you're even human at all. Just leave us alone, you sick monster!"

Big Boss eyed me with an air of warning. "I'd be very *very* careful about what you say next, Capricorn."

Kitty grabbed my arm pleadingly. Tears formed in her sad brown eyes. "Please don't make him mad," she whispered. "I don't want him to hurt us again."

"You should listen to kitty-kitty," Big Boss advised. "She's a smart kitty cat." Then his face broke into a sudden malicious grin. "Or, maybe I should say, Kit-Cat. Isn't that what Allie used to call you, Kitty? Kit-Cat?" His eyes flashed pure malevolence.

At these words, Kitty burst into abrupt sobs.

I spun towards him. "Don't you dare speak her name! Don't dare even mention it. I will not let you disgrace her memory by having her name come from your lips!"

"Ouch," Big Boss scoffed. "Too soon?"

I threw my arms around Kitty and hugged her tightly, doing what little I could to comfort her. We both knew what was coming next. From over Kitty's shoulder, I saw Big Boss unlocking the door of our cage, advancing towards us menacingly with a metal object in his hand. I buried my face in Kitty's shirt and tried to force my mind to transport itself to a happier time. I frantically grasped at a moment to zero in on, remembering again the day we found out Big Boss knew our secret. I could faintly hear the sound of Allie's sweet, cheerful voice…

Chapter 6

"Hey, Kit-Cat! Want a piece of candy?"

Allie bounced around like a kangaroo, zig-zagging between us, passing out candy from a bag on our walk home from school. As we moved closer to our front yard, we noticed Big Boss standing on the path outside his house. He was trying his best to look nonchalant, but it seemed he was waiting for us, a suspicion confirmed when he looked directly at us as we approached.

"Just ignore him," Justin mumbled, as we realized we were going to have to pass right by him. We had every intention of following Justin's advice, but as we moved closer, as if on cue, Big Boss spoke up.

"Why if it isn't my little neighbors, the Munch children. On your way home from school? And how was your day today?"

Breezy called from the sidewalk. "CC told us not to talk to you."

Big Boss did his best to look a little hurt. "Oh really? That's too bad. Why's that?"

"I'm guessing it might have something to do with the psycho neighbor act you pulled on us last week," Allie said.

Big Boss glared at Allie in an unnerving manner. "Yes, well,

I wanted to talk to you about that. I believe we may have gotten started on the wrong foot the other day."

"Oh really, you think?" Allie said derisively. "Gee, you don't think that has anything to do with the fact you called us names, attacked Becky, and then declared us your enemies, do you? I know it's a long shot, but some of us may frown on that kind of thing."

"Enough with the sarcasm, Allie," Big Boss directed. "I take your meaning."

"And you still never explained how you know my name," Allie responded. "Or CC's name. Or our last name."

"Like I already told your father, Allie," Big Boss said with a slight hint of annoyance, "It isn't very hard to find anything online."

"No, I get that, but what I don't understand is *why* you were looking us up in the first place," Allie said.

"If you brats hadn't smashed my window, I wouldn't have reacted so defensively," Big Boss declared, narrowing his eyes.

"So now we're back to being brats?" Allie asked, raising one eyebrow. "And there you go again with sidestepping my question by subtly veering off-topic. You've never given us a straight answer by using that trick."

"You're quite observant, aren't ya, Allie?" Big Boss challenged.

Breezy pulled Allie to the side, whispering to her not to engage him. She took hold of Allie's elbow and guided her away. I felt Big Boss's eyes on us as we walked towards the paved path leading to the front of our Victorian bluish-gray house. We had just reached the concrete steps to our white-pillared wraparound porch when Big Boss gave us a final call out.

"Hey, Munch brats!" We let out a collective sigh and slowly turned around. I don't think any of us were prepared for his next words.

"The next time your ball goes over my fence, you can save yourselves a lot of trouble by just...Poof!" He snapped his fingers in the air dramatically. "Beaming another baseball into existence."

His laughter washed over our shocked faces as we stood fixed to the ground in staggered silence. We stayed planted there like stone statues long after Big Boss left. Fittingly, Allie finally broke the spell taken hold of us. She turned to Breezy and Hazy with her arms half-cocked and nodded at them.

"Congratulations," she said, her voice a little shaky. "Your theory has just been proven true."

Chapter 7

The weeks turned into months and thankfully there was no sighting of Big Boss anywhere. Things quickly returned to our version of normalcy.

I walked into the kitchen and found Allie and Ryan doing dishes. Due to the extremely large size of our family, we maintained a tight division of labor in our house. We kept a strict chore chart where we split the chores equally amongst ourselves, that way no one was stuck with more than their share of the work, and it allowed CC to concentrate on running his nonprofit from his home office while being free from doing chores for thirteen kids. CC made it unequivocally clear the chore chart was not up for negotiation. It was one of the tricks he used to keep him sane.

At the far end of the kitchen, I saw Breezy, Hazy, Chase, and Kevin doing homework together at the table. Chase, Kevin, and Ryan hung out with each other constantly. Kevin had a round face, thin eyes, short black hair, and light beige skin, and again, none of us knew our ancestry, but Kevin's seemed to be an Asian country. Chase had light skin, blonde hair, brown eyes, and a gentle face. As for myself, my appearance suggests some indigenous background: straight black hair, dark eyes, and rosy tan skin. I wandered to the refrigerator to find myself a snack and stopped short at what I saw at the sink. The sponge was moving by itself, up and down under the running water, scrubbing the dish under it as if by phantom hand. Once the dish was clean, Allie handed it to Ryan and Ryan placed it in the drying rack.

"Allie!" I yelled. "What are you doing?"

Allie and Ryan spun around in surprise, guilt written on their faces at being caught in the act. Allie rushed to put her finger to my lips, motioning at me wildly to be quiet.

"Shhhh!" Ryan whispered. "Just chill. Don't say anything."

I was not in the mood to be silenced. "Are you doing that with magic?"

"Shhhh!" They both hissed, looking over at the kitchen table frantically.

"Are you doing what with magic?" Breezy inquired from across the room, instantly raising her attention from her math book to our hushed commotion.

At the sound of Breezy's voice, Allie threw her hands up and handed me an exasperated look. "The jig's up, Rye Bread," she declared to Ryan with defeated assurance.

Ryan huffed. "Great. That's just great. Thanks a lot, Capricorn!"

Breezy's focus fully shifted to us. "What are you guys doing? I thought you were washing dishes. Are you doing something with magic you're not supposed to?" she gently chided as she headed towards us.

Allie whirled her finger in a circular motion through the air to represent lights on a police car, making a blaring sound in imitation of a siren. "Woo woo woo woo!" she rang. "Stop right there. Step away from the dishes and come out with your hands up. This is the magic police."

Ryan snickered. "Seriously."

Breezy saw the sponge moving by itself and immediately surmised their scheme. "Allie! Ryan! Are you serious? Do you know what CC would say if he saw this?"

"Wow, what a cool and innovative way to take care of the daily drudgery of washing the dishes?" Allie retorted.

Breezy laughed. "Come on, guys. You better stop before CC sees you. You're lucky it was Capricorn who caught you instead of him."

"Wait," Chase piped up from across the room. "Are you saying you're using magic to wash dishes? This I've gotta see!" The three at the table rose at once and sprinted to the sink.

"Whoa," Kevin said when he saw the self-possessed sponge. "Check that out! That is so cool!"

"That's brilliant!" Chase cried. "I've been scrubbing dishes myself this whole time like a sucker." Out of all the household chores, Chase despised doing dishes more than anything and dreaded when his turn came up on the list.

"Wait, hold on," Ryan said. "Something has always been bugging me. Why is this automatically a misuse of magic? We have these powers and we barely get to use them. It doesn't make any sense."

"Yeah!" Chase said, jumping to hang on to the possibility of a life free of washing dishes. "Why can't we use our powers to wash dishes? We definitely should!"

"Okay, that's it," Allie said. "For Christmas this year, we're getting Chase a dishwasher."

Everyone laughed then Allie directed her attention to Ryan. "Can I give you some advice, Rye Bread? Let it go. Cut your losses and move on. You're not going to win this one." She reached out to emit a beam of light and instantly ceased the sponge's continuous movement. It collapsed to the floor of the sink like dead weight.

"Nooooo!" Chase cried out. "Why did you do that?"

Allie put her arm around Chase. "It's going to be okay. You'll get through this. Life goes on."

"No, wait," Ryan said. "I really want to talk about this. I still say there's nothing wrong with using our powers to do chores. What makes one thing a misuse of magic and not another?"

"Haha," Allie said, the corners of her mouth forming into a tiny smirk. "Rye Bread, are you seriously about to engage in a philosophical debate with *Breezy*? Yeah. Okay. Good luck with that."

Ryan deliberated on this a moment then nodded. "Okay, Breezy. Explain to me what makes this a misuse of magic."

Breezy wasted no time. "Because it's not necessary. You don't need a self-scrubbing sponge. To be perfectly honest, it's just laziness. You don't save anybody by not doing dishes."

"Speak for yourself," Chase said sadly.

"Oh, won't somebody please buy this poor child a dishwasher!" Allie cried.

"Okay, but along with all the necessary uses, what's so bad about using powers for convenience?" Ryan countered.

"Nothing," Breezy responded. "If using powers didn't zap so much energy, there would be no problem. But the powers have limitations. We can't afford to waste them on things like getting out of chores."

"Yeah, I get that," Ryan said. "But we have thirteen people with powers. It's not like we're going to run out."

The rest of us intently watched Ryan and Breezy, looking back and forth between them as if watching a tennis match. I could tell everyone's side in this argument by reading their faces.

Kevin and Chase were on Ryan's side, and Hazy was on Breezy's side of course. The only one I wasn't sure about was Allie. I figured she was with Ryan since she was in cahoots with him with the sponge, but she seemed to think it was inevitable Breezy would win. She stood watching them closely, leaning against the sink with her arms lightly crossed, an amused smile on her face. As for my position, I'm a little ashamed to say I was with Ryan. I understood Breezy's argument, I just thought there was nothing wrong with using magic for fun every so often. I was wrong. Boy was I wrong.

Breezy forged forward to argue Ryan's last point. "Ryan, look at how Chase and Kevin reacted when they saw what you did with the sponge. They want to do it too. And it won't stop with dishes. Pretty soon everybody would use magic to do chores. Do you really think you're the only one who doesn't want to do housework?"

Ryan said he'd do it without telling anyone, and Breezy asked how long does he think he could keep that a secret, and how that's fair. "Why should you get to use magic like that and nobody else can?"

"They can if they want to," Ryan said. "Everyone should be able to choose to use their magic however they like."

"And if everyone chooses, as I'm sure they will, to use their powers as carelessly as you'd choose to?" Breezy challenged.

"Well that's fine," Ryan said. "That's their right."

"Which would mean suddenly no one can use a power in an emergency. We wouldn't be able to help each other and it would put everyone at risk. What then?" Breezy contested.

Ryan struggled to come up with an argument to counter Breezy's ironclad logic but couldn't generate anything.

Allie's smile swelled into a radiant grin as she looked at Ryan. "I believe that's check and mate, Rye Bread," she trumpeted. "I told you you're not going to win this one."

Later that night, I caught Allie at a rare moment when she was alone. It was my chance to find out what I had questioned earlier. "Hey Allie, I'm curious. What was your position on that whole debate in the kitchen today? Did you take Ryan's side or Breezy's?"

Allie looked surprised I would even ask her that question. "You're kidding, right? Breezy's right, Cap. Squandering magic isn't smart. Worst case it's dangerous. We have to be able to use our powers if we need to."

"But wait, why did you use magic to do dishes with Ryan then?" I asked.

"It was Ryan's idea, but I went along with it. I thought I'd give it a shot and see if I'd get caught. Turns out I did, thanks to you," Allie said, elbowing me in the ribs playfully. She shrugged and gave me a wry smile. "So sue me."

"Sorry I blew your cover," I replied.

"That's okay, Cap," Allie said. "Like Breezy said, you probably did me a favor. Better you than CC. But wasn't that fun today? Poor Ryan. He never knew what he was walking into. I tried to warn him. He made a rookie mistake. You never actually try to debate Breezy. He should have just done what I always do."

I gave Allie a quizzical look. "What do you do?"

Allie paused, looked around the room to see if anyone was listening, then suddenly burst into a great big, conspiratorial grin. "Avoid the argument entirely with entertaining one-liners and quick wit, of course."

Oh God, how I miss Allie.

Chapter 8

Kitty sat next to me at the breakfast table, pulling her long hair back behind her ear. "Good morning," she said softly.

"Good morning, Kitty," CC greeted.

There were six at the table so far, including me. CC was reading a hardcover book titled "The United States of Inequality" while sipping coffee from a blue mug, with a pictured baby seal, from the Save the Seals Society. He was wearing a green T-shirt he bought on a thrift store trip he snuck in while we were in school.

Allie bounced into the dining room, followed by Hazy and Breezy. CC put different cereal boxes in the middle of the table. Allie scanned through the choices in front of her and frowned. "Hey, do we have any boxes of cereal that don't have ten boxes of sugar in them?" she asked.

Ryan and Ashley sniggered. From behind his book, CC sighed.

"Well there are lots of different choices," Justin replied.

"There is? Because all I see is the same cereal with different names," Allie replied. "See look, there's Sugar O's, Sugar Smack, Sugar High, Sugar Shock, Sugar Overdose, Diabetes in a Box...."

CC looked up from his book. "If you're not happy with the cereal choices, Allie, make some oatmeal."

"Can I have a grapefruit for breakfast instead?" Allie asked.

"We're out," CC replied.

"What? Arrgh! Can you buy some more?" Allie said.

"Sure, I'll just run out and buy you a grapefruit right now," CC said in a dry tone.

"Well can I make a grapefruit?" Allie asked.

"You already know the answer to that," CC said, returning his gaze to the book.

"Please?" Allie pleaded. "I haven't used any magic in a long time and…"

"There's no reason you can't eat cereal," CC interrupted.

"Because I don't want sugar for breakfast," Allie protested.

"Allie!" CC scolded. He dropped his book with a thud. "I said no."

Allie lowered her eyes away from CC's and pulled a bowl towards her.

There was thumping on the stairs and Twisty and Carlie entered the room.

"Cereal again?" Twisty groaned.

"I'm tired of cereal," Carlie whined.

"We already did this," Allie said to them. "CC said you must eat your sugar."

CC fixed Allie with a stern look. "It's cereal for breakfast today, take it or leave it," he said to Carlie and Twisty.

"Leave it," Twisty said, making a face.

"Can I have something else?" Carlie asked.

CC repeated the option of making oatmeal. Carlie stuck out her tongue and slumped down in her seat.

Allie picked up her spoon and dinged it against Hazy's spoon. "Hey, Haze? Want to have a spoon fight? The first one to drop their spoon loses. Go!" Allie and Hazy banged their spoons against each other as if in a swordfight.

"CC, I want something else for breakfast," Carlie moaned.

"Just eat cereal, Carlie," Ashley said. "Cereal isn't going to kill you."

"Hey, she doesn't have to eat it if she doesn't want to," Twisty said, jumping to defend Carlie.

"You dropped your spoon! I win!" Allie sang victoriously between laughs. "Okay, let's go again. Ready, set, go!" The two resumed whacking spoons in the air.

Breezy rested her hand on Hazy's arm to calm her, but Hazy was already far lost in the joyful world of Allie's silliness.

"I'm hungry. I want something else for breakfast," Carlie pouted, beating her feet under the table.

"Be quiet!" Ashley and Kevin yelled at Carlie.

"Don't tell her to be quiet!" Twisty shouted at them.

CC slammed his book on the table. "That's it!" He turned towards Carlie and Twisty, who shrank back from him. "We," he said, with stress on each word, "are having cereal for breakfast today. That's it. This isn't a restaurant. I'm not going to start fulfilling individual orders for each of you." He turned to the other side of the table. "Allie! Hazy! Put the spoons down now. Spoons aren't swords."

Hazy looked like she just realized what she was doing, and hastily dropped her spoon. Allie set her spoon down with a clang, giving a rueful grin. "We were just playing, CC," she said, her hands held out entreatingly.

"Mhm," CC grumbled as he picked his book back up.

"Can I have tofu scramble?" Carlie asked CC.

All ten other kids at the table gave Carlie the same look, including Twisty. It was a look that, translated into words, said, "You've got to be kidding me!"

CC wasn't amused. "I'm not making you anything else, Carlie. Either eat cereal or don't eat breakfast."

"What if Kitty makes it for me?" Carlie asked. Kitty was the best cook in the house, which included CC, so this request wasn't exactly shocking.

"Wow, Kit-Cat," Allie said, looking at Kitty with a growing smirk. She put on her most saccharine tone of voice. "How kind of you to volunteer to cook for Carlie! That's so generous of you! I didn't hear you make the offer, so you must have done it telepathically!"

Kitty and the rest of my siblings exploded into riotous laughter, except for Carlie, who sat at the table, glowering.

"No, Kitty will not make anything for you," CC rebuked. You didn't even ask her, as Allie just pointed out. Kitty isn't your personal chef. I'm getting very tired of this, Carlie."

"But I don't want stupid cereal," Carlie whined.

"CARLIE!" CC snapped, fixing Carlie with a forceful glare. Everyone exchanged low whistles and wide-eyed expressions. Twisty snatched the nearest box of cereal in front of her and dumped it into her and Carlie's bowls. She slid a spoon into Carlie's hand, eyed her tensely, and mouthed the word "eat." Twisty started eating her cereal with deliberate ambition.

"Fine, I'll eat stupid cereal then," Carlie muttered.

CC let out a loud exhale of exhaustion and looked up at the ceiling. "Can I just get one day?" he asked. He flung his book down. "I give up! That's the tenth time I've tried to read this book and I can't get off the first chapter." He quickly surveyed everyone in the room. "Where's Chase and Becky? Still sleeping? They need to get up or they'll be late for school."

We looked at each other with small smiles and chuckled softly.

"What?" CC asked, understanding immediately there was some inside joke.

"It's Saturday, CC," Breezy explained.

"Oh, for Pete's sake!" CC exclaimed. "I can't even keep the days straight anymore."

"I'll get them," Ashley announced, popping up from the table.

"You know what you need, CC?" Allie said. "You need a vacation."

"Yes, thank you, Allie, I agree," CC said. "Wouldn't that be nice? I'd love to take a vacation. Or go out and see friends, or even do something fantastical like go on a date. But I can't, because I can't hold down a babysitter if my life depended on it because no one in their right mind wants to watch thirteen kids. Not that I blame them, but I don't know what that says about me. I must be completely insane!"

Allie widened her eyes and raised her eyebrows. She sat in awkward silence before continuing. "Um…Okay. Wow. Well, you don't need a babysitter. We can watch ourselves."

CC burst into boisterous laughter. "Right. That's funny. Nice try though, Allie."

"No, I'm serious," Allie said. "We're responsible."

CC chortled.

Ashley came back with Becky treading groggily behind her. "Chase was too tired to come down," Ashley announced.

"What else is new?" CC muttered. "If he's not up in two hours, I'm dragging him out of bed."

"I'm hungry," Becky said, becoming more alert as soon as she sat down. "Oh good, cereal!"

"At least someone here likes my cereal," CC said, delivering a critical expression towards Carlie and Allie. Allie held up her spoon to indicate she was eating. CC couldn't help but smile.

"Hey, Allie," Becky said. "I need the soymilk."

"Oh, do you?" Allie answered her. "That's nice. I need lots of stuff too. I need to study for a test this weekend. And I need to eat a healthier breakfast, like a grapefruit. And I need more sisters with manners."

Everyone tittered as they took Allie's meaning. Becky didn't get it.

"No, I mean give me the soymilk," she ordered.

"You want to try that again?" CC directed, making eye contact with Becky. "And this time try asking a little more politely?"

"Oh," Becky said. Her cheeks flushed a little. "Really? Oh, brother." She turned to Allie and painted on a courteous smile. "Allie, may I have the soymilk, please?"

"Of course you may, Becky," Allie said, using the same imitated genteel tone. She picked up the container and passed it to her. "All you have to do is ask."

CC rolled his eyes and shook his head. "It's going to be a long day," he sighed. He looked out the window and immediately brightened. "Why don't you go outside and play? It's going to be a nice autumn day. And rake some leaves while you're out there."

Ryan moved to ask a question. "Can we use…"

"No," CC responded before he could finish.

"You don't even know what I was going to say!" Ryan complained.

"I do know, Ryan. The same thing you always ask. Can we use magic?" CC replied. "And my answer is always the same. No."

CC took Ryan by the shoulders and directed him to the kitchen, pointing at the back door. "Go. Go play. All of you. Please. Have fun. I need to get some work done."

Chapter 9

Freshly-fallen leaves painted our backyard vibrant auburn and brilliant gold. Acorns from our towering oak tree lay scattered across the grassy floor, and we heard their soft crunch under our feet as we stood together in the backyard. We were immersed in animated conversation, discussing CC. Breezy was trying to convince us CC badly needed some help and we should work to make things easier for him. Ashley claimed because some of us used our powers so irresponsibly, CC didn't trust us to be alone. To prove her point, she brought up Ryan's bewitching of the sponge to wash dishes.

"You're not going to tell on me are you?" Ryan asked Ashley.

Ashley shook her head, but a devilish gleam suddenly came into Twisty's eye. "That depends," Twisty said. "How much is it worth to you?"

"Oh come on, Twisty. You're really going to tell on me?" Ryan cried.

"For the right price I won't," she said boldly. "How about if you do my chores for a month, then I don't say anything. Otherwise, I go straight to CC."

My siblings delivered Twisty disdainful glares, showing

they didn't approve of her bullying behavior.

Ryan looked like he had just been struck. "Chores for a *month*? I'm not doing your chores for a whole month!"

"Well, then I guess I'm going to talk to CC," Twisty menaced.

"No! Don't! Come on, Twisty, please," Ryan pleaded.

Allie was swinging playfully around the oak tree, taking in the beauty of the changing leaves. Now her focus fully shifted towards us. She came towards Ryan and Twisty and tapped Ryan on the shoulder. "Don't worry, Rye Bread. I got this."

Allie stood to meet Twisty eye to eye. "So Twisty, when you tell CC about Ryan and the sponge, are you also going to tell him about all the times you've misused magic? Or do you want me to go ahead and do that for you?"

"When have I misused magic?" Twisty asked, her smile fading.

"Let's see," Allie said. "There was the time you made a book fly across the room, where you replicated a whole pizza for yourself, oh and the baseball bat, and...How about I just make a list for you?"

A slow grin spread across Ryan's face. Twisty's smile, however, was now completely gone and replaced by a blank stare. "You-you know about all that?" she stammered.

Carlie ran up to Twisty, coming to her favorite sister's rescue. "What Allie isn't telling you, Twisty, is she and Ryan used magic to do the dishes together. So she's just as guilty as Ryan is," she announced with a smug expression.

Twisty's face morphed into a triumphant grin. "Is that true? So that's the reason you don't want me to tell on Ryan, isn't it? Well, I'll tell on Ryan *and* you."

Allie folded her arms and tilted her head towards Carlie with a smirk. "Thanks, Car," she laughed. "You would sell me up the river in a second, wouldn't you? Well, at least I know where we stand." She looked back at Twisty. "I never said I wasn't in on it with Ryan. I'm not going to deny it. Go ahead and tell on me. Just know if you tell on me or Ryan, I will tell CC everything you've done. And trust me, Twisty, I've got a lot more on you than you have on me. But if you want to play this game, go ahead, make the first move," Allie challenged, her eyes sparkling.

Twisty and Carlie exchanged sunken faces. Twisty's whole body quickly deflated like a balloon. "Fine. I won't say anything," she conceded.

"Good," Allie smiled. "I thought as much."

Ryan's face burst into a victorious grin. "Thanks, Allie! You're amazing." They exchanged a high-five.

"No problem. Told you I got this," Allie said.

Chase laughed like he just witnessed the funniest thing in the world. "Oh, man! That was awesome!" he crowed. "Serves you right for trying to browbeat Ryan!" Twisty looked like she could swat him.

"Can we get back to our main discussion? We've gotten completely off topic," Breezy said.

Ryan suggested CC should get multiple babysitters so they can divide the work. "Done. Easy."

"Haha, easy. Anyone who thinks that's easy obviously hasn't met us," Ashley said. "It's not just the number either. We have a reputation."

"That's your fault, you know," Becky said, pointing at Twisty. "If you hadn't scared away the last babysitter, CC would still have one."

"Hey, all I did was ask her if she wanted to see a magic trick," Twisty responded.

Allie laughed. "Right. That's all you did. What Twisty is

conveniently neglecting to mention is she not only asked her if she wanted to see a trick, but she showed her the trick. And the trick involved shooting a fireball across the room."

Twisty smiled wickedly. "Well, it was a magic trick. I didn't lie."

Kevin cracked up at the memory. "I've never seen anyone run so fast. That's the closest thing I've ever seen to those human-shaped holes through doors you see in cartoons."

"Gee, I can't understand why CC doesn't trust us with our magic," Allie said. "It's a complete mystery to me."

Breezy frowned. "It's not funny, guys." She sighed. "Let's just focus on solutions. What can we do to make things easier for CC?"

"Have Twisty adopted to another family?" Allie offered. Twisty whirled on Allie, her dark eyes blazing with fury. Allie held up her hands in a defensive posture. "Kidding. Kidding. I'm just kidding."

"Well, it's not funny!" Twisty yelled.

"Oh, you don't like it when *you're* the target, do you?" Allie responded.

"Come on, Allie, enough. Maybe we can try to cut down on the constant fighting and bickering?" Breezy suggested.

"I think that's a good idea, Breezy," I chimed in. "But judging from what just occurred in the last fifteen minutes, I think that would be difficult."

Breezy sighed. "Can everyone just try? For CC's sake. Or at least not fight when he's around? That's all I'm asking."

When we went in for lunch we knew we were in danger of breaking the agreement we just made if we talked to each other, especially since Twisty was already itching for a reason to go after Allie. We somehow unanimously decided the best way to keep to Breezy's "no fighting" rule was to eat in virtual silence.

The problem was since this was so unusual for us, it only resulted in utterly dumbfounding CC. He stared at us in blinking confusion through nearly the whole meal. "Is something wrong?" he asked at last. "Everyone is awfully quiet. Did something happen outside?"

"No," we responded in perfect unison.

"Thanks for lunch, CC," Allie said as we finished, quickly clearing the table to go back outside. Everyone followed Allie's lead in a chorus of thank-yous and polite nods towards CC.

"Who are you and what have you done with my children?" CC said.

When we got back outside, Breezy pointed out CC's obvious state of astonishment at our behavior.

"Well at least we didn't fight," Justin said.

"Perfect," Allie said. "So all we have to do is eat every meal together like monks who have taken a vow of silence."

All of a sudden a small bird swooped in front of us and to our horror, whammed into the kitchen window. For a brief second, the little bird hung in the air, stunned from the blow, then plunged to the ground, lying motionless.

We hurried over and crowded around the bird. Allie pushed her way to the front and scooped the bird's tiny body up in her hands, cradling him to her chest.

Breezy walked up to Allie with her hands clutched to her heart, looking solemnly at the little creature in Allie's arms. She petted the top of the bird's head. "Poor little guy. Is he dead?" she asked tearfully.

Allie looked at the bird and shook her head. "No, I think he's alive." She held the bird gently, caressing his feathers. "It's okay, little one," Allie cooed. "You're going to be okay. I'll make sure of it." She kept stroking the bird and cupped him close, as the yellow light glowed over the bird's little body. We moved in around Allie to watch, and I was close enough to feel the warmth on my face as the beam grew in brilliance. The bird looked up and fluttered his wings, suddenly unsure where he was, appearing startled. "There you go, little guy," Allie whispered to the bird. "You fly off now. And be careful of windows." The bird flapped his wings more vigorously. Allie held her hands open and lifted him to the sky, giving the creature a little toss into the air. The bird caught the idea, lifted his wings, and took to the air soaring. We stood silently with our heads raised upwards as the bird flew farther and farther into the sky, until he became just a speck. Allie smiled into the sky with pure joy, her light-toned freckles becoming fully manifest, shimmering like little drops of sunlight.

"Very impressive, Allie," said a cold, icy tone behind us.

I knew at once that voice didn't come from my siblings. I whipped around towards the fence at the same speed as Allie, who looked jolted from being suddenly ripped from her blissful moment. There he stood, slowly tapping his fingers against the fence, staring at us. "Hi," Big Boss greeted mawkishly.

"Oh good, you're back!" Allie returned in a sugary tone. "We were worried you were gone for good."

Big Boss ignored Allie's comment and its sentiment. "That was a pretty neat trick you did there with the little birdie, Allie. Thought that bird was a goner for sure."

Allie scowled. "Where have you been anyway? Hiding out somewhere doing intel on us?"

Big Boss turned to the rest of us. "So what other kinds of things can you brats do with those special powers of yours?"

"How did you know about that, anyway?" Ryan frowned.

Big Boss smiled wide like the cat who ate the canary. "Oh, that's my little secret."

"What does that mean?" Kevin demanded.

Big Boss smiled ominously. A cold chill ran through me. Breezy picked up on my fear and secured my hand in a protective grasp.

"Okay, goodbye," Becky said, retreating to the house and away from Big Boss as fast as she could. Kitty and Carlie quietly followed her.

"What other kinds of abilities do you have?" Big Boss asked again. "Besides making objects appear from thin air and bringing animals back from near death."

"How dumb do you think we are?" Twisty said. "We're not telling you anything."

"Well then show me. Now's your chance to show off those powers. How often do you get to do that? I'm betting no one else outside your little family knows about them, do they?" Big Boss sneered.

"Oh, well if it's a chance to show off, why didn't you say so?" Allie said. "We won't *tell* you anything, but *showing* you is a whole other story. Of course, that's okay. Why don't you come over and we'll give you a personal demonstration? Then we can fill you in on all the details of our lives you somehow still missed. We'll go around in a circle and read entries out loud from our private journals, and you can collect notes about us you don't yet have in your own personal records."

Big Boss set dead eyes on Allie. "Hey Allie, you brazen little brat. Did you ever try nixing that cocky little attitude of yours and just say what you really think?"

Allie stared back at Big Boss with a severe expression. "I don't think you want me to say what I really think, Big Boss, because you wouldn't like what I have to say," she stated starkly. "And if you call me or any of us a brat one more time, we'll give you a *real* demonstration of our powers. And I promise you,

you'll regret asking for one."

Big Boss laughed contemptuously. "Are you threatening me, Allie? Well, what do you know! She's not only got a smart little mouth on her but the guts to match. Okay Allie, if you insist, go ahead and show me what you got."

Justin stepped out in front of Big Boss. "Hold on, this is going too far. We don't want any trouble," he said with a tight voice. "There's no reason for anyone to attack anybody here."

"Attack?" Big Boss questioned. "I wasn't attacking anybody, nor did I have any intention to. I was simply curious about your powers, that's all. The only one here trying to escalate this into a fight is Allie."

"No one is falling for your innocent act!" Allie shouted at Big Boss. "You're spying on us, refusing to say how you know so much about us, insulting us..." Allie hammered off. "You lied to our father when you met him. Oh, and really nice too saying you couldn't have hurt Becky that badly because there was no mark left on her wrist when *clearly* you knew about the magic, so you knew very well her arm was healed. Yeah, don't think we missed that one."

Big Boss lifted his eyebrows, appearing impressed.

"One of the first things you do after meeting us is hurt Becky," Allie continued, "and then you say you have no intention to attack us? And *I'm* the one escalating this into a fight? You have done nothing but work to escalate this as much as possible since the moment you met us. This isn't harmless curiosity. This is intimidation. We have shown nothing but the utmost restraint by not using our powers against you yet to defend ourselves. But I think I speak for everyone when I say we are losing our patience. There. How's that for saying how I really think?" Allie delivered.

"Boom!" Chase roared, pointing at Big Boss. "I think you

just got served. And Allie just dropped the mic!"

Big Boss's expression turned downright hateful. "That was quite a rousing speech, Allie. Would you like to come accept your award? I can see you're the brains in this group. Of course, that's not saying much for a pack of foolish little children."

"What's wrong with you, Big Boss?" Allie shouted. "What's in you that's so demented you pick on a bunch of kids? I mean really, do you even hear yourself?"

"A bunch of kids with some *very* powerful abilities," Big Boss stressed. "Quite frankly, I'm a little concerned about the safety of this community with a gang of reckless children possessing such dangerous power. That's why I want to know what you're capable of and how much damage you can cause."

Ashley peered over her glasses at Big Boss. "Oh, please," she scoffed. "Do you expect us to believe you care one iota about anyone in this community? We've managed to live here for years without anyone being none the wiser about our powers. We've never hurt anyone and we never would. We don't need you to come along and start policing us, thank you very much."

"So *you* say," Big Boss responded. "Something tells me the residents of this neighborhood might feel differently if they knew how serious a threat you posed. For instance, how do we know you won't decide on a whim to make half the people in the neighborhood disappear? What's going to stop you?"

"That's impossible," Kevin said. "We can't make anyone disappear. Plus anyway, we can't use a power on more than one person at a time and once you use a power you can't use another one again for…"

Allie scrambled to Kevin and clasped her hand tightly over his mouth, cutting him off mid-sentence. "What are you *doing*?" she said in a harsh, urgent whisper. "Don't tell him *anything*!"

Kevin blushed deeply, turning a shade of pink against his light tan skin, as he realized what he did. Big Boss gave us a smug grin at Kevin's inadvertent disclosure of some of the limitations of our powers. It dawned on me Big Boss just tricked us into revealing information about our powers. I suppressed a shiver as I became more fully aware of how cunning and manipulative Big Boss is.

"So, Kevin," Big Boss gloated. "What were you saying? About how long does it take before you can use a power again?"

"Wait," Ryan said in staggered bewilderment. "How do you know his name is..."

"I'm-I'm sorry," Kevin mumbled to us. "I didn't…I didn't mean to, I mean, I didn't think…"

"It's okay, you didn't do it on purpose," Allie said to him gently. "He tricked you," she revealed, looking at Big Boss accusingly.

Big Boss spoke in a tone so polished and smooth it made my skin crawl. "So I'm going to go ahead and guess what Kevin was going to say was there's a waiting period between using those powers. Right? Which means once a power is used for some purpose, let's say, healing an animal," he stated, looking straight at Allie, "you can't use another power again for a while. And with doing something as powerful as healing a mortal wound, we're not talking a period of just a few minutes here either, are we?" He strummed his fingers against the fence in a rhythmic manner that was so discomposing I felt I'd become unhinged. For some reason, the image came to my head of a ticking clock relentlessly counting down to our impending doom. "How close am I so far?" he asked, slightly leaning towards us. "Am I in the ballpark?" We could only stare back at him, momentarily numb. "Judging from your faces I'd say I'm right on the money."

Allie suddenly turned her head towards me and gave me a weak smile, but there was a desperation in her eyes I couldn't miss. She was trying to send a one-word message that was unmistakable: Help. At first, I was puzzled, but then I recognized why. Allie used all her power to save that bird, so she was unable to defend herself right now. Which was exactly what Big Boss had already realized. Allie was afraid Big Boss would take advantage of her temporary vulnerability.

Big Boss bore his eyes down on Allie. "So, Allie, what was that you said to me before? About how I'll get a demonstration of your powers if I call anyone a brat one more time? And that I'll regret asking for one?" Allie's eyes grew big. Big Boss leaned forward like a predator preparing to pounce on his prey. "You still want to stick by those words, Alll-ieee?" he taunted, drawing out Allie's name in a scathing tone. "You still going to give me a demonstration? Huh, Allie?"

Allie backed away from the fence and scanned her eyes frantically among us, looking for assistance. Big Boss advanced aggressively, moving as close to the fence as he could, gripping it tight. "You still planning on following through with that threat, Allie, you audacious, precocious, insolent little brat," he snarled, firing each word like an assault weapon.

That was when Breezy broke ahold of my hand and stepped boldly forward in front of Allie to face Big Boss. "Allie just saved that bird's life, so she can't do this right now, but I can," she declared. Breezy held out her hand palm straight out as if she was giving a stop signal. All at once, the yellow light radiated from her hand, and a ray shot out like a laser beam through each finger. The five points merged as one great big wall of light, where it became so blindingly bright we had to cover our eyes, right before it quickly flickered and dimmed out. In its place stood a long, tall, gelatinous wall, higher than the fence, fully transparent, but completely impenetrable.

Breezy walked up next to the wall and looked straight through at Big Boss on the other side. Her soft and airy voice took on a commanding yet still somehow calm tone I had rarely heard before. “This, Big Boss, is a shield. It serves as protection so you can’t hurt us and we can’t hurt you. Nothing will get through it and nothing will break it. It will last about an hour. Now here’s what’s going to happen now. We’re going to go in our house and you’ll go in yours. You’re not going to talk to us anymore and you’ll leave Allie and the rest of us alone. If you continue to try to intimidate us, harass us, or threaten us in any way, there will be consequences. Do you understand?”

Big Boss stood listening to Breezy and nodded at her like one would when meeting a worthy adversary. “Sure, Breezy,” he crooned. “But for the record, I wasn’t going to hurt Allie or any of you. I certainly hope you weren’t thinking of hurting me. This shield isn’t necessary. The fence alone sufficed. However, if you feel it’s needed, suit yourself. I’m going in my house. Have a good day.

Big Boss smiled stiffly and walked away. We stood watching safely behind the protective barrier, almost glowing in tune with the warm, benevolent, viscous membrane, which at that moment sheltered us all.

Chapter 10

That evening, I sat in our living room watching TV with Breezy and Hazy. For once it was free. Usually one of my siblings monopolized it or CC was engrossed in one of his serial dramas or social documentaries. Our living room was wide, open, and had lots of natural lighting from the big picture window on the main wall. The long sectional couch in the middle of the room was everyone's favorite place to sit, which was surrounded by cushioned armchairs. CC tried to design every room to be calm and relaxing with lots of earth tones. I was trying my best to sit and rest contently, but the events from earlier still troubled me.

Breezy gave me a concerned look. "Are you okay, Cap? You seem a little anxious." That was the one problem with Breezy. Hiding your feelings from her wasn't an option.

"Oh, no, I'm fine," I said, trying my best to sound convincing.

Breezy did one of her quick silent exchanges with Hazy.

"Are you sure, Capricorn?" Hazy asked. "You do seem a little lost in thought." I smiled at Hazy's stuffy pronunciation.

"Are you thinking about what happened today? With Big

Boss?" Breezy questioned. So much for my fake act.

"I just can't stop thinking about what would have happened if you didn't put up that shield," I finally admitted.

"I don't know, but I wasn't going to wait to find out," Breezy said. "I wanted to make sure nobody got hurt. I was afraid Big Boss would retaliate if someone attacked him."

The sweet-salty aroma of freshly-popped popcorn drifted into the air. Allie bounced into the room, holding a big wooden bowl filled to the brim with popcorn, and waltzed over to the couch, plopping down next to Breezy.

"What are we watching?" she asked, munching.

"Um, I think it's some kind of cop show," Breezy said.

Allie made a face. "Ew. No. Sorry, but no. Where's the remote?" Allie flipped through the channels, finally settling on a rerun of a popular sitcom. "Let's watch this."

Now it was Breezy's turn to make a face. "This isn't much better, Allie."

"No, it's funny. Give it a chance," Allie insisted. "Here. Eat popcorn. Be happy," she said, holding out the bowl to Breezy.

We delved into the bowl and munched blissfully. I let the buttery kernels melt lightly on my tongue.

Allie tossed a kernel in her mouth. "So what were you guys talking about since you obviously weren't paying attention to the TV?"

Breezy raised her eyebrows. "What makes you think we weren't paying attention to the TV?"

Allie smiled slyly. "Come on, Breeze! When have you ever been interested in a cop show?" I swear between Allie's masterful observation skills and Breezy's psychic abilities, my sisters could've easily subbed for CIA agents.

Breezy laughed. "Well, I'm not the only one here, Allie."

Allie snorted. "Right, because we all know Hazy is a huge

fan of crime dramas and Cap just can't live without seeing a criminal chase-down at least once a day."

"We were talking about what happened today. With Big Boss," Breezy revealed.

"Oh yes, our oh-so-friendly next-door neighbor," Allie remarked with a slight eye roll. "By the way, that reminds me, I owe you one for today," Allie said to Breezy, tapping her arm. "Thanks for putting up that shield."

"Of course. But honestly, Allie, I found myself wanting to do *a lot more* than just put up the shield," Breezy admitted. "I had to stop myself from doing something much more serious."

Allie gaped at Breezy. "Breezy! *Breezy*! I can't believe *you* just said that!" She turned to me and Hazy with amazement. "Did you just hear that? Breezy has a dark side! Who would have guessed it?"

I was just as surprised to hear Breezy confess to any desire to use non-peaceful means of resolution. Like Allie, I always thought Breezy wasn't even capable of thinking that way.

"Can you believe it? Saint Breezy!" Allie exclaimed, pressing her palms together upward as if in prayer. "Sweet, angelic Breezy who is all about empathy, love, and compassion." Breezy swatted Allie with one of CC's tan squishy throw pillows. "Shalom. Om Mani Padme Hum," Allie chanted, closing her eyes and holding her hands out in a meditative posture.

Breezy tossed another pillow playfully at Allie. "But in all seriousness, Big Boss made me really angry. I didn't like the way he was talking to you at all, Allie."

Hazy frowned. "Me neither. He's a very mean man." She looked at Allie. "Are you going to tell CC what happened?"

"No," Allie answered flatly. "I'm sure he'd say this is my fault."

Becky, Twisty, and Chase walked into the living room and immediately spied the bowl of popcorn on Allie's lap, making a beeline towards it. Chase dipped his hand in the bowl and grabbed a fistful. Twisty and Becky also scooped servings greedily.

"Help yourselves. Really. Don't trouble yourselves with asking first," Allie jabbed.

Chase gave Allie a sheepish smile. "Hey, Allie, I meant to tell you. You absolutely *slayed* it today with that Big Boss guy! That whole speech you gave him was *fire*! And then, Breezy, when you threw up that shield-"

"You put up a shield?" Becky interrupted, looking at Breezy. "What happened after I went inside?"

"You should have stayed. It was awesome!" Chase proclaimed to Becky.

"Awesome is not the word I would use," Allie started to say, but Chase steamrolled ahead, explaining what happened with animated energy. He babbled breathlessly, speaking as if he was describing an exhilarating ride on a roller coaster.

"It was just *amazing*," Chase finished.

"Again, I don't think amazing is the word-" Allie tried a second time.

"Wow! You actually did that, Breezy?" Becky asked. "I don't believe it."

"Believe it. She did," Twisty confirmed, giving Breezy a rare look of respect. "It was pretty cool. Although if it was me, I would have shot him with a fireball or something to really shut him up."

"So why didn't you, then?" Chase challenged.

"Well I'm glad she didn't," Breezy cut in. She explained how badly it could have ended if Big Boss attacked in retaliation.

Twisty waved her hand dismissively. "If he tried anything, we'd just hit him again with another power. It would be no contest."

"Yeah," Chase agreed. "He wouldn't stand a chance against us."

"I wouldn't be so overconfident," Allie said quietly.

"Well, as a precaution, I'm going to keep putting up shields every time we see him," Breezy declared.

Twisty repeated, "We don't need shields."

"No," Breezy professed. "We are using the shields."

"Whatever. I still say we go on the offense and strike hard," Twisty said, grabbing fistfuls of popcorn and stuffing them in her mouth.

"Here, Twisty," Allie said, holding out the bowl to her. "Why don't you just take the whole bowl for yourself? And I'll go in the kitchen and make a whole second bowl of popcorn just for you."

Twisty scowled. "Keep your stupid popcorn," she grumbled, pushing the bowl back.

Allie shrugged and threw a kernel in her mouth. "Okay, if you insist. I'll eat my stupid popcorn with everyone else then." Allie held out the bowl towards the rest of us, one by one. "Hey Chase, would you like some more stupid popcorn? Want some stupid popcorn, Becky? Haze, do you like stupid popcorn? Breezy? Cap? Stupid popcorn? Or do you like intelligent popcorn better?"

Chase nearly choked on his popcorn laughing. Twisty looked daggers at Allie until she exploded in rage. "You think you're so smart, don't you Allie? You think you're just so funny! I'm getting tired of you and your stupid jokes! I should hit *you* with a fireball! It would be payback for earlier today."

"Earlier today?" Allie repeated. "Oh, you mean when you

were acting like a terrible person."

"I'll show you a terrible person!" Twisty shouted. She lunged towards Allie, but Breezy stood up, using herself as a barrier to block Twisty from going any further.

"Stop it," Breezy ordered. "Stop fighting. Don't make me put a shield between the two of you too. Twisty, don't even think about using magic against Allie! How could you? Just stop."

"I don't want to fight her," Allie stated. "I don't understand why you're getting so upset, Twisty. I said you were *acting* like a terrible person, not that you are one. And you were. What you tried to do to Ryan today wasn't cool. You're capable of being nicer, you just choose not to be."

"Oh, don't give me some high-and-mighty lecture like you're better than me, Allie," Twisty said. "You're not better than me."

"I never claimed to be," Allie returned. "What the heck, Twisty? Defensive much? You have a lot of issues to work out, you know that?"

Before Twisty could respond, Breezy put her arms out to separate the two of them. "Enough. Twisty, go take some time to cool off. If you keep fighting like this, I'm going to get CC."

Twisty put her hands up and backed off. "Don't get CC. I'm leaving. She's not worth getting in trouble over." She left the room.

Chase approached Allie and cupped his hand around his mouth in a stage whisper. "If you and Twisty fight, you could totally take her."

"Chase, don't encourage her," Breezy said.

"Okay," Chase laughed. "But don't worry about that Big Boss guy. We could take him down in no time flat," he said, walking away.

Breezy, Hazy, and Becky left.

“So do you think we really could take Big Boss down no time flat?” I asked Allie. “I bet you could do it all on your own,” I laughed.

Allie didn’t laugh back. She looked down at the floor, then looked up and gave me a wan smile. “I don’t like him, Cap. I don’t like him at all. I think Becky’s right. I think he’s dangerous.”

Chapter 11

A few nights later, during dinner, Ashley announced it might snow.

"I want it to stay warm so we can play outside," Carlie whined.

"Well if that Big Boss guy is out there again, I won't stay outside no matter how warm it is," Becky stated.

"Well if he is," Chase laughed, "we'll just have Allie slay him with one of her epic takedowns while Breezy throws out a shield just like before!"

Chase looked up just in time to see Allie wildly shaking her head and frantically waving her hands no in Chase's direction. Too late. CC was already staring intently at Chase with an inquisitive expression and a deep frown. The room grew silent as everyone realized what just happened. Allie brought her waving to a grinding halt and slapped her forehead down in her hand in resigned irritation.

"When was this?" CC demanded.

Chase realized what he had done and now looked like he wanted to sink into the floor. "Umm...it was...it was just the other day," he replied, clearly embarrassed.

"Big Boss was out there the other day?" CC questioned. "I thought he disappeared." He met our uncomfortable silence with a severe look. "And why am I just hearing about this now?"

Breezy spoke up and told CC the whole story. CC sat stunned for a moment, then spoke. "Why didn't you come and get me?" He turned to Becky, Carlie, and Kitty. "And you three, you didn't think when you came into the house to come and tell me what was happening outside?"

Becky, Carlie, and Kitty, who were preening like proud peacocks because they were sure they were off the hook, now looked away from CC and slumped guiltily in their chairs.

"Well, we...didn't want to bother you," Kitty mumbled.

CC made a face like he didn't buy that excuse and sighed heavily. He told us to ignore Big Boss when he's outside, and if he doesn't leave us alone, to come and get him no matter how busy he is. Breezy asked about using the shields, and CC told her it was smart to keep using them as a precaution. He warned us not to engage or antagonize Big Boss, looking directly at Allie.

Allie appeared incredibly irritated. "Why are you looking at *me*? CC, he started with me."

"Allie, you got smart with him, gave him attitude as you're fond of doing, which only antagonized him further," CC admonished.

Allie insisted she was only standing up to him. Everyone apologized except for Allie.

"I don't think we should let Big Boss intimidate us, but you obviously disagree!" Allie shouted at CC.

CC scolded her, and the argument escalated until Allie yelled, "You always blame me for everything!" She ran to her room in tears.

Chase looked like a puppy who got caught having an

accident on the rug. He hurriedly left the table. CC said he'd talk to Allie and suggested we give her some time to calm down.

I waited a few hours, then went to talk to Allie. I stood in front of our bedroom door, deciding whether to knock or enter. There were 5 bedrooms in our house, and no one except CC had their own room. Breezy, Hazy, Allie, and I, the Four Musketeers, shared a bedroom. There were two sets of bunk beds in our room. Breezy and Hazy had one set, and Allie and I had the other. The other group of four sharing a room with bunk beds were Ryan, Kevin, Chase, and Justin. Twisty, Carlie, and Becky had the third room, and Ashley and Kitty had the fourth. The fifth bedroom belonged to CC.

I finally came to a decision and rapped lightly on the door. Allie greeted me with a small smile.

"Hi, Allie," I murmured. "Can I come in?"

"Of course. It's your room too," Allie replied.

I walked in and glanced around the room awkwardly. Some board games, puzzles, and craft supplies were strewn all over the blue fluffy carpet. A laundry basket filled with clothes overflowed onto the floor. The corner bookshelf had chapter books and stuffed animals smushed together like marshmallows in a bag. I suddenly felt a little out of place. I was not used to Allie displaying raw emotion and was uncertain how to broach the subject with her.

"Um, how are you doing, Allie?" I mumbled.

"Fine," she answered. She tossed some cards into a game box.

"Do you want some help?" I asked.

"No, I got it," she responded.

"Are you sure?" I was clearly stalling and I was positive Allie knew it.

"Yep."

I looked down at the ground, feeling very uncomfortable. "So, you're okay then?"

Allie dropped puzzle pieces into a box with a flourish and looked up at me. "Cap?" she said with a twinge of a smile. "If you want to ask me about dinner, just go ahead and ask."

Now I really felt dumb, but I also had to somewhat appreciate Allie's forthrightness. "Okay, fine. What happened there? You were really upset."

Allie looked up at the ceiling and sighed deeply. "I'm just tired of CC blaming me every time something goes wrong."

"I understand. But we all got the blame for not telling him about what happened."

Allie spotted some stray playing pieces and threw them in the box with force, creating a jiggling sound. "So, are you all grounded for a week then too?" She looked up at my surprised face and let out a bitter laugh. "No, of course you're not."

"He grounded you for a week? That's not fair. He shouldn't have singled you out."

Allie said CC told her she was grounded because of her disrespectful behavior. Allie apologized to CC for being disrespectful, and CC apologized for upsetting her. CC told her she had to try to ignore Big Boss, but she couldn't agree. "I'm not going to stand there and do nothing while he intimidates us."

There was a low knock on the bedroom door. Allie answered it and found Hazy and Breezy standing in the hallway.

"Hi, Allie," Breezy said softly. "Um, can we come in?"

"Why is everyone asking me for permission to come into their own room? Nope. You can't. New policy: I'm now charging admission to enter your room. That will be five dollars, please," Allie teased, holding out her palm.

Hazy reached into her pocket and pulled out a five-dollar

bill, placing it in Allie's hand. Allie looked at it in half-amazement and immediately handed it back to Hazy. "No, no," she said, shaking her head. "Put this away. You think I would make you pay to come into your room? But wow, Haze, next time I need someone to spot me five bucks, I know who to come to."

Breezy and Hazy walked into the room. Hazy asked Allie if CC talked to her.

"Yeah, he said I'm grounded for a week," Allie said.

"He grounded you for a week?" Breezy and Hazy both cried in unison.

Allie laughed and turned to me with a big grin. "I love it when they speak in stereo."

"Allie, no. That isn't fair. Let me talk to CC for you. Putting up that shield was a very risky move. I should be equally punished," Breezy reasoned.

"No, it's okay, don't do that. He said I was grounded because I was disrespectful anyway," Allie said.

We heard a small knock and Chase stood in the doorway. "Hi," Chase said. He looked at Allie then quickly at his feet. "Allie, I um...I know you probably hate me right now..."

Allie shook her head and gave Chase a reassuring smile.

"I uh...I just wanted to tell you I'm sorry," Chase continued. "I wasn't thinking when I....said that stuff. I forgot about CC. I'm so stupid. I'm really sorry, Allie."

"It's okay, Chase, I know you didn't do it on purpose," Allie replied. "And you're not stupid. Don't say that about yourself."

Chase's face immediately brightened. "Really? So you forgive me?"

"Yes, of course, but Chase? The next time you're talking, and you see someone wildly waving their hands no back and forth like this," Allie said, flapping her hands in front of Chase's face in demonstration, "take the hint. Okay?"

"Okay, got it," Chase laughed. He asked if we all got in trouble with CC, and Allie told him she was grounded, but no one else.

"So nobody got in trouble for not telling CC about what happened with Big Boss before I opened my dumb mouth? That doesn't seem fair. Okay, I'll fix it. I'm going to make it up to you," Chase said to Allie, walking away.

"Chase, wait! What do you mean you'll fix it? How?" Allie called down the hallway.

Little did I realize then the chain reaction Chase was about to set in motion.

Chapter 12

As the four of us got up the next morning, Ryan knocked on our open door with an announcement. "Chase told CC to ground everybody," Ryan revealed. "We're all grounded. And it was because of you, Allie."

Breezy nodded. "Okay, so last night when Chase left our room, saying he'd fix it, he went to see CC."

"To see CC? And then he went to DDD?" Allie quipped.

Ryan snorted and Breezy laughed. "He probably told CC it wasn't fair to ground Allie and no one else," Breezy said.

"Is Chase in your room right now?" Allie asked Ryan.

"Yeah, he was getting up, but he may have fallen back asleep," Ryan answered.

Allie suddenly shouted out to Chase next door, making me jump. "Chase? Chase!"

Ryan rubbed his ear. "How about a word of warning before you do that?"

Allie smiled apologetically. "Sorry."

"Yeah?" Chase's groggy voice called back through the wall.

"Come here!" Allie yelled.

Chase appeared at the doorway in his red flannel turtle

pajamas, rubbing his eyes. "What?"

"Did you talk to CC last night?" Breezy asked.

"Oh," Chase yawned. "Yeah, I did." He rubbed his head, trying to wake himself up. "I told him he should ground us *all* for keeping what happened with Big Boss from him."

"See?" Ryan said. "Can you believe him? Why on earth would you tell him to do that, Chase?"

"I thought we should all be punished. It's only fair," Chase answered.

"Chase, you give new meaning to the phrase 'glutton for punishment,'" Allie laughed.

"I know," Ryan agreed. "Why would you ask to be punished? Who does that?"

"I wanted to make it fair!" Chase repeated. "I'm kind of responsible for getting Allie in trouble, so I should be equally punished."

"Well, then you should have asked CC to punish *you*. Why did you have to drag the rest of us down with you?" Ryan whined.

"Because we all did it!" Chase cried. "CC agreed with me."

"So there you go," Ryan said, throwing up his hands. "And now we're all grounded because Chase actually asked for us all to be. Nice going, Chase!"

"How long is everyone grounded for?" Hazy asked.

"A week," Chase replied.

Allie suddenly realized she's going to be grounded for two weeks instead of one because of the additional punishment.

"Well, at least everyone is grounded now, not just you," Chase said.

Allie broke into laughter. "So now I'm grounded twice! Thanks for fixing it, Chase! You really made it up to me!"

"Aren't you mad?" Ryan asked Allie. "He just got you punished *even longer*."

Allie laughed so hard she could barely get her words out. "Don't worry, I'll help you out! Now you have two weeks instead of one. You're welcome!"

"Um, I just wanted to make it fair. I was trying to help," Chase mumbled.

"Oh, I know, and that's what makes it so *perfect*!" Allie giggled. "Thanks, Chase. You've helped me enough. I'm good!" She turned to Hazy. "Hey, Haze! He fixed it!" They exploded with heavy laughter.

A short while later we were gathered together around the breakfast table when CC made his announcement. He explained it was unacceptable to keep important things from him, and after speaking with Chase, who had similar concerns, he decided to ground everyone for a week with no screen time.

Across the table, my siblings erupted into howls of protest.

"But CC!" Twisty cried. "I thought we were going to the movies on Friday!"

CC said the movie will have to wait, and Twisty whined she'd been waiting to see it for months and it ends this week. Twisty cast her eyes towards Chase and shot him a death glare I couldn't miss.

Later on, the four of us Musketeers were playing a game on the floor of our bedroom. There was a knock on the door and I opened it. Chase stood there, his appearance very different from this morning. His cheeks were red and his lip had a slight tremble. It looked like he had been crying. His left eye was swollen and there was a dark bruise forming under his lower eyelid. I gasped.

"Hey, Capricorn," he said in a shaky tone. "Can I talk to Allie?"

I nodded. Allie saw Chase and her face froze.

"Hi, Allie," Chase quivered. "I just wanted to say again

how sorry I am about all this. I really screwed up. Stupid me. I got everyone grounded, and now everyone hates me."

Allie stared at Chase's face. "Chase, what happened to your eye?"

Chase shifted, covering the blemish. "Oh, it's nothing."

"What do you mean nothing? Chase, it looks like you got a black eye. Did someone hurt you?" Allie asked.

"Well, it's just…people are really angry I got them all grounded," Chase answered.

"Chase, how did you get that black eye?" Allie asked again, more insistently.

Chase looked down at his feet. "It was Twisty. She's really mad. Furious actually. It's not like I didn't deserve it."

"Twisty hit you?" Allie shouted.

"Uh, yeah, but it's okay. I can heal it. I'm just waiting for my power to recharge. No big deal," Chase said.

"Chase, it's not okay for Twisty to hit you. It's never okay for anyone to hit you," Breezy stressed.

"Where's Twisty right now?" Allie demanded

"I-I think she's in her room," Chase answered.

Allie went off like a rocket, out the door, and down the hall. The rest of us hurried after her. Breezy called for Allie to wait, but Allie was already heading into Twisty, Carlie, and Becky's room. Allie barged in and found Twisty standing with her back towards the door, talking animatedly to Carlie and Becky. Allie, in a state of fury, stormed towards Twisty, and shoved her hard in the back, sending her flying forward, arms flailing, painfully into the side of the bed.

Twisty wheeled on Allie, her face contorted in rage. "What do you think you're doing, Allie?"

Allie's eyes burned into Twisty's with sheer ire. "What do you think *you're* doing!" she shouted back. "You hit Chase? You hit Chase! What's wrong with you?"

Twisty glanced at Chase, who was frozen in shock at the back of the room, where Breezy, Hazy, and I had also become temporarily glued. Becky and Carlie appeared as stunned as the rest of us. "He got us all grounded!" Twisty shouted. "He deserved it! If you were smart, you'd be just as angry. But instead, you rush to his defense. Figures!"

"Oh, boo-hoo you got grounded!" Allie yelled. "So what? Suck it up and take some responsibility for what you did like the rest of us! You don't get to hit Chase just because you're mad you're missing your stupid movie, you selfish, mean, nasty little--"

"You're going to call *me* names?" Twisty screamed. "That's rich! You, Allie, are the queen of nastiness. Always going around with your snide little comments. Look! You just came in here and pushed me!"

All the screaming had attracted a crowd. We all stood and intensively watched the fight between Twisty and Allie.

Allie clenched her fists at her sides and fired back at Twisty. "I pushed you because you hit Chase! Look at Chase's eye! You gave him a black eye! How is that okay?"

"It's not okay for you to push Twisty either, Allie," Carlie interjected, walking between them.

"Stay out of this, Carlie," Allie warned, staring at our tiniest sister. "This has nothing to do with you."

"It does if you're going to go after Twisty," Carlie challenged.

"I'm not going after her. She's the one who goes after people!" Allie cried with heated fervor. "I'm getting really sick of you bullying our brothers and sisters, Twisty! First, it was Kit-Cat, then Ryan, now Chase? I mean, seriously, what's your problem?"

"Why do you always need to jump in and fight their battles for them?" Twisty seethed. "Why don't you let them defend themselves?"

"Why don't you stop acting like a mean-spirited, awful, nasty, little twit?" Allie slammed.

Twisty boiled with hot rage, her eyes wild. She gritted her teeth and spoke in a threatening snarl. "What did you just call me?"

Allie looked directly into Twisty's eyes and repeated the insult, enunciating each word. "I said you are a mean-spirited, awful, nasty, little twit."

Twisty hurled herself at Allie, and grabbed her by the ears, pulling on them viciously. Allie squealed and flung her fists at Twisty to attempt to make her let go. Twisty released Allie's ears and tried to hit her, but Allie drew back, and the back of Twisty's hand caught Allie's cheek, scratching her. Allie cried out and punched Twisty's nose. Twisty shrieked, holding her nose, and seized on Allie's hair, pulling it forcefully. Allie screamed and grabbed Twisty by the back of her hair braid, yanking it just as fiercely. The two stood screaming, pulling on each other's hair, trying to kick and claw each other.

The rest of us were watching this in open-mouthed amazement, too stupefied to intercede. CC rushed into the room, with Breezy and Hazy behind him. In all the chaos, I didn't even notice Breezy and Hazy had left. Of course, that made sense. If they had been present one of them would have stopped this altercation before it became physical. They must have foreseen how ugly this would get and went to find CC in his office.

"What's going on in here?" CC roared. He marched straight to Allie and Twisty and pulled them apart. "Break it up! Break it up right now!"

They both stood panting and glaring at each other.

"What are you two doing?" CC yelled. "What's going on? Why are you fighting?"

Twisty instantly tried to play the innocent victim, giving CC a pitiful look, her brown eyes filled with tears. "Allie came in here and pushed me into the bed. She called me names and punched my nose! I think my nose is broken!"

Allie snorted. "That's a nice version of the truth, Twisty. Of course, you left out everything *you* did. Like scratching me and pulling my ears and hair!"

"Enough!" CC shouted. "I want to know who started this fight. And remember your sisters and brothers were here to witness this, so don't even try to lie."

"Twisty attacked me first," Allie said. "We were arguing, then she grabbed my ears and pulled them. She scratched me, and I punched her. Then she pulled my hair, so I pulled hers back."

"Is that true?" CC demanded of Twisty.

Twisty faltered. "Yes, but, but I got mad because she called me a nasty little twit. Plus, she came in here and shoved me from behind into the bed!"

CC turned back to Allie. "Did you push her?"

Allie nodded. "Yes, I did, and I called her a nasty little twit too. I'm sorry. But CC, the reason I did was because she hit Chase!"

CC widened his eyes in surprise and wheeled back on Twisty. "You hit your brother?" he thundered.

Twisty didn't say anything and looked down at the floor guiltily. Slowly, she nodded her head.

"You hit Chase?" CC repeated. CC looked up and found Chase in the room. "Come here, Chase," he said, beckoning with his finger.

Chase walked over to CC a little apprehensively. CC took Chase's face in his hand and got a good look at his eye. "Did she punch you in the face?" CC asked. Chase nodded solemnly.

CC turned on Twisty, his voice filled with anger. "Take a good look at your brother! Look what you did to his eye! Why did you punch him, Twisty? Because you were mad about being grounded?"

Twisty continued staring at the ground, unable to speak.

"Answer me!" CC demanded.

Twisty nodded again, on the verge of tears.

"You owe your brother an apology. A big one," CC asserted.

Twisty looked up at Chase tearfully. "I-I'm sorry, Chase. I'm sorry I hit you. I shouldn't have done that."

"No, you absolutely shouldn't have," CC said. He moved to Chase again. "Are you able to heal yourself?"

"Um, no, I can't right now. I have to recharge," Chase admitted, with a shamefaced expression.

CC stared at Chase. "I'm not even going to ask why you don't have enough energy left. Let's just get that fixed." He addressed Twisty. "How about you? You have enough power to heal?"

Twisty nodded. CC directed her to heal Chase's eye.

Twisty approached Chase, shaking nervously, and placed her hand under his eye. The beam of light surrounded her hand, and within seconds Chase's eye was good as new. "Thanks," Chase said to Twisty. Twisty looked down.

"You don't have to thank her," CC said to Chase. He looked at Twisty. "Now, you're going to make it up to your brother for hurting him. You're going to do his chores for him for the next two weeks."

Chase beamed brightly. I wondered if in Chase's mind it

was worth getting hit to not do dishes.

"Two weeks!" Twisty cried. "I'm not doing his chores for two whole weeks!"

"Excuse me?" CC said. "Would you rather I make it three?"

"No," Twisty replied gloomily. "Two weeks is fine."

"Yes, it is," CC said. "And you, Allie, do not take it upon yourself to come in here and confront Twisty over hitting Chase. You should have let me handle it. And pushing Twisty, Allie? That was definitely not the way to handle it. You could have really hurt her. What were you thinking?"

"I *wasn't* really thinking," Allie replied honestly. "I was really angry she punched Chase. Plus, she's been bullying everybody lately, and I'm just tired of that too."

"What do you mean she's been bullying everyone? Bullying how?" CC asked.

From behind CC, Twisty glared at Allie with sheer scorn. "She's been calling people names, making them feel bad, trying to threaten them into doing her chores," Allie revealed.

"Is this true?" CC asked Twisty. "Have you been bullying your brothers and sisters?"

Twisty looked at CC imploringly. "No! I was just messing around. I didn't mean anything by it!"

"Maybe you should ask Kit-Cat and Ryan and everybody else you picked on if *they* thought you meant anything by it," Allie replied.

"Maybe *I* should ask the people *you* always pick on if they think *you* mean anything by it!" Twisty fired back. "You're so quick to defend all your friends, Allie, all the people in your little crew, Ryan and Kitty and Chase and especially those 3 over there you're practically chained to (of course she pointed to me, Breezy, and Hazy). No one dare go after them or they'll feel your wrath, but go outside your little circle, Allie, and then you're not so nice. Just ask Carlie or Becky what they think of you!"

An introspective look flashed briefly on Allie's face, then it was gone. "You know what? You do the exact same thing. Also, I never punched anyone."

Twisty let out a spiteful laugh. "You just punched me in the nose! You're going to stand there and say you never punched anyone?"

"I punched you because you attacked me first! That's not the same thing. I never hit anybody unprovoked," Allie defended.

"Unprovoked?" Twisty shouted. "You pushed me!"

"Because you punched Chase!" Allie cried. "What part about that aren't you getting, you twit?"

CC caught Twisty mid-leap before she lunged at Allie again. "Hey!" he shouted. "That's enough of this!" He handed Allie a severe look. "Allie, you just apologized for calling her that name, and you just did it again! Right in front of me, Allie? Really?"

Allie shrank back. "I-I'm sorry. It's just...she makes me so mad," she explained weakly.

"Nowhere near as angry as you make me," Twisty muttered under her breath.

"I said that's enough!" CC shouted. "This fighting ends this instant! Until further notice, you both need to stay away from each other. You're not to be in the same room together. Is that clear?"

"That won't be a problem," Twisty said. "I don't want to be anywhere near her."

"The feeling's mutual," Allie said in a droll tone.

"And you're not speaking to each other either," CC ordered. "I need to think about appropriate punishment for the two of you because this fighting is absolutely unacceptable. You'll both be grounded for a while."

Allied nodded resignedly, but a woeful expression took over Twisty's face. "Grounded?" Twisty cried. "I already have to do Chase's chores for two weeks! Why am I grounded too?"

"Are you really asking me that, Twisty?" CC railed. "You don't want to argue with me about this. You punched your brother and got into a fight with your sister. Hurting your siblings is a serious offense and there are serious consequences."

Twisty looked up at CC pleadingly. "I'm sorry," she choked out.

"Yes, I hope you are. But sorry doesn't cut it, Twisty. Not for this," CC stated. As he left the room, he asked the rest of us to keep an eye on them and let him know if there's any more trouble.

Twisty stood, a mixture of depression and fury swimming through her, tears brimming from her eyes. Slowly, shaking with anger, she lifted her head and fixed her sight on Allie with deadly precision, like an archer with a drawn bow. She bore her eyes into Allie, burning with venomous rage, her hands clenched into iron-tight vises. "I hate you, Allie," she spat.

Chapter 13

"Repeat after me," Allie directed Chase, once we were back in our room. "I am not stupid. I don't deserve to get hurt. It's not okay for anyone to hurt me."

Chase laughed, but Allie stared solemnly back at him and shook her head. "I'm completely serious. Repeat after me."

Chase seemed momentarily embarrassed, then repeated Allie's words in a monotone voice.

"Okay. Now say that again like you believe it," Allie pressed.

Chase repeated the words with more gusto.

"Good. Now remember that, because it's true," Allie said. "And don't let anyone push you around or say otherwise. Promise?"

Chase smiled. "Okay, I promise."

"And if Twisty ever hits you again, hit her right back," Allie added.

"Allie, that's terrible advice," Breezy admonished.

Allie smiled slyly at Chase and they both laughed.

After our week of punishment was over, we were ready to burst with the worst case of cabin fever. I felt a pang of guilt for

Allie, still confined to our room for two more weeks, as I dashed out the house, embracing the fresh air. I happily ran to meet my siblings (sans Allie and Twisty) in the yard, aware of the biting sting now carried in the cool breeze.

We started playing Hide and Seek, but as I rounded the corner, I stopped short. Big Boss stood at the fence. He stared at us with a deep intensity in his eyes, like we were a secret code to crack. I quickly found Breezy and pulled her to the side, motioning with my eyes towards Big Boss. "What should we do?" I whispered.

Breezy looked at Big Boss and frowned. The others spotted Big Boss and quickly moved towards Breezy and me. We huddled together in a group and spoke in hushed tones.

"Should we get CC?" Chase asked.

"He hasn't said anything to us," Ryan replied. "CC said to ignore him."

We decided to put up a shield, and Breezy turned towards the fence, throwing her hand forward to create the jellied force field. Big Boss lingered there a minute, then turned on his heel and left the yard.

The next day we were back outside and Big Boss was at the fence again. Breezy put up another shield, and Big Boss left without speaking a word. This pattern continued daily for the whole week. By the weekend, Breezy automatically put up a shield when we got outside.

By the following week, we had gotten used to the pattern. We were throwing a ball around the yard when I noticed Big Boss still there from behind the shield. This was a little disquieting, but I shook it off and ignored him, as we started a game of Monkey in the Middle. I threw the ball to Kitty, and everyone else scrambled to catch it as she threw it back to me. As everyone charged towards me, I made a fake-out throw, then barreled the ball back to Kitty. Kitty caught it, laughing at my deceptive move. Carlie wailed I tricked them and she wasn't going to play anymore.

"I wish Twisty was here. Then we could play our own game!" Carlie cried.

"Well good luck playing Monkey in the Middle with only two people," Ryan laughed.

"Yeah, I think that's called catch," Kevin said.

"Well other people can play too, as long as they play by the right rules," Carlie insisted.

"Well you're going to be waiting a while to play that game, Carlie, because Twisty's been grounded for a month," Kevin hooted.

A voice cut in amongst the arguing. "So where's Allie?"

It took me a minute to realize Big Boss was the one who asked the question. We turned towards him in surprise.

"Um, what?" Ryan finally muttered.

Where's Allie?" Big Boss repeated. "I haven't seen her out here lately and I definitely haven't heard her spouting her cocky little mouth off."

"None of your business where she is," Ashley snapped. "You're not supposed to talk to us."

Big Boss pointed to Kevin. "So you said Twisty's been grounded for a month?" He whistled. "Wow, that's rough. Is Allie grounded too? Is that why she's not here?"

"Allie got Twisty in trouble. That's why Twisty's grounded," Carlie blurted out.

All at once, we jumped on Carlie, shouting the same words at her. "Don't talk to him!"

Big Boss looked at Carlie. "What happened, Carlie? Did they get in a fight or something?"

"Don't answer him, Carlie," Breezy directed. She

approached the shield and looked Big Boss in the eye. "Big Boss, I'm giving you a warning. You were told not to talk to us several times. If you try to talk to us again, I'm getting our father."

Big Boss smiled smugly. "I'm just making friendly conversation, Breezy. I thought we could bury the hatchet, but I can see you're not interested in that. I don't know what you're so afraid of. You've already got this shield up, isn't that enough? If you really don't want me to speak to you, fine. Just one thing I want to say before I go." His eyes searched our yard and fell on Becky. "Becky, is it? I wanted to apologize for hurting you. Your father's right, I had no right to do that. I'm frankly ashamed of myself for hurting a child. So I'm sorry. Anyway, that's all." He walked away from the shielded fence.

I waited till I was sure he was back in his house before I announced I didn't believe him.

"I don't either," Breezy said. "He's not sincere." I knew Breezy well enough to know she was stating a fact, not her opinion. Becky nodded to indicate she agreed.

"And what the heck were *you* thinking?" Ashley asked, pointing her finger at Carlie. "Telling him Allie got Twisty in trouble?"

"Allie did get Twisty in trouble. Who cares if he knows," Carlie cried.

"That's not even true. Twisty got herself in trouble by hitting Chase," Ryan stated.

"No, Allie told on Twisty and got her punished," Carlie replied.

"Yeah, Chase," Kevin laughed. "If only Twisty was able to hit you and get away with it. Then poor Twisty wouldn't be grounded right now. Darn Allie for telling on poor Twisty."

Ryan and Chase laughed. "Right, because Twisty is the real victim here," Ryan ribbed.

Carlie glowered at them. "Let me guess, you're on Allie's side. Well, that's no surprise." She argued Chase should have told CC himself Twisty punched him. "Then Allie wouldn't have gotten into a fight with Twisty and gotten her in trouble."

"Because Twisty's never responsible for her actions. It's just Allie that makes her do bad things," Ryan snarked.

"And Allie told CC Twisty was bullying people. There was no reason for that," Carlie added.

"Except for the fact Twisty was actually bullying people," Kevin said dryly.

"Twisty wasn't bullying anybody. Allie made that up," Carlie argued.

Ryan snickered. "Um, yeah, okay. You're kidding, right? So trying to force me into doing her chores for a month? What do you call that?"

"That's not bullying. She didn't mean it," Carlie replied.

"Haha, right! It sure seemed like she meant it to me!" Ryan laughed.

"Oh, come on, Carlie! You're saying if Allie didn't jump in to stop her, Twisty wouldn't have gone through with making Ryan do her chores?" Kevin asked incredulously.

"Allie's one to talk," Becky huffed. "She bullies people all the time."

That's when I broke in. "Allie's *not* a bully." I was slightly surprised by the amount of anger in my voice.

Becky snorted. "Oh please. Yes, she is. She's always making sarcastic remarks about people. Even you have to see she isn't the nicest person sometimes, Capricorn."

"Well, you're not the nicest person sometimes either, Becky!" I shot back. "You're always bossing everyone around!"

Becky fired back in defensive outrage. "You're not very nice either, Capricorn! You make excuses for Allie. You don't even care she picks on people!"

"She doesn't pick on people," I said through clenched teeth. "Allie's my best friend. I know her better than anyone. If you think that, you got her all wrong!"

"The very notion of Allie being a bully is beyond ridiculous," Ashley scoffed.

Chase, Ryan, and Kevin nodded emphatically.

Carlie rolled her eyes. "Of course you three don't think she's a bully. You always take Allie's side."

"Maybe we do because she knows what it means to be a good sibling, something you could learn a lot more about, Carlie," Kevin threw back.

"Ooh! You just got burned!" Chase laughed at Carlie.

Justin, who shrunk back and became a ball of anxiety since this argument began, put his hands up. "Stop it, guys. Stop it! This is getting completely out of hand!"

"I think we should end this argument right now, especially since Allie isn't even here to defend herself," Breezy asserted.

"Neither is Twisty," Carlie noted.

"Good. I think that's a great idea," Justin cried.

"Hey, brats! Can I weigh in on this debate?"

I jerked my head in horror. We had become so immersed in our dispute we didn't even notice, at some point during the squabble, Big Boss returned and was quietly hiding in the shadows of his yard, listening to us. My heart sank deep in my chest. He may have heard that whole argument. I don't know exactly why, but somehow I knew this was really bad.

Chapter 14

Allie ran towards us as we stepped into our room. She leaped into Hazy, linked hands with her, and spun her around. Hazy giggled wildly.

"Thank God you're here! It's so good to see other human faces. What's it like on the outside? Tell me everything!" Allie squealed.

"Al, we've only been gone a few hours," Breezy laughed.

"I've been so bored!" Allie cried. "I'm here alone with no one to talk to. I spend every day after school here reading. I've reread *Charlotte's Web* three times! I'm going to tear out the pages of all the books I've read and make 1000 paper airplanes. I'm going crazy! You'll see me in the corner trying to convince the spiders to write 'Free Allie' in their webs."

"Allie," I chuckled. "You're never going to believe what happened outside."

I started telling Allie about what just occurred in our yard. She rolled her eyes over Carlie's usual stubborn behavior, but her eyes widened as I continued.

"Why was Big Boss asking about me?" Allie interrupted, a little rattled.

"I think he's just trying to get to us. To show he knew you were missing," Breezy replied.

Allie nodded. "So is this just something he does now? Watch us? We've all just accepted this?"

"Well he was out there every day last week, but I put up a shield and he left," Breezy said.

"Whoa!" Allie exclaimed. "What? Back up! What do you mean he was out there every day last week?"

Breezy explained what happened. Allie gaped at Breezy. "He was out there at the fence *every single day* last week just staring at you guys? That's…not okay. Did you tell CC?"

"No, because Big Boss left us alone," Breezy answered.

Allie vigorously shook her head. " Staring at you isn't leaving you alone. It's uber-creepy."

"Yes," Breezy sighed. "But it's not like he'd stop if we asked him."

"Well here's a thought," Allie said. "*Tell CC.* He needs to know. And I have a feeling he won't agree that staring at you like a big creep meets the definition of leaving you alone."

I continued the story and deliberately stopped right before Big Boss interrupted us. I knew Allie would comment first on the argument about her.

Allie smiled warmly at me. "Thanks for sticking up for me, Cap. I know how hard it is for you to put yourself out there like that."

"You're welcome," I mumbled, blushing a little. "I didn't mean to get upset. But Carlie and Becky were making me so mad, saying you're a bully. Ashley's right, that's ridiculous."

"That's crazy," Allie said. "Right, I'm a bully. Meanwhile, Twisty is literally going around punching people."

"Well, why do you think they think you're a bully?" Breezy posed.

"Let's see…" Allie said. "Becky is rude and doesn't like being called out on it, Carlie is Twisty's lapdog and goes along with whatever Twisty says, does, or thinks, and Twisty is the actual bully. So there you go. Any other questions?"

Breezy frowned. "Come on, Allie. Don't you think that's just a little reductive? You're completely minimizing their views."

Allie held out her hands in a helpless gesture. "Breeze, what do you want me to say? I can't help how they feel."

"No, but maybe you can act a little nicer towards them," Breezy offered.

"So the next time Twisty hits Chase, you want me to go up to her and say…" Allie put on an exaggerated smile and a high-pitched, sugary-sweet tone. "Excuse me, Twisty. If you don't mind, I would very much appreciate it if you didn't hit our brother. Would you be so kind as to refrain from doing that? Thank you so much! Have a great day!"

Hazy and I cracked up and Breezy couldn't help laughing too.

"Capricorn," Hazy said. "Aren't you going to tell Allie what happened at the end with Big Boss?"

"I was just getting to that," I nodded. I explained how Big Boss cut in at the end of our argument. I watched the apprehension come back into Allie's eyes.

"So did he hear that whole fight?" Allie asked.

"We think he did," Breezy answered.

"Um, okay, soooo…..that's not good," Allie said, shaking her head.

"Yeah, I know," I said. "I thought so too. But I can't figure out exactly why."

"I don't know why either," Allie answered. "All I know is something is instinctively telling me the less he knows about us, the better."

"He keeps eavesdropping on our conversations, watching us," Breezy commented. "At this point, I have to wonder what he *doesn't* already know about us."

Allie cringed. "Did you tell CC about this?"

"No, but I'm going to," Breezy said.

"Good," Allie responded. "Because if you don't, I will. This is really important."

Breezy nodded. "I know. Don't worry. We'll go talk to him right now."

Some minutes later, Breezy, Hazy, and I were in CC's home office, where he waved us in while on a call with a Shelter for All steering member. CC served as a distant head of the organization, rarely meeting anyone in person, and managed all business remotely, everything from interviewing housing applicants to fundraising. CC had few friends or social connections because of us and the need to guard our secrets. I glanced around the room at the towers of files stacked high on CC's desk and chairs. CC ended his call and I commented on the number of files as he moved them from the chairs to the floor so the three of us could sit down.

"I've been backed up on work for months. My children keep me very busy," he said with a wry smile, nodding at us to sit.

We told CC the whole story of what happened. He listened to us without interruption, and as we finished, he looked at us with deep concern. He paused to collect his thoughts before speaking.

"Well, first of all," CC said at last, "Thanks for coming to me about this. Although I really wish you would've come earlier."

Breezy explained her reasoning for not coming sooner.

"When I said come to me if he doesn't leave you alone, I meant if he does anything other than ignoring you," CC clarified. "And staring at you is not ignoring you. In no way is that acceptable."

"CC?" I asked timidly. "What do you think Big Boss wants from us? Why does he keep bothering us?"

CC let out a long, slow exhale. "I don't know. At first, I thought he was just a nasty man who hated kids, but now I think there's more to it. I have no idea why a grown man would pick on a bunch of kids, but he seems to be getting a real kick out of it."

"Allie said she thinks he's dangerous," I revealed. "Do you..." I swallowed and forced myself to plow through my question. "Do you think he would ever try to hurt us?"

CC tried to give me a reassuring smile, but I could see a glint of fear in his expression. "In all honesty, Capricorn sweetheart, I don't know. I want to say of course not, but then he already attacked Becky, so I don't know what he's capable of. I will promise you all one thing though: I'll do everything to keep you safe."

I gave CC a loving smile and was stunned to find tears welling up in my eyes. CC smiled gently and handed me a tissue from his desk. I wiped away my tears with shaking hands. Breezy reached over and rested her hand lightly on the top of mine. I didn't realize till then how much fear I was holding in.

"CC, what should we do if we go outside tomorrow and he's out there again?" Hazy asked.

"Come and get me," CC said without hesitation. "Come and get me no matter what. Tomorrow or whenever you next see him. Okay?"

The three of us nodded. CC stood from his desk chair and hugged me. "I know you're scared, Capricorn, but don't worry. Everything's going to be okay."

I swallowed and hoped to God he was right.

Chapter 15

"It's gotten a lot colder since the last time I played out here!" Allie exclaimed, as she ran outside, overjoyed to finally be free.

"Well it is November now, Al," Breezy reminded her.

"That's so sad. I missed so much of Fall," Allie said. "The next time I'm about to get in a fight with Twisty, do me a favor and punch me instead."

"Well look at it this way, Allie," Chase said. "You're out here and she's still inside for another week."

"That's true," Allie smiled. "Yay! A whole week of Twisty-free play!" She raised her arm in a cheer and jumped.

Chase cracked up. "It's good to have you back, Allie."

"Is she still doing your chores for you?" Allie asked Chase.

"No, that ended a week ago," Chase answered.

"I bet you're sad that's over, huh, Chase?" Allie asked, nudging him with a knowing grin.

"Would I be a bad person if I said I thought about provoking Twisty to hit me every week, just so she'd never stop doing my chores?" Chase asked with a sheepish grin.

Allie burst out laughing. "No, but I think CC would get

wise to your con pretty fast."

"Well, you could always get lucky and she could hit you again," Ryan laughed. "Since it's Twisty, that's pretty much inevitable."

"I wouldn't bet on that, Rye Bread," Allie said. "I've got a feeling Twisty isn't going to hit anyone anytime soon. A month is a long time to spend indoors. I did three weeks and it felt like an eternity. I was ready to crack and write repeatedly on the walls 'All inside and no outside makes Allie a dull girl.'"

A little later we were deciding on a game to play together. Allie handed her water bottle to Kitty to pass around. Becky insisted we play soccer and Allie called Becky out on her bossy behavior. Carlie complained it wasn't fair Allie was there while Twisty was still grounded for another week.

"If it makes you feel better, Carlie, I'd gladly trade Allie for Twisty to be out here instead," Becky said.

"And I would gladly trade you, Becky, for a kinder sister," Allie shot right back.

"Stop fighting," Justin said. "We always fight anymore. Remember what CC told us the other day. We need to work on getting along better. We're all on the same side."

Becky walked up to Kitty and handed her Allie's now empty water bottle. "Kitty, go in the house and refill this," she ordered.

"Why does she have to refill it? Why can't you?" Allie asked Becky.

"Because I asked her to," Becky responded.

"You didn't ask her. You commanded her," Allie corrected. "She's not your water girl. She doesn't have to follow your orders."

"Allie, it's okay, I don't mind..." Kitty said meekly.

"Kit-Cat, you don't have to do what she says. You're

allowed to tell her no. She wasn't even the slightest bit polite," Allie advised Kitty gently.

"Oh brother. Fine, Allie, if you care so much, you go do it!" Becky snapped.

"No. I won't. You can't push me around," Allie responded. "If you want more water, then you go get it."

"You are so annoying! If you aren't willing to do it, why did you even butt in in the first place?" Becky moaned.

"Because I don't like the way you treat people, Becky," Allie answered.

"The way I treat people? How about the way you treat people? If it was anyone else who asked Kitty to get water, you wouldn't have said a word. But because it was me, you jump all over me," Becky accused.

"Apparently you need to work on your understanding of the definition of the word 'ask,'" Allie retorted.

"Allie," Breezy warned. "Remember what we talked about."

Allie threw up her hands and let out a long breath. She looked back at Becky and held out her hand. "Just give me the bottle."

Becky looked surprised at this sudden turn-around, then handed the bottle to Allie. Allie headed for the house. "You're welcome, by the way," she called back over her shoulder.

As the back door slammed behind Allie, Big Boss popped up at the fence.

"Excuse me," Big Boss said. "I was just in my yard doing work and I couldn't help overhearing some of that." He pointed towards the house where Allie was. "I don't know how you can stand her. I'm with you, Becky, she is extremely irritating. Don't you all get tired of her? How do you deal with her snarky comments all day?"

"I know, she's so annoying," Carlie said.

"*What are you doing?*" we shouted at Carlie. "Stop talking to him!"

I reacted fast. I held out my hand and cast the shield along the fence. Allie came out the back door, heading towards us with the water bottle. She saw Big Boss and stopped short. Breezy told Allie to tell CC Big Boss is outside. Allie nodded and hurried back.

"You know what amazes me about all of you?" Big Boss said. "You have these special powers, yet you hardly use them. You won't even refill a water bottle automatically. It just astounds me. What's the point of having those powers if you never use them? You mind as well be like everybody else."

We stared at him, waiting for Allie and CC to get there.

"Is it your father?" Big Boss continued. "Does he not let you use your powers? Boy, he's got you all on a very short leash, doesn't he? Did you ever consider he doesn't allow you free use of your own powers because he doesn't like them? He knows those powers make you more powerful than him, and he's scared of them. He may even be jealous. I have to say if it was me, I'd use my powers however I wanted. After all, it's my power and it belongs to me. You might want to think about it. Ah, speaking of your father, here he comes now."

CC and Allie came through the yard. Allie headed towards us, while CC stormed up to the shielded fence to face Big Boss for the second time.

"Casey, we meet again," Big Boss said, smiling at CC affably.

CC looked like he could spit fire. He pointed to the shield. "You are very lucky this is here because I don't think I can restrain myself from what I want to do to you right now," CC growled.

"Wow. Well, you're obviously angry, Casey. Have I done something wrong?" Big Boss asked.

"Have you done something wrong?" CC shouted. "I'll tell you what you did wrong! You need to leave my children the hell alone!"

"I didn't touch your kids, Casey," Big Boss said. "I've never laid a hand on any of them since that warning you gave me. I even apologized to Becky for hurting her."

CC appeared like he wanted to rip through the shield and ring Big Boss's neck. "Don't even try to hand me this innocent act! You've been out here harassing my children!"

"How am I harassing them, Casey? All I've done is talk to them," Big Boss claimed.

"Let me run through the list for you," CC stated. "You're stalking them, eavesdropping on their conversations, *staring* at them! One week you were at the fence staring at them every day. What kind of grown man stands there and stares at children?"

"I wasn't staring at them, Casey," Big Boss defended. "I may have stayed and looked at them for a few minutes, but I wasn't staring."

"Don't you dare even try to imply my children are lying! You were staring at them!" CC screamed. "You repeatedly insult them, you threatened Allie…"

"I didn't threaten Allie," Big Boss interrupted. "*She* threatened to use her powers against *me*."

"You threatened her!" CC shouted. "You made it appear like you were going to attack her. Plus, you called her names like "brazen little brat" and "cocky." Don't you dare insult my daughter!" CC thundered. "And she threatened to use her powers against you because you've been intimidating them."

"Casey," Big Boss said. "First of all, you need to calm down."

"Don't tell me to calm down!" CC shrieked.

Big Boss continued as if CC said nothing. "Second, I wasn't going to attack Allie. I was only trying to scare her a little for threatening to use her powers against me."

CC narrowed his eyes at Big Boss. "That's another thing, how did you know about their powers anyway? And no, you didn't find it online. No one knows that outside our family. It's a closely guarded secret. So how on Earth did you know?"

Big Boss gave CC an evasive smile. "Maybe more people know about that closely guarded secret than you realize, Casey. Or maybe I saw the kids using their powers."

CC glared at Big Boss. "Are you playing games with me? Are you going to give me a straight answer?"

Big Boss laughed. "Okay, Casey. I admit it. I saw your kids use their powers."

"When?" CC demanded.

"The day I met them. I saw them use them to make a bat and ball," Big Boss revealed.

My siblings looked at each other in disbelief. We whispered amongst ourselves that that happened right before he first talked to us, so he must have been hiding somewhere in the yard. I shuddered because that meant he was spying on us before he even met us.

CC fixed Big Boss with a steely expression. "I'm going to have to talk to my children later to verify whether that's true," he said, looking over towards us with a frown. "But if it is, it means you've been spying on them. They would never use their powers knowingly in front of someone else."

"I wasn't spying on them. I was in my backyard and looked over and saw them do it. It's the truth, Casey. Take it or leave it," Big Boss said.

"Here's some truth for you, Robert," CC said severely.

"The next time you harass my kids, I'm calling the police."

"The police?" Big Boss scoffed. "On what charge? Talking to my neighbors?"

"No, you arrogant dirtbag! I'll report you for harassing my children!" CC shouted.

"All I did was talk to them, Casey. That's my worst crime," Big Boss insisted.

"Fine. Then let me make it easy for you," CC hissed. "Don't speak to my children ever again. Don't even look at them. Just stay away from them."

"Fine, Casey. But there's really no reason for all this animosity," Big Boss stated.

CC studied Big Boss, looking him up and down. "You should know I'm giving my children full permission to use their powers against you to defend themselves if necessary. Just keep that in mind. You've been warned."

Big Boss gave CC a small smile. "It sounds like *you're* threatening *me* now, Casey."

CC met Big Boss's smile with his own wider one. "Oh, I am. You better believe I am."

Big Boss nodded. "Got it, Casey. I understand."

"Understand this, Robert," CC said, dropping his voice to a low growl. "If you hurt my children, I'll make you sorry you were ever born."

Big Boss appeared irritated. "Why would I want to hurt your children, Casey? What possible interest could I have in harming a bunch of ten-year-olds?"

"I don't know, Big Boss," CC said evenly. "I don't know what your intentions are, but you're obviously interested in my kids. So you tell me. What do you want with my children?"

"I don't want anything from them, Casey," Big Boss asserted. "What kind of monster do you think I am? You think

I would hurt a bunch of innocent children?"

CC stared Big Boss in the face. "Yes, Robert. I think that's exactly the kind of monster you are."

"Well, then I'm sorry you feel that way," Big Boss said with a cold glare. "Besides, I wouldn't dare hurt them even if I wanted to. I know they can attack me with those powers. I'll keep away, don't worry."

Back in the house, CC told us he didn't think it was a good idea to play in the backyard right now. We squealed loud vocalizations of protest, but CC insisted it was necessary since it seemed Big Boss was eavesdropping on us in the backyard. He gave us the park close to our school as an alternative place to play, and we brightened a little.

CC asked us if it was true we used our powers to make a bat and baseball. We looked at him like thieves caught red-handed. Becky, who couldn't believe after all this time she was going to get caught, had a countenance of nausea on her face. Allie turned Twisty in without hesitation, and CC asked for the other culprit.

Becky made herself as small as possible. "I did it, CC," she mumbled.

"Becky?" CC questioned. "Becky, I'm surprised at you. That was the day Big Boss hurt your wrist. So how did you heal it?"

Becky looked at the floor. "I didn't. Breezy did."

CC tipped up on his toes and exhaled. "I see." He gave us another short lecture on the importance of using our powers only when necessary and making certain when we do use them that we're not seen by anyone. He told Becky she and Twisty were losing all privileges for a few days as a consequence. Becky nodded morosely but Carlie protested on Twisty's behalf.

“What’s the big deal about using magic to make a bat, anyway? Why do we get punished for using our own powers?” Carlie demanded.

“Carlie, enough. You know the rules. It’s not up for discussion,” CC scolded.

Carlie stomped her foot and scowled at CC. “We should be able to use our powers however we want! They're ours, not yours!” she shouted. She ran out of the room, flew upstairs, and slammed her bedroom door so loud it echoed like a gunshot.

Chapter 16

"Here, Breezy, catch!" I threw a small pink ball into Breezy's open hands.

It was an unseasonably warm November day at the park. Twisty was back, much to Allie's chagrin.

"Let's play ball tag," Ryan said.

"I don't want to play that game," Carlie whined.

"Here we go." Allie rolled her eyes.

"I want to play something else," Carlie said.

"Of course you do. I think we'd be shocked if you did want to play. What game are you playing instead? The stand around and argue about what game to play until you run out of time and don't get to play anything game?" Allie retorted.

Twisty jumped to Carlie's defense. "So we're supposed to do whatever you want instead, Allie?"

"I don't care what we do. Anything's better than arguing," Allie answered.

Carlie motioned for Twisty to come close, and she whispered in Twisty's ear. Twisty stood up, wearing a mean smile.

"Carlie and I are going to go play our own game," Twisty announced.

Twisty and Carlie stalked off, speaking in hushed voices to each other. They suddenly stopped and turned around, gesturing at Becky.

"Hey, Becky!" Twisty called out. "Do you want to play with us?"

"We're going to play soccer!" Carlie added.

Becky smiled, running off to join them.

"Hey, dumbos!" Kevin yelled out to the three of them. "You can't play soccer! You don't have a soccer ball!"

Twisty, Carlie, and Becky ignored Kevin. They went to the other side of the small park where we could still see them, but they were no longer within earshot. The rest of us started playing ball tag, then in the distance, Carlie made a burst of spherical yellow light: A soccer ball. We stopped playing instantly. The ten of us scanned the park for observers, then hurried to the other side, shouting at our three sisters.

"Are you guys nuts?" Ashley whispered. "You can't use magic! What if somebody saw you?"

"Nobody saw us," Twisty reported dismissively. "There's no one here. And if they did, all they saw was a flash of light, which could be anything. No big deal."

"No, it is a big deal," Breezy frowned. "Not only because you're using magic in public, but you're using it unnecessarily."

"We wanted to play soccer," Carlie said. "We needed a soccer ball. Problem solved."

Allie snickered. "You just got in trouble for using magic to make a baseball bat," she said to Twisty. "You just never learn, do you?"

Twisty advanced on Allie and got up right in her face. "Are you going to tell on us, Allie? Are you going to run off and tell CC about this too? Are you going to be a snitch?" she snarled through clenched teeth.

Allie boldly met Twisty's eyes and lunged forward, forcing Twisty to stumble backward. "Back off!" she ordered. "I'm not a snitch!"

"Hey guys, come on!" Justin moaned. "Don't start this again. Enough with the fighting!"

"Forget Allie, Twisty," Carlie sneered. "Let's just play soccer."

"With your contraband soccer ball," Kevin chuckled.

"All of you need to mind your own business," Becky said. "Just stay on your own side and leave us alone."

The three of them returned to kicking the soccer ball between them.

Oh, I get it!" Allie exclaimed with a fake grin. "It's the I Hate Allie Club! Members only. The only requirement is you have to hate me. Well, I've had it with all three of them!"

"Me too," I agreed. "I'm so sick of Twisty and her nastiness. And Carlie and Becky are her little minions."

"Come on, that's not very nice," Breezy disapproved. "They might say the same thing about the four of us."

"They're being very mean, Breezy," Hazy said. "There's no excuse for how they're acting."

Hazy had just taken the counter-argument to Breezy, which rarely ever happens. Allie gave Hazy a double-take.

"Don't worry, you've made your point!" Allie shouted out at Twisty, Carlie, and Becky. "I won't talk to any of you ever again."

"Hallelujah!" Becky shouted back. The three gave a boisterous cheer.

"The three of you are so mean!" Hazy suddenly shrieked.

"Oh look," Becky called back. "Hazy's taking Allie's side. Color me unsurprised. Can we extend the no-talking-to-us-ever-again rule to all of Allie's friends too?"

Hazy looked hurt. Allie's protective instincts for Hazy took over and she shouted back at Becky with fierce, renewed energy. "Leave Hazy out of this! She did nothing to you! You're just being mean out of spite!"

"I thought you weren't talking to us anymore," Twisty yelled. "I knew that was too good to be true."

Then Chase joined in the fight. "Are you sure you don't want any of Allie's friends talking to you? You'll regret that really fast. All of Allie's friends are here. All you'd have is each other to talk to!"

"That would be more than fine with us," Twisty yelled back.

Ryan snorted. "Okay then. I'm done talking to you all too!"

Ashley, Kevin, Chase, and I all shouted our agreement.

"Well this is going to make mealtimes together very awkward," Allie said.

Justin approached all of us and spoke loud enough for everyone, including the three quickly becoming outcasts playing soccer, to hear him. "Come on, everyone! This is crazy! Are we really not going to talk to each other anymore? What are we even fighting about? Does anyone even know?"

"Yes," Twisty answered. "There's Allie's side and our side. Which side are you on?"

"What do you mean Allie's side and your side?" Justin cried with his hands on his temples. "We're really going to split our whole family apart over a personal feud you have with Allie?"

Suddenly, Becky put her hand out and a tube-shaped light appeared.

"Becky, what are you doing?" Ashley cried.

Becky held a full water canister in her hand. She took a long swig and passed it to Twisty. "What?" Becky asked Ashley in an obstinate tone. "We were thirsty. And I thought you weren't talking to us anymore."

"There is literally a water fountain right over there," Allie said, pointing to the back of the park.

"We wanted our own water," Becky cried. "And when do you actually stop talking to us, Allie? Or is that just another thing you're not serious about?"

Twisty held out her palm to make a cylinder beam, forming a full soda can. Having spent all their magic, the three announced they were leaving and headed towards the path home. The rest of my siblings didn't want to leave, but we had to go regardless since CC told us to all come back together. We trailed behind our three wayward siblings, winding by the shrubs and pine trees, past our school, through the meadow, across the street, and down the sidewalk to our house. Then Twisty suddenly turned around and looked back at us.

"There was no reason for you to follow us," Twisty said. "We wanted to walk home alone."

"We wanted to stay, but we had to leave because of you dumbos!" Kevin yelled.

"Stop calling us dumbos, Kevin!" Becky shouted.

"No, that's what you are. Dumbos, dumbos, dumbos," Kevin taunted.

Everyone came to a standstill in front of our house.

"If you call us dumbos one more time, I'm telling CC," Becky cried.

"Ha! No, you won't. Because if you do, I'll tell CC you just used magic to make a water bottle, soccer ball, and a soda," Kevin crowed.

"I only made the water bottle," Becky said. "And you wouldn't dare."

"Try me," Kevin challenged. "If you tell on me, I'll tell on you."

"He won't tell on us," Twisty said. "If he does, he'll be sorry."

"Are you threatening Kevin now?" Allie questioned. "Is he your next target?"

"What are you going to do, Allie? Push me?" Twisty shouted with intense fury.

"Oh, I'll do a lot more than push you this time, you twit!" Allie shouted back.

"Allie!" Breezy cried. "Stop!"

Twisty charged towards Allie with her fists balled up.

Kevin stepped out in front of Allie. "Hey, look what I can do that you can't," he said to Twisty.

Kevin stuck out his finger, and little sparks of electricity came shooting out. Twisty came to a grinding halt, but it was too late. Some of the sparks hit Twisty's arm, giving her a burning shock. Twisty screeched in pain.

"Kevin! What did you just do?" Breezy cried, running over to Twisty.

"She threatened me," Kevin said. "And she was going to hit Allie. I gave her a taste of her own medicine."

Carlie ran up and punched Kevin clear in the stomach. Kevin bent over in pain.

"Don't you ever hurt Twisty again!" Carlie screamed.

"You're lucky I don't have any magic left or I would get you too," Kevin wheezed, holding his stomach.

Justin ran in and pushed Kevin away from Carlie. "What are you doing?" he yelled at the two of them. "Stop attacking each other! Kevin, how could you use magic to hurt your own sister?"

"Um, Kevin," Allie mumbled. "I think you may have just gone a little too far."

"You think so, Allie!" Carlie shouted. "All of this is because of you in the first place!"

"Because of me? No, it's Twisty!" Allie cried. "Twisty

punched Chase, came after me repeatedly, and just now threatened Kevin. Face it, Carlie, Twisty's a bully. She's a mean, nasty bully. And maybe she got what she deserved."

"Take that back or I swear to God, Allie, I'll punch you too!" Carlie threatened.

"You might want to rethink that, Carlie!" Allie roared. "Because unlike you, I didn't squander my magic. I still have mine!"

"Stop it!" Breezy suddenly screamed out, piercing through all the shouting. "Just stop! All of you! Twisty's hurt! And you're all standing around fighting each other! What's wrong with all of you?"

Breezy turned to Twisty on the ground. Tears ran down Twisty's face and she cried her arm was burnt. Breezy laid her hands gingerly over Twisty's burns and the warm healing light emerged from her fingertips. As the pain melted away, Twisty's face went from contorted to relieved. She straightened up, wiped away her tears, and smiled.

"Thanks, Breezy," Twisty said. "You're the only decent person of Allie's friends." She stuck her finger in Kevin's face. "You better watch your back, Kevin. I'll get you for that." She spun towards Allie and stood eye to eye with her nemesis. "Allie," she said through grit teeth, "I hate you. I hate you more than anyone and anything. And you better sleep with one eye open. Because this means war."

Twisty and her posse smiled viciously at Allie, then moved as one, heading inside the house.

"You want a war?" Allie shouted after Twisty. "Don't worry, you got one! And I've got more soldiers on my side. So good luck with your lousy two minions!"

My siblings went inside the house, and I stood alone. I bent my head down and closed my eyes, upset at what just happened.

Then I looked up, and my breath caught in my throat. There, standing in the shadows, was Big Boss. One look told me he had just witnessed that entire scene. The smug, diabolical smile on his face said it all. He suddenly locked eyes with me, and his smile grew wider. I felt all the blood drain from my face as I became paralyzed with terror. Big Boss held my gaze fiercely with his cold eyes. Then, just when I thought I couldn't stand one more second, he lifted his hand and waved at me.

"Hi, Capricorn," he gloated. Then he shot me a downright malignant look and dropped his hand, sauntering away.

Chapter 17

The atmosphere in the room at dinner was extremely uncomfortable. My siblings traded evil eyes with each other and only spoke to those on "their side." Breezy and Justin hadn't said a word through the entire meal and sat with sorrowful expressions.

"So, how was the park today?" CC asked. "Did anything happen?"

Immediately I flashed on the fight in the park and front of our house. Then my mind drifted off to Big Boss and that terrifying smile. What was it about the way he smiled that made every drop of blood in my body instantly freeze? And he knows my name, I thought, shivering. *Hi, Capricorn.*

I was vaguely aware of Ashley answering CC's question, saying we played ball tag.

CC lifted his eyebrows. "So everyone got along fine then? No problems?" CC seemed suspicious, rooting for answers.

Kevin's small eyes went wide. Chase covered his face and slouched low in his seat. Breezy kept her head down, knowing her guilty expression would be an instant tell.

"No problems, CC," Twisty said.

CC lifted an eyebrow at Twisty. "Did you and Allie get into any more fights?"

In the back of my head, I thought CC is definitely on to us. Twisty should give up the ghost right now, but she won't.

"No," Twisty lied. "We stayed away from each other."

Well, that was at least partly true, I thought to myself.

"And nobody else got into a fight?" CC pressed. "Nothing else happened today? Nothing?"

Panicked silence followed. CC put down his fork with a clink and looked at us. "Kids," CC said sternly, "I'm going to ask you one more time, and this time I want an honest answer. What happened today? You could cut the tension in here with a knife."

I could almost see the wheels turning in my siblings' heads, deciding just how little they could say while still telling the truth. Ashley said we got in an argument over the game we played. Kevin added some people went off by themselves because they didn't want to play.

CC looked at each of us again. "If that's all it is, can we resolve this, please? I don't know why everyone would hold a grudge against each other over a game, but it seems nearly half the table isn't speaking to the other half."

"It got out of hand," Ashley said. "We'll fix it."

Hi, Capricorn. Big Boss's words incessantly rang through my head like an alarm. The way he smiled. What did it mean? I'm sure he saw us fight. Was he happy about that? Yes, but there was something more...Through my clouded mind I became aware of my family focusing on me and I thought I heard my name called. It wasn't just that he was happy, I thought. He was proud. Yes, that's it! Proud of something he did.

"Capricorn?" Out of the fog, I heard CC's voice, like it was coming from somewhere far away. "Capricorn?" Slowly I swept away the mist, emerging from the murky haze.

"Capricorn!"

CC's firm tone finally sliced through my reverie. Abruptly, I re-focused my attention on the physical present in the dining room. It was then I realized everyone at the table was staring at me. CC was looking at me with an expression of deep concern. All my siblings were gaping at me with questioning looks. Even Twisty and Carlie were eyeing me curiously. Next to me, Allie sat with her elbow resting on the back of her chair, staring at me with a quizzical expression. She waved her hand in my face to assess if I was present.

I was suddenly mortified and felt my face flush. "I'm-I'm sorry. I didn't hear you. Were you calling me?"

"About five times!" CC exclaimed. "Capricorn, honey, are you alright? You seemed to be in your own little world there."

I knew there was no sense in trying to hide it, so I told the truth. "I saw Big Boss today. I can't stop thinking about the way he smiled at me. It was scary."

"You saw Big Boss?" CC asked, his voice tight with worry. "Where? At the park?" He scanned his eyes to each of my siblings, and they shook their heads and held up their hands, indicating they knew nothing about this.

"I was the only one who saw him," I explained. "When we came back from the park. In front of our house." I wisely skipped the part about the fight and told them about Big Boss's smile and what he said. "It's creepy he knows my name."

"Capricorn, he's done much worse than that," Ashley said.

"That's true, but Capricorn is obviously shaken up about this, Ashley," CC said. "I'm sorry he scared you, Capricorn. Next time something like that happens, I'm calling the police."

Carlie laughed. "CC, you can't call the police because

someone said hi to Capricorn. The police would laugh you off."

CC eyed Carlie sharply. "Carlie, you know very well this isn't just a matter of someone saying hi. There's a pattern of harassment here."

"Okay, but still, all he did was smile and say hi," Carlie insisted. "Why is that bad?"

Was Carlie actually defending Big Boss? My siblings stared at Carlie with their mouths agape, including Becky.

"Are you for real?" Ashley asked Carlie with a raised eyebrow.

"He didn't just say hi!" I exclaimed. "It was the way he smiled. Like he was really happy and proud."

"Wow, he was happy and proud so he smiled? Imagine that," Carlie said sarcastically.

Twisty snorted with laughter.

CC looked at the two of them harshly. "There's nothing funny about this. Capricorn is very upset."

CC reassured me we'll call the police if this happens again. It was family movie night and CC headed to the living room to set everything up. Most of my siblings scurried out of the room, racing to get a good seat on the couch. Hazy, Kevin, Chase, Allie, and I remained at the table.

"Hey, Cap, are you okay?" Allie asked me. "That was weird before. You were completely gone! CC kept calling you and you didn't even hear him!"

"I know, I'm sorry," I said. "I'm okay now. I know it sounds like nothing, but it wasn't just smiling and saying hi like Carlie said. It was the *way* he was smiling."

"Carlie's a brat," Allie said. "Just ignore her. You know she's just saying that to try to get to you, right?"

"And what the heck was all that about smiling and saying 'hi' isn't a bad thing? Like Big Boss was just trying to be friendly or something!" Chase exclaimed. "Is Carlie actually defending Big Boss?"

"I know!" I shouted, happy to have my thoughts validated. "What was that?"

"After what he did to Becky, I'm surprised she'd say anything like that," Allie said. "Carlie should know better. Becky was looking at her like she had three heads." She got up from the table and turned to Hazy on the other side of her. "Hey, Haze, you've been so quiet. Are you mad about what happened today too, like Breezy?"

"No," Hazy said quietly. "I'm just sad that happened. I know Twisty's mean, but Kevin, you shouldn't have used magic to hurt her. I don't think we should ever use magic on each other."

Allie raised an eyebrow at Kevin. "You did go a bit too far there, Kev. Even if Twisty kind of deserved it. That was a little much."

"Yeah, I know," Kevin moaned. "I realize that now. It's just, argh! I can't stand Twisty sometimes!" he cried, throwing up his hands.

"Yeah, I know the feeling," Allie nodded.

"And she was seriously going to attack you again, Allie," Kevin added. "And she threatened me. That was the last straw."

Allie nodded. "I understand, believe me. Still, be a little more careful with that trigger finger, Kev. Sometimes you get too carried away."

" I know," Kevin admitted. "Sometimes though, I just can't help myself."

Allie smiled. "We better get to the living room before they start the movie without us. Are you coming, Cap?"

"Yeah, I'll be there in a minute," I said.

Allie and the rest of my siblings left, and I sat alone at the table. Again I thought about Big Boss's smile. What was it that disturbed me so much? Some primal instinct deep within me urged that *our lives* depended on figuring this out. Was he proud of the fight we had? But why would he be proud unless he caused it? That fight was largely over Allie, and Big Boss did tell us he doesn't know how we could stand her. And he overheard that argument we had over Allie not being a bully, I remembered. So Big Boss knew there was friction there and stirred the pot. He *is* the source of the fighting, I suddenly realized. And there's something else…the magic. Big Boss told us we should use it however we want and not let CC stop us. Now Carlie, Twisty, and Becky are freely using their powers. So Big Boss…deliberately put the idea in their heads. My mouth snapped open at the revelation. And then I grew aware of the question at the root of this that was the true cause of my terror. *Why?*

Chapter 18

Over the next few days, things seemed to go from bad to worse, and I viewed each event with a growing sense of fretful trepidation. Twisty, Carlie, and Becky were now using their powers freely for just about anything, flaunting their use in front of us.

One day, I was in the kitchen with Allie helping her with dishes, and Ryan was sweeping the floor. Ryan suddenly threw down his broom, and Allie and I twirled around, startled.

"I'm sick of doing this by hand like a sucker, while Twisty, Carlie, and Becky go around using magic however they want," Ryan declared. "I'm using magic to sweep this floor."

"No, don't," I cried. "Don't start using your magic too, Ryan."

Ryan looked at me and nodded towards the dishes. "You could use magic too, you know. Use it to wash dishes. You don't tell on me and I won't tell on you."

Allie laughed. "Ryan's like the serpent in the Garden of Eden." She imitated the sound of a snake hissing. "Ussssse the powerssss. I won't tell sssssssssC sssssssssC."

Ryan chuckled. Allie saw my angst-ridden expression, and quickly changed her tone. "Rye Bread, in all complete seriousness though, that's a bad idea."

"What if someone tries to attack us and we can't defend ourselves? Like Big Boss," I blurted out.

Allie and Ryan stared at me in surprise.

"He wants us to use our magic. Maybe that's so he could easily attack one of us," I elaborated.

I explained to Allie what Big Boss said about our magic.

Allie's eyes nearly popped from her head. "He said that?"

Ryan cleared his throat. "Well…he kind of has a point."

"What do you mean he has a point?" I shouted.

Ryan jumped back. "Well, I know Big Boss is awful, but that doesn't mean he can't still be right about this. It's our magic, not CC's. We should be able to use our own powers."

Allie pointed out it's suspicious Big Boss made a point to say that to us. Ryan considered this, then agreed, picking up the broom.

On another day, we were walking home from school together, when suddenly Twisty and Carlie ran ahead of us. We let them go, remembering what happened last time we insisted on all walking together. Breezy, Hazy, Allie, and I were the next behind them, so we sped up so there wasn't a huge gap between them arriving home and us. We arrived on our street, ahead of the rest of the group, and slowed down to give them a chance to catch up. However, as we approached our house, we not only slowed but stopped dead in our tracks at what we saw. There, in front of us, Big Boss stood in his front yard. But what made us freeze on spot was who was also there, deep in hushed conversation with Big Boss: Twisty and Carlie. Big Boss stopped speaking when he noticed the four of us standing there in shock. Twisty and Carlie saw us, turned back to Big Boss, smiled, and began walking away.

Allie pointed to Twisty and Carlie. "What did you just say to them?" she demanded of Big Boss.

Big Boss gave Allie an elusive grin, then turned and headed to his house. That icy prick of terror returned to the base of my spine.

Allie darted toward Twisty and Carlie before they could get in our house, stopping in front of our porch like a roadblock.

"What did he say to you?" Allie shouted. "What were you talking about?"

"None of your business, Allie," Twisty said. She and Carlie pushed Allie aside and walked up the porch steps.

Allie stood limp in stunned silence. The rest of our siblings reached the house and curiously looked at us.

"What's going on?" Chase asked.

"Twisty and Carlie were just talking to Big Boss," Allie said with a blank expression. "They were whispering together."

"What?" Half our siblings exclaimed at once.

"What were they saying?" Ashley asked, wrinkling her brow.

"I have no idea," Allie said. "They said it was none of my business."

"Are you serious?" Ashley cried. "Ho-ly crap! What's wrong with those two?"

"We have to find out what they said to him," I said. I pointed to Becky. "Can you ask them? You're one of the only people they'll talk to."

Becky seemed extremely disturbed by just the *idea* her roommates spoke with Big Boss. "This has to be a mistake," she muttered. "They wouldn't do that. He probably said something to them as they walked by and they answered him back."

"No, they were whispering with him," Allie said. "It looked pretty friendly to me."

"Well, you're wrong, Allie!" Becky shouted. "They

wouldn't do that!" She stomped into the house.

Later that day, I found out the nature of that conversation Twisty and Carlie had with Big Boss. Allie, Ryan, Chase, and I were watching TV together in the living room while CC was helping our other siblings with homework. Ryan had a gnawing craving for chips, but we were out. Then Twisty and Carlie walked into the living room.

"What are you doing here?" Chase groaned.

"It's our living room too," Twisty said. "We want to watch TV."

"No, we're already watching it," Chase responded. "Go away."

Carlie suggested to Twisty that they use magic to make their own TV.

"If you're using magic anyway, can you make me a bag of chips?" Ryan asked half-jokingly.

"Chips?" Twisty said. "That sounds good." She held out her hand and manifested a full bag of potato chips, opened them, and started eating them in front of Ryan tauntingly, crunching loudly.

Ryan begged for some but Twisty refused to share.

"Ryan, if you want chips so badly, make your own bag," Twisty said. "You have enough energy to do it, don't you?"

I broke in immediately to protest this, and Allie quickly backed me up, again trying to make the case to Ryan that squandering magic is a bad idea.

Twisty scoffed. "Ryan, here's my advice: Use your magic however you want. It's yours, and you shouldn't let anybody stop you."

"So," Allie smirked. "Is that your opinion, or Big Boss's?"

The temptation to easily satisfy his craving got the better of Ryan, and despite my and Allie's persistent warnings, he gave in to Twisty's pressure and created his own bag of chips. Chase watched the whole scene play out with intense interest, and announced he wanted to use magic to wash dishes. Twisty and Carlie swooped in to swiftly convince him to do this.

"So did you complete your mission?" Allie asked Twisty and Carlie accusingly. "Or are there still others you have to recruit? Was that the top-secret conversation you had with Big Boss today? Get everyone to start overusing their magic? How dumb are you two, anyway? Did it ever occur to you to wonder why he suggested you use your magic more often? Maybe so he could easily attack you? He is playing you two for suckers! And you're falling right for it!"

I knew instantly Allie was right: That's exactly what Big Boss told Twisty and Carlie to do. A sharp pang of fear raced through me as I wondered again *why*.

A chain reaction began. Once the word got out Ryan and Chase joined the rebellious ranks of the magic mavericks, everyone quickly followed them, progressing one after another like dominos. The act of using magic freely, an idea I was now convinced Big Boss had planted in everyone's heads, spread like wildfire.

Kevin was the first to jump on the magic bandwagon, eagerly following Chase and Ryan, his fellow partners in crime. Next, I caught Ashley using her magic heedlessly. Ashley was a huge video game buff, and she badly wanted a new game she saw advertised. She begged CC to buy it for her, but outside holidays, CC rarely bought us gifts. He was always afraid of spoiling us. Since CC had money, he didn't want us to become another bunch of "selfish, self-entitled, rich kids." He always said our society had too many people like that already, and they never do the world much good. In fact, they're to blame for many of its problems.

One day, while she was on her laptop, the advertisement for the video game popped up. Ashley placed her hand on the screen, concentrated very hard, and with some strained physical effort, made the video game appear in her hand.

"Do you have any idea how much energy you just zapped from yourself to create that game?" I practically shouted at Ashley. "It's probably going to take a whole week to recover your energy!"

Ashley argued she felt it was worth it and it was her choice.

"But your choice affects the rest of us!" I cried. "Having a new video game is not an emergency!"

Ashley snapped her laptop closed with decisive finality, moving away from me. "I'm sorry, Capricorn, but who died and made you the magic police?"

As she bounded away with her new game, in my head I heard the clicking down of another domino.

Besides Breezy, Hazy, Allie, and me, Justin and Kitty were the last two still keeping to CC's rules. I decided to take some proactive measures and went to talk to Justin on my own before he could follow the rest of the wayward pack. I knocked on the door of the boys' room at a time when I saw Justin in it alone, working on one of his nature sketches. The walls of their room were covered with his drawings. He also had his own bookshelf by his bed that was filled with titles like "Kids Can Save the World" and "Anti-racist Kids." Justin looked up at me from his bed in surprise.

"Hey, Capricorn," he said. "If you're looking for Ryan, Chase, and Kevin, they're downstairs."

I winced, realizing even Justin knew I didn't frequently seek out his company. "Actually Justin, it's you I want to talk to," I said awkwardly.

"Really?" Justin replied with piqued curiosity, pushing his

sketchpad to the side. "Okay. What's up?"

I explained my motivations for being there and asked Justin not to give up on CC's rules.

Justin broke eye contact with me, his cheeks flushing a little under his dark skin. "Um, are you sure I haven't *already* given up on the rules?"

By his reaction, I knew I was already too late. I asked why he had given up.

"I just thought since everybody had, why not? To tell you the truth, Capricorn, I never really agreed with CC's rules. I think they're a little too strict. These powers were given to us for some purpose, I think we should use them. We could use them to help people, like people who are hungry and don't have money. Or we could go into hospitals and heal people. We could be saving a lot of lives. I never understood why we keep these powers a secret and use them all for ourselves on, well, kind of silly things. When we could be doing the world so much good. And the world really needs it. Just think of the things we could do, Capricorn!"

For a moment I forgot what I came in for and let my mind wander with Justin's utopian visions of what that could look like. I saw us traveling around the world, going into war zones and gang territories, and disappearing weapons. I saw us working to put ecosystems back together and disappearing toxic chemicals. I saw us going into slaughterhouses and labs and freeing all the animals. Imagine. We could eliminate so much suffering.

"Hey, Capricorn, you still with me?" Justin's voice broke into my daydream. Oops. I must have zoned out again. I really need to stop doing that.

"Oh, sorry, I was just thinking about what you said. It sounds amazing! We could save the world."

"Well, I wouldn't go that far," Justin said sensibly. "There's a lot we wouldn't be able to do too. We couldn't end white supremacy. We couldn't end greed. We can't get rid of all pollution or fix the climate. There would still be a lot of problems. But we could definitely help."

I gave Justin an impressed grin. "Wow! You've thought a lot about this. You're right, there are limits on what we could do. And I just thought of another one: We can't create or replicate money." This was true. For some reason we could never understand, our powers did not work on money. And believe me, we've tried.

Justin told me he wanted to approach CC with his idea, but he knew CC would never go for it. "CC doesn't want anyone to know about our powers, so doing those things would be impossible. But I can't have all this power and just do nothing. So I decided to do something, even if it's pretty small. Every day I make a peanut butter and jelly sandwich and a veggie and hummus sandwich. Then I use magic to replicate them a few times. I wrap them up and take them down to a park bench for people to eat. One day I came to the bench and someone had left a nice thank you note under a rock. It was from a mother with two children. She said she has a really hard time making ends meet and her kids sometimes had to skip meals. She brought her children to the park to play and found the sandwiches. She felt like it was a miracle, and her kids got to eat dinner that night. She keeps coming back to the park for more sandwiches when her kids are hungry and they're short on food. She said the sandwiches have been a godsend and whoever I am, I'm an angel. I don't know if CC would approve of me spending magic like that, but I can't take the chance he'll say no, and those people need me. Please don't tell CC."

I threw my arms around my incredible, kind-hearted

brother in a giant hug, completely abandoning my plan to stop him from freely using magic. How could I tell him to stop doing something as beautiful as that?

The last person on the list was Kitty. I was sure she'd be easily persuadable. One evening, CC surprised us all with chocolate chip cookies he baked for us, telling us to take one each. Everyone dove for the cookies, and with mouths full mumbled thanks to CC as we rushed off. I followed Kitty to the living room, seeing my chance to talk to her. She was chatting with Ashley, holding her still uneaten cookie in her hand. Ashley sat on a cushy chair with her legs folded. Her thick black hair was styled in two puffy buns that framed her brown face perfectly. Kitty touched the cookie, creating a zap of yellow light, and now there were five cookies in her hand. She gave two cookies to Ashley, saving the other three for herself. I cried out in disapproval.

"Uh oh, here comes Capricorn," Ashley said. "Don't let her catch you using magic. She'll practically have you arrested."

"Kitty," I said. "You can't use magic on things like that!"

"See?" Ashley murmured to Kitty. "Apparently Capricorn thinks she's been deputized as the magic sheriff."

I explained to Kitty and Ashley that if everyone squanders magic, no one will have any left in an emergency.

"Capricorn, I hear what you're saying, but the probability all thirteen of us will have no power left at the exact same time is slim," Ashley replied. "But if that happens, we'll deal. There is such a thing as first aid. It's what the normals without healing powers do. Also, hospitals exist."

I revealed my fear that Big Boss told Twisty and Carlie to convince everyone to overuse their magic.

Kitty contorted her face. "I don't understand, Capricorn," she murmured. "Even if that's what Big Boss told them, why would Twisty and Carlie go along with that?"

Ashely agreed even though Twisty and Carlie can be unbearable, she didn't think they'd do that. "Listen, Cap, I really wouldn't worry too much about Big Boss," Ashley reassured me. "Try to take it easy. And please, for the love of God, stop playing magic police."

I burst out laughing and felt relief wash over me like a warm bath. Safe and sound in our warm house, laughing with my sisters in the living room, munching on homemade cookies, the smell of melted chocolate still lingering in the air, I felt all was right with the world. For the first time in months, it seemed everything was going to be okay.

Oh God, I was so wrong.

Chapter 19

Breezy, Hazy, Allie, and I were sprawled out on the floor of our bedroom amongst a sea of papers, coloring books, and crayons. An aura of calm was present in the room as we were spending a relaxing Sunday afternoon coloring. Allie, Breezy, and Hazy were laying down on their elbows, filling the spaces of various shapes and figures with bright colors, quietly listening to me as I shared Justin's utopic dreams for our family. Serene smiles appeared on my sisters' faces as I spoke of mine and Justin's majestic visions. For a few minutes, the soft whisk of crayons to paper and the sound of my voice were the only things heard in the room, which had the effect of putting us all in a tranquil and meditative state.

When I finished, Allie rolled over on her back and stretched her arms out wide in the air, as if she were embracing the sky. She closed her eyes, and let out a long, peaceful exhale. "Ahhhh, world peace."

"Well, Justin would say not quite. But, yes, close," I said. I asked why this idea isn't possible. "I think CC would approve of using magic like that."

"Oh, he'd definitely approve," Allie confirmed. She rolled

back over on her stomach and looked at me with her hand cupped under her chin. A tendril of her straight golden-brown hair fell over her cheek. "Are you kidding? That's right up CC's alley! But Justin's right, CC would never let us."

I scrunched my face. "You just said he'd approve of using magic to help others."

"Yes, but that's not the issue," Allie clarified. "CC would never let us do anything that would put us in danger."

"Danger?" I questioned. "We wouldn't be doing anything dangerous."

"Um, Cap, somewhere along that whole thing didn't I hear you say something about going into war zones?" Allie asked with a crooked grin. "Yeah, that might be a little dangerous."

Breezy, Hazy, and I snorted with laughter.

"It's not just that though," Breezy added. "To do what you and Justin are suggesting, Cap, it would involve going public with our magic abilities. Which is exactly what CC doesn't want and what he's most afraid of."

"Plus, I'm sure there'd be a lot of people who wouldn't like what we're doing and would try to stop us," Allie pointed out. "And that would be a whole other danger."

"What people wouldn't want to help save the world?" I asked.

Allie looked at me like she was surprised I could be so naive. "Um, military and government leaders, executives of giant industries, people whose profits and power depend on others' suffering, and other miscellaneous forces of evil. I mean, have you taken a good look at the world lately, Cap? There's a reason why we *don't* have world peace."

"That's very true," Breezy nodded solemnly.

Allie added people also might try to get us and use our powers for themselves. Allie saw the disappointment in my face and tried to hearten my spirits. "Don't despair, Cap. We could still help others. We just have to do it on the down-low."

That made me remember the other amazing thing Justin told me. I told my sisters all about Justin's kind deed with the sandwiches.

Hazy turned to a blank picture in her coloring book of a group of children. She picked up a light brown crayon that matched her sandy-colored skin and shaded in one of the girls on the page. "This is me," she said quietly. "Why is Justin afraid to tell CC he's feeding people?" she asked me. "I think CC would be proud of that."

"Yeah, I think he's being a little over-cautious," Allie agreed. "He's keeping everything secret and replicating the sandwiches at home. CC would probably hold him up as a shining example of how we *should* use our powers."

"I think that's my fault," I said. I explained I wanted to convince Justin not to use his powers needlessly. "But when he told me *that*, there was no way I could tell him to stop."

Hazy reached for a dark brown crayon to color two boys on the coloring page she decided were Justin and Ryan. "You went to convince him not to use his magic?"

I told them about my failed efforts to persuade everyone to stop squandering magic.

Breezy let out a long disapproving sigh and shook her head. "I don't know what makes them think they can just stop following CC's rules. There's a reason the rules exist. They can't just choose to stop following them! They are going to get in so much trouble if CC finds out."

Allie elbowed me and cupped her hand over her mouth to speak in my ear. "I think CC's already here," she said in a stage whisper, pointing repeatedly at Breezy.

I slapped my hand over my mouth to keep from spurting

into uproarious laughter. Breezy playfully smacked Allie's arm, and Allie, giggling, tried to dodge her. "Very funny, Al, but I'm being serious here," Breezy laughed. "If everybody is using magic all the time now, that puts us all in danger. And I think Big Boss deliberately put this idea in their heads too, like Cap said."

"Well, I'm not squandering my magic for that very reason," Allie said. "And I know you guys aren't going to be breaking CC's rules anytime soon. But maybe you should tell CC what they're doing."

Breezy said normally she doesn't feel it's her place to snitch on anybody, but this might be important enough to make an exception. Allie responded she felt the same way.

"Why don't we make a pact?" I suggested. "For now let's not say anything to CC, and just depend on the four of us for magic if there's any trouble. But the minute we think there's any danger the four of us alone can't handle, we go to CC."

Allie, Breezy, and Hazy agreed to this proposal. We resumed coloring, considering the matter settled, and pushed it out of our minds.

Chapter 20

The day before Thanksgiving, CC rushed to prepare for tomorrow's meal. We were eager to celebrate, but CC told us to do our homework before we play. For the gazillionth time, we questioned why we had to go to school anyway. We frequently debated this issue. Since we have that unusual condition of not aging due to our powers, CC planned to have us go to school up to the point where Ashley (the oldest) reached high school level again, then he would hire private tutors for us, as moving further up was highly likely to arouse suspicion. In fact, when CC discovered our condition, he had us all repeatedly transfer to small private schools. We've asked CC what will happen once people notice we don't age. CC rumpled his brow, clearly not liking that question, and said we'll eventually have to move.

CC didn't like to show it, but the question that worried him the most was who would take care of us after he's gone? Even if we could take care of ourselves, once the state found out a family of kids was living by themselves, we would be back under their care again before we even realized it. Sometimes we talked together about this dreaded question, but we figured it was so far in the future, it wasn't worth worrying about. But for CC, this question, more than anything, kept him up at night.

I sometimes felt sorry for CC because he took on a lot more responsibility than he bargained for by adopting children with such extraordinary anomalies. I wondered if he would have adopted us if he knew his life would become ruled by hiding our secret. I felt like we were a rope around CC's neck, tied down with an anvil. I sometimes wondered, but I'd never dare to ask if he longed to be free of us. Then again, it wasn't really our fault he held such a heavy burden either. We never asked for these powers. And the thing I realize now that none of us fully understood before, but of course, CC knew, was those powers were a huge weight on us too. And as much as CC's life was controlled by those powers, our lives were even more restricted by them. We knew we were never going to grow up and drive a car, for instance, or go to college, have a career, vote, drink alcohol, get our own place, fall in love, get married, or have children. We also knew we'd have to live constantly on edge of the possibility of people finding out about us, like we were permanent members of the witness protection program, and be ready to uproot our whole lives, over and over, when necessary. And it's for these reasons I think CC felt even more sorry for us than he did for himself, and even though we didn't have the maturity to realize the absolute extent of what we lost, CC did, and I think privately he grieved for us.

I sat at the dining room table with Allie, Breezy, Hazy, and Ashley, lost in the mind-boggling confusion that is middle school math. Ashley was a real math whiz, and since she was technically the oldest, she's had more practice doing advanced math, so the four of us gravitated toward her when we saw her at the table, studiously working on solving equations. Allie scrunched her face in frustration, writing and erasing answers, then flung her paper in Ashley's face, looking for help.

Ashley took the paper, pushed her glasses down to examine it closely, and handed it right back to Allie. "The answer is 8."

"How does that help me?" Allie moaned. "The answer is 8," she imitated in Ashley's assured tone. "Okay, great. But how do you get that answer?"

"It's easy," Ashley stated. "You solve for x." She gave a lengthy explanation of how to solve the formula.

"I don't understand anything you said. And why is there an x anyway? X is a letter, not a number," Allie said.

Ashley sighed. "X is a symbol that stands for the unknown."

Allie wrinkled her face. "The unknown?"

Ashley yanked her glasses off her face, squeezed her eyes shut, and held her forehead. "Allie, haven't you been paying attention in class?" she muttered through her teeth.

"Yes, but I don't get it!" Allie whined. "This stuff doesn't make any sense to me!"

"I don't get it either," Hazy admitted in solidarity.

Breezy suggested Allie work on the poem for homework instead.

Allie grinned ear to ear, causing her freckles to come out of hiding. "Okay, how about this?" She flourished the math paper, clearing her throat. "An Ode to an X." She went on pretending to read in an over-polished accent. "To be known or to be unknown? That is the question. Whether it is better as a letter to remain in the alphabet where you are well-known or to live amongst the numbers. Perhaps the x is unknown because it does not belong amongst the numbers. The letters call the x home, but the x does not hear. The x has become unknown. But what does it mean to be known anyway? Can any of us ever *really* be known?"

We laughed so hard we wiped tears from our eyes. CC walked into the dining room and saw the five of us bent over in hysterics. "This doesn't sound like homework."

"Oh, sorry, CC," Breezy laughed. "It's just Allie started..."

"Being Allie?" CC finished. He hesitated, deliberating on asking us a question. "Can I trust the five of you to do me a favor?" he finally said. "I'm preparing for dinner tomorrow and I don't have everything. You know the grocery store a few blocks down? Can you all walk there together and buy potatoes, green beans, corn, and the other items on this list?"

"Of course, CC," Ashley answered.

"I'm trusting you to do this," CC said.

"Okay, potato chips, green jelly beans, and candy corn. Got it," Allie said.

"You know what?" CC said. "Never mind. I'll do it myself later."

Allie held out her hands to prevent CC from leaving the room. "No, no, stop, CC. I was just kidding. I'm sorry. Look. Potatoes, green beans, and corn. See? I know."

CC crossed his arms. "How do you expect me to trust you to do this if you won't be serious, Allie?"

"CC," Allie cried. "My whole point is you're being silly! Of course we can handle getting groceries. We're not babies. You should give us stuff like this to do more often. We could help you out a lot more. So give us some credit!"

"Okay," CC said. "We'll see how you do with this trip." He pulled out his wallet and handed us three twenties. "Oh, and here," he said, reaching into his pocket. He pulled out his cell phone and handed it to Allie. "Take this. Just in case you need it."

Chapter 21

We walked down the sidewalk, heading towards the store. "I don't get it," Allie said. "He's been letting us go to the park by ourselves, we walk to school and back by ourselves. What's the difference between that and going to the store?"

Ashley shrugged. "I don't get it either. Does he think we'll screw something up?"

"How do you screw up getting groceries?" Allie laughed. "I mean really, what does he think is going to happen?"

Then we saw something that stopped us in our tracks: Big Boss was walking directly towards us. He reached us before we even had time to think about turning around and finding another way to the store.

"Why, hello little Munch neighbors!" Big Boss said. "Fancy seeing you out here. Are you all getting ready for Turkey Day tomorrow?"

Ashley made a face. "You mean Thanksgiving?" she asked in a disgusted tone.

"Yes, Thanksgiving. It's also called Turkey Day. After all, you eat turkey on Thanksgiving," Big Boss said.

Allie shook her head. “Not us. We don’t eat animals. We’re vegan. We don’t support violence towards other living beings.”

“Really? Well, how noble of all of you!” Big Boss took a few steps around us and stood at our side. The five of us turned to face him, not trusting to take our eyes off him for a second. ”Is that your rule or your father’s?”

“It’s both,” Allie answered. “And it’s not a rule. It’s a principle. And how are you spending the holiday tomorrow, Big Boss? Are you having friends over for dinner, then going off to celebrate by bashing in the heads of kittens and finding a litter of puppies to poison?”

Ashley snorted and put her hand to her face to hold in laughter. Big Boss took a giant step towards us, and we automatically backed up. That was a mistake. Directly behind us was a brick wall of a large office building. I noticed it just as Big Boss advanced towards us again, and we had no choice but to move backward or be plowed over. Our backs pressed up against the wall. I scanned my eyes, surveying my surroundings. We were on a public sidewalk with little foot traffic, especially in late November. But on the street to the right of us, cars drove by fairly frequently. No good. We couldn’t risk using magic right now. Big Boss stood in front of us, blocking the way forward. I anxiously assessed we were trapped.

Big Boss handed Allie a scornful smile. “So bold,” he chided. “You got me all wrong, Allie. I’m not an evil person. I would never do something like that.”

Allie crossed her arms, raised an eyebrow, and sized up Big Boss squarely. “Right. You’re not an evil person. You’re only a complete psychopath.”

As soon as Allie said it, I knew the term fit Big Boss perfectly.

Big Boss frowned. “You really shouldn’t say things like

that, Allie. That's nothing to joke about."

"Oh, I'm not joking," Allie responded. She bravely locked eyes with Big Boss and spoke slowly. "You are a complete and total psychopath. You are the very definition. If you searched the word psychopath, there'd be an image of you."

Big Boss appeared insulted but there was something in his face that showed he was impressed. "Psychopaths hurt people, Allie. I don't hurt people."

Allie scoffed. "Except for our sister Becky. And how do we know you never hurt anyone else? Has anybody ever checked your basement for severed heads?"

Ashley burst into fresh laughter, but I was too tense to laugh along. Part of me wished we were near a more secluded street so we could use magic, and part of me wished it was more crowded because it made me extremely uneasy being this close to Big Boss with so few people around.

Breezy tugged on Allie's arm anxiously, leading her forward. Big Boss took a giant step directly in front of them, using his broad body as a barrier to prevent them from going any further. Breezy moved towards the opposite side, but Big Boss blocked them again. Like a bully on a playground taunting his victims, Big Boss rapidly moved back and forth to each side, refusing to let us pass. Breezy began to tremble.

"I've already apologized to Becky," Big Boss said. "And I assure you, Allie, I have never hurt anyone else."

"Haha, right," Allie replied. "I wasn't born yesterday."

Big Boss looked at the rest of us. "You brats are adopted, right?" he sneered.

Anyone who took even a passing glimpse at us could tell we were adopted. Except for Breezy and Hazy, from hair color to body shape to skin tone, we looked nothing like each other. When CC occasionally took us all out in a public place together, we'd laugh as people would see us and do a double-take. Some people assumed we were on a class trip, but others quickly realized we were a family, and decided it was their business to come up and ask CC rude questions like, "Are they all yours?" "Are they *all* adopted?" and "How do you stay sane with that many kids?" (I kid you not.) Allie got fed up with these intrusive questions, so she started responding to them with her signature snappy retorts. My favorite one was when a woman came up to us in a restaurant while we were eating. She marched up to CC and loudly proclaimed, "My! You sure do have your hands full!" She waved her finger broadly over us. "Adopted, right?" she asked CC in a condescending tone. "No," Allie said. "We're actually the newest campaign models for a brand-new diversity ad for The United Colors of Benetton." We burst out laughing so hard Ryan spit out his soda.

None of us responded to Big Boss's question since the answer was a given. Big Boss turned back to Allie. "Do you even *know* when you were born, little orphan Allie?" he smirked.

"No, but I know it wasn't yesterday," Allie answered without fully registering what Big Boss said. "And I'm not an orphan! We have a father!"

Big Boss's smirk stayed frozen on his face. He seemed to be waiting for Allie to process what he said. For once I was ahead of her in figuring it out. Big Boss's question indicated he knew we didn't know when we were born.

Allie finally came to the same realization. "Hey, wait a minute! How did you know that?"

Big Boss gave a scoffing laugh. "I'm surprised at you, Allie. You're usually much quicker than that. I keep telling you, Allie, I know all about you brats. When are you going to believe me?"

"But, *how* do you know all about us?" Allie asked shakily. "And stop calling us brats!"

Big Boss pretended not to hear Allie. "It must be hard going through life never knowing your birthday. You never get to have a birthday party or presents and birthday cake."

Ashley huffed. "Not that it's any of your business, but we celebrate our birthday together as the day we were adopted," she said curtly.

That was true. Adoption Day, as we called it, was celebrated as a collective birthday for all thirteen of us. CC threw us a giant party with games, food, cake, and lots of presents. At our house, Adoption Day was bigger than Christmas.

"Well that's nice," Big Boss said. "Still, aren't you at least the slightest bit curious when your *real* birthday is?"

"Well since you seem to already know everything else about us, Big Boss, maybe you could tell us," Ashley replied crisply.

"Maybe I could," Big Boss teased.

There was a moment of restless pause, then for the first time ever, Hazy timidly addressed Big Boss. "Um, Mr. Big Boss sir, we need to go. We have to walk to the store. Can you let us by so we can go?"

Big Boss flashed Hazy a big, malicious grin. He responded in a tone of mimicry, imitating Hazy's unique muffled voice, cruelly mocking her. "Oh, do you need to goed, Hazy? You need to woke to the sto-wa? You need to get boy so you can goed to the sto-wa?"

Breezy's mouth dropped open and Hazy looked ready to burst into tears. Allie threw her arm around Hazy in a fiercely protective grasp and pulled her down the wall away from Big Boss.

Breezy held her hands out towards Hazy. Allie relaxed her grip, and Hazy dashed into Breezy's open arms. Breezy made eye contact with Big Boss and spoke to him in her rare firm and forceful tone she had come to use with him. "Big Boss, don't you ever speak to my sister like that ever again."

Big Boss took an intimidating step forward. "Or you'll do what, Breezy?"

"Big Boss, you are aware we can still use our powers against you, right?" Breezy reminded.

"I thought you brats don't believe in violence," Big Boss scoffed.

"We don't. But we do believe in self-defense!" Allie shot back.

Big Boss laughed coldly. "Okay. So show me what you got then," he provoked. "Come on, brats, aren't you going to use your powers against me?" He pointed to the street parallel to us where cars were passing. "Except you won't. Because you won't dare use them in public, will ya? You would have done it already."

"You need to move out of our way and let us by this instant!" Breezy demanded.

"Go ahead and move me then," Big Boss taunted. "Go ahead. I dare you to. Let's see what you brats can do *without* your powers. Not so powerful, are ya?"

"That's it! That's it!" Allie shouted, shaking in rage. "I'm calling the police!"

Allie pulled CC's cell phone from her pocket (which I had completely forgotten she had) and dialed 911. "Hi, I want to report my next-door neighbor for harassment," Allie said into the phone. "My name is Allie Munch, er, Allison Munch."

Allie gave some identifying information into the phone. Big Boss stood watching Allie. "My neighbor's name?" Allie said into the phone.

"Go ahead," Big Boss hissed at Allie, loud enough so only we could hear him. "Tell them my name is Big Boss. See how far that gets you."

Allie boldly looked Big Boss dead in the eye as she spoke into the phone. "His name is Robert Wheeler. And for some reason, he calls himself Big Boss." She held the phone down at her side and shouted at Big Boss triumphantly. "That's right! I remember your real name! I'm not as stupid as you think I am, Big Boss!"

Big Boss gave Allie an almost praiseworthy smile. "Quite on the contrary, Allie," he said in a slow, slithery tone, "I think you're the brightest crayon in this whole entire box," he said, waving his hand in a sweeping motion over all 5 of us, then pointed his hand out towards our house, indicating our whole family. "That's why I've already determined you're going to be my biggest challenge," he said chillingly.

A powerful shiver rippled through my body at Big Boss's words. Breezy and Hazy actually went pale, which is difficult to do with their complexions.

Allie's eyes clouded over in fear. "Your biggest challenge to do *what*?" she asked Big Boss, her voice higher than usual. She was shaking again, but it was no longer with rage.

Big Boss just stood facing her with that insidious smile back on his face.

"Big Boss! Your biggest challenge to do *what*?" Allie squeaked.

"Allison? Allison!" the voice from the phone called.

Allie lifted the phone back to her ear. She gave more details to the police, then hung up the phone and flashed a victorious smile at Big Boss. "The police are coming right now."

"There was no reason to call the police, Allie. It's not a crime to talk to your neighbors," Big Boss said.

"No, but it's a crime to harass and intimidate them," Allie cried. "And what do you mean I'm your biggest challenge? A challenge to what? What are you planning?"

"Wouldn't you like to know," Big Boss responded in a low, sinister tone.

Allie stared at Big Boss and with trembling hands dialed another number on the phone.

"Who are you calling now, Allie?" Breezy asked, her voice shaking.

"CC," Allie answered firmly.

I moved closer to Allie so I could hear the conversation on the other end.

"Hello?"

"Hi, Ryan? Is that you?"

"Allie?"

"Yeah. Hey, is CC there? I need to talk to him. It's really important."

"Yeah, hold on."

There was a lot of commotioh on the other end and I heard Ryan talking to CC: "It's Allie. She says it's really important." After a moment's pause, I heard CC's voice.

"Allie, what's wrong?"

"CC! We were on our way to the store like you asked, and then Big Boss stopped us and he won't let us leave-"

"WHAT?"

"Big Boss is here. And I called the police…"

"Big Boss is there right now?"

"Yes, he's still here. I called the police and they are on the way."

"Allie, where are you?"

"On Elmer Street. We're standing against a wall of an office building."

"Stay right there! I'm coming down! I'll be there in a few minutes."

Allie hung up and gave us a reassuring smile.

"Well, I'll be seeing you soon, Munch brats." Big Boss turned and walked away.

"Wait, are you leaving?" Allie shouted after him. "You're leaving *now*? Sure, you can pick on a bunch of kids, but you can't handle anyone your own size, can you! You coward!"

"Allie, just be glad he left," Breezy said.

"Thank God," Hazy whispered, tears in her eyes.

"Ho-ly crap!" Ashley cried. "When he made fun of Hazy...I couldn't believe it. And what he said to you, Allie! That whole 'you're my greatest challenge?' What did that mean?"

Allie shook her head. "I don't know. But I'm positive it was a threat."

A cop car sped down the street, siren blaring. Two officers got out of the car and approached us, just as a blue minivan squealed up to the curb. The van door slammed as CC raced over to us.

Chapter 22

We were giving our statement to the two cops. One of the officers, Officer Clarke, took down notes on her notepad.

Officer Maddow asked if Big Boss attempted to hurt us or hold a weapon on us. We shook our heads.

"I have to say while this man sounds like quite a bully, if that's all he did no crime has been committed," Officer Clarke stated.

"That's not all he did," CC cut in firmly. "This man has been harassing my kids for months. This is not an isolated incident." He filled the officers in on what Big Boss had been doing. "I want to file a police report for harassment."

"Okay, Mr. Munch," Officer Maddow replied as Officer Clarke hurriedly scribbled everything down in her notepad. "Why don't you all come down to the station and we'll file a formal report. When he attacked your daughter, did you take her to the hospital?"

"No," CC answered. "The injury wasn't severe enough. But there was a visible wound on her wrist."

"When did this occur?" Officer Maddow asked.

"May of this year," CC replied.

"So six months ago. Did you take any photographs or video of the injuries?" Officer Clarke asked.

CC sighed. "No. I guess I should have."

"Why didn't you call the police immediately after this occurred?" Officer Maddow queried. "If he wounded your daughter, that's assault. Why didn't you report it?"

"I don't know," CC lied. "I didn't hear about it until after it happened. I talked to the man and warned him to stay away from my children."

Officer Maddow exhaled loudly. "Mr. Munch, I hate to break this to you, but if you have no physical evidence of this attack, you don't have much of a case. From what you've described, I can tell you it's going to be your word against his."

"Fine," CC sighed. "I still want to file a report. Let's go to the station."

We started walking towards the car, accompanied by the two officers. Then, unbelievably, Big Boss came down the sidewalk with a big, charismatic smile on his face. My sisters and I froze. Big Boss walked up to the two police officers.

"Hello, officers," Big Boss greeted warmly. "I believe you may be looking to speak with me."

Instinctively, CC pulled the five of us closer to him, glaring at Big Boss. "This is him," CC stated. "This is the man who has been harassing my children."

Officer Clarke looked up at Big Boss in surprise. "Are you Robert Wheeler?"

"Yes, I am," Big Boss smiled, holding out his hand. "Pleased to meet you, officers. Who do I have the pleasure of addressing?"

"I'm Officer Clarke and this is Officer Maddow," Officer Clarke said without returning the smile. "We have some questions for you, sir."

"Yes, I'm sure you do," Big Boss nodded. "First of all, I must apologize to you. When young Allie here called the police, I must admit I got a little panicked and left. But then I realized I had no reason to run because, you see, this whole thing has been a giant misunderstanding, and I'll be happy to clear it all up. I feel really silly for running off like that. I hope you forgive me."

Big Boss's genteel manner gave me a bad feeling from the start. CC wasn't about to let him get the upper hand. "No, there's been no misunderstanding," he said bluntly, not taking his eyes off Big Boss. "He keeps saying that, but make no mistake, he is harassing and intimidating my children."

"Now, Casey, I know you're upset, but there's no reason to make such outlandish charges against me," Big Boss said to CC. "This *has* been a misunderstanding and I'll tell you why if you allow me a few minutes to explain."

"Before he spins you his story, just know everything he is about to tell you is a lie. He is a good liar," CC said to the officers.

"I'm afraid Mr. Munch and I never got started on the right foot," Big Boss said. "He is under the impression I am intimidating his children. But I assure you, I am doing no such thing. I was simply trying to be friendly and get to know them. Apparently, that makes Mr. Munch uncomfortable. But honestly, it's not a crime to talk to your neighbors, is it?"

"Mr. Wheeler, let me ask you a few questions," Officer Maddow cut in. "Have you been stalking Mr. Munch's children?"

"Stalking?" Big Boss questioned with a puzzled look. "No, of course not. I live next door so of course, I'm close to them, and I have run into them a few times outside the house naturally, but I don't think that constitutes stalking."

"Stalking as in spying on us!" Allie suddenly yelled. I saw the smoldering anger in her eyes rising with every word out of Big Boss's mouth. She turned towards the officers with her hands outstretched. "He knows things about us we never told him! He knew our names, our last name, he even knew the nickname for our dad!"

CC rested a hand on Allie's shoulder and lightly drew her back. "Allie, honey, let me handle this. I don't want you talking to him," he said quietly.

Big Boss smiled at the cops. "I already told Allie and her father I overheard them talking. The children play in the backyard quite frequently, and often I am working in my yard at the same time. The children are rather loud, not exactly their fault, mind you, there are thirteen of them. I can't help but overhear what they say sometimes."

"Wow," CC said acridly. "This is quite a stretch of the truth he's giving you. In addition to spying, he also leers at them."

"I'm sorry, Casey, but you are mistaken like I told you before," Big Boss said. "I may have stopped to watch them while I was in my yard, but I didn't mean to stare at them. If I did, I sincerely apologize. I didn't mean to make the children feel uncomfortable."

CC scoffed. "Oh, you are really laying it on thick, aren't you?"

Officer Clarke asked about the attack on Becky.

"See, this is where I think this whole misunderstanding started," Big Boss said. "The day I met the children they were playing baseball in their yard, and their ball crashed through my window. I confronted the children with the ball, and I may have used some harsh words with them because I was pretty upset. Then little Becky boldly asked for the ball back, and I'm sorry to say, I sort of lost my temper. She reached for it and, without thinking, I grabbed her rather roughly. Then I immediately came to my senses and let her go. I'm so ashamed because I never handled a child like that in my life. I apologized to both Becky and Mr. Munch since then. I never meant to hurt the little girl. I did leave a small mark on her, I'm sorry to say, but thankfully it wasn't a serious injury. It had already faded away by the time Becky went to her father about it."

I swallowed hard and a cloud of dread fell heavily in the core of my stomach. It was amazing how Big Boss kept that story so close to a real version of the truth, and yet by deliberately leaving out the most important detail, Breezy was able to heal Becky's wrist, it was a huge lie. I don't know what frightened me more: How smoothly Big Boss was able to lie, or the fact he was diabolical enough to plan all this going his way so far ahead of time.

"Wait a minute," Officer Maddow said. "Are you saying Mr. Munch never actually saw the injury on his daughter's wrist? Mr. Munch, is that true?"

CC sighed wearily, already knowing where this was going. "Yes, it's true, I didn't see it. But all thirteen of my children did, and they all describe it the same way. It sounded like a pretty serious injury to me."

"How long was it after the incident occurred that Becky approached you about it, Mr. Munch?" Officer Clarke asked.

CC sighed again. "They came to me shortly after it happened."

Out of the corner of my eye, I saw a smug smile appear on Big Boss's face.

"It couldn't have been that bad if it faded away before you even saw it, right after it happened," Officer Maddow half-laughed. "Mr. Munch, is it possible your children elaborated the severity of the injury a tad? And I'm just throwing this out there because I have kids myself and I know how it is, maybe your children were afraid of getting in trouble with you over Mr. Wheeler's broken window, and they knew they could deflect your attention from it by playing up the injury?"

"I know that's how it sounds, and that's exactly how he banked on it appearing, but I assure you that's not the case," CC said, glaring at Big Boss accusingly. "Look, what about today? He practically held my daughters hostage against that wall today. I'd love to hear how he's going to twist the story on that one," CC declared, folding his arms across his chest with a hostile stare at Big Boss.

"All that happened today was I ran into the children as I was out walking," Big Boss began, spinning a new tale. "I tried to engage in some friendly conversation about the holiday tomorrow, and Allie responded with some pretty rude and sarcastic remarks, which is quite a habit of hers. I found her snide comments completely uncalled for, and to be quite honest, I was a little tired of the smart-alecky attitude. So I tried to teach her a little lesson in respect, and yes, I pushed the children up against the wall a bit. In retrospect, it was a rather dumb and childish thing to do. I had no intention of keeping them there long, just enough to make my point, but then Allie overreacted and called the police. I got scared, thinking I crossed the line, and took off. When I realized I hadn't committed any crime, but I would look guilty regardless by leaving the scene, I decided the best thing to do was come back and explain."

Allie shot daggers at Big Boss the whole time he spoke. When he finished, she exploded with heated conviction. "That's not how it happened *at all*! And he's conveniently leaving out the part where he threatened us! And where he made fun of Hazy!" This time CC didn't stop Allie, only stared at Big Boss furiously.

"I didn't make fun of Hazy, Allie," Big Boss said. "And what do you mean I threatened you? In no way or manner at any point did I threaten you."

The bald-faced lie he didn't make fun of Hazy made the rest of us jump in with loud protestations.

"Look," Officer Clarke said. "While it's wrong to make fun of a child, I'm more concerned about the accusation of a threat being made here. Mr. Wheeler, did you threaten these children?"

"No, of course not," Big Boss replied immediately. "I don't know where on earth they got that idea."

"You told me I was the brightest crayon in this whole entire box and you already determined I was going to be your biggest challenge!" Allie cried.

"Oh, that?" Big Boss laughed dismissively. "Allie, you misunderstood me again. All I meant was because of your smart attitude, out of all your siblings, you are the most challenging to get along with. I can't believe you took that as a threat."

"Maybe it's because of the creepy way you said it, and when I asked you what you meant you said, 'Wouldn't you like to know,' in an even more creepy way," Allie said tartly.

"There, you see?" Big Boss said to the officers, his hands splayed towards Allie. "She just proved my point exactly. She's a real pistol, isn't she?" he chuckled.

"This is just unbelievable," CC broke in again. "I hope after shoveling through all this BS he's feeding you, you're able to see there is an ongoing pattern of harassment here."

"Mr. Munch, with all due respect, the only thing you have here is hearsay and what appears to be fabricated stories," Officer Maddow expressed. "However, you are welcome to come down to the station if you are still interested in filing a report."

"Yes, I absolutely want to file a report," CC said without faltering.

Just then, a black Jaguar came rolling down the street and pulled up at the curb. The car door opened, and an unknown man emerged from the vehicle, moving with confidence, heading directly towards us.

Chapter 23

The man had light skin, a broad belly, a brown goatee, and a bald head. He approached the officers with a self-assured swagger. "I'm Chief Donald Seager, and I have the direct authority to take over this investigation. Thank you for your work in this matter officers, but I'll be taking over from here," he said with an air of bravado.

"I think there must be some mix-up," Officer Maddow said. "We were merely responding to a simple complaint of harassment."

"No, no mix-up," Chief Seager asserted forcefully. He turned to CC. "You are Mr. Casey Munch, correct?" he asked in a gruff voice.

"Yes," CC replied, looking as confused as the officers. My sisters and I also traded bewildered expressions.

"And these are your children, right? Some of them anyway. The other eight are at home, I presume?" Chief Seager asked CC.

CC blinked. "I'm sorry, who did you say you were again?"

Chief Seager turned on his heel, stretching his arm out to meet Big Boss in a handshake. "Mr. Wheeler, it's a pleasure to see you again," he said heartily with a big smile.

Big Boss warmly shook Chief Seager's hand. "Chief Seager, the pleasure's all mine," he proclaimed. "I hope your family's well."

"Wait," CC said, staring at the two in awestruck daze. *"You know him?"*

Chief Seager ignored CC and turned to the two officers. "May I have a word with both of you a moment?"

With puzzled faces, the officers followed Chief Seager over to his car to speak privately. CC and all five of us turned to watch them, gobsmacked by this recent turn of events.

From the distance, we saw Chief Seager pull out his wallet and flash some sort of ID. All at once, the officers changed their demeanor, becoming more subservient. The three had a hushed conversation, and every so often the two officers looked back at us with curious expressions. Watching them, I felt even more unnerved than I did before. Something about all this felt so surreal. What was going on? Who is this man?

CC turned around to glare at Big Boss. "So who is he?" CC snarled at him. "A buddy of yours?"

Big Boss met CC's question with his unsettling smile.

Chief Seager and the two officers returned from their private meeting. "Mr. Munch," Officer Maddow said. "I'm sorry, but Chief Seager will be taking over your case. This investigation is no longer under our jurisdiction. We'll be leaving now and Chief Seager will take it from here."

CC gaped at Officer Maddow. "No, he will *not* be taking over this case! Chief Seager obviously has some sort of relationship with Mr. Wheeler. He can't investigate this! It's a complete conflict of interest!"

"I'm sorry, Mr. Munch," Officer Clarke replied. "But our hands are tied. We have orders from forces much higher up than this department. You must direct all future business with Chief

Seager. Good day to you, Mr. Munch. And to the children. And Happy Thanksgiving!"

As soon as the officers were gone, Chief Seager turned to CC and spoke to him in a brusque tone. "All right listen up, Mr. Munch. I think Mr. Wheeler has been more than patient with you, too patient if you ask me, but this comes to a stop now. I will not allow you to besmirch this man's good name any longer. You will drop these false allegations against him, and we will consider this matter closed. Is that clear?"

CC's mouth flew open. "What? Are you kidding me? I don't even know who you are, and how do *you* know Mr. Wheeler? Or Big Boss, the ridiculous name he calls himself. Besmirch his good name? Don't make me laugh. He's a liar, he's manipulative, and he's been harassing my children."

"That's quite enough, Mr. Munch!" Chief Seager barked. "I know all about your so-called case. Mr. Wheeler approached me in advance. He was concerned about how such outrageous allegations could harm him. I listened to everything he said and two things were very clear. First, these claims are based on lies and trumped-up accusations. Second, your children are the ones harassing Mr. Wheeler, not the other way around. Mr. Wheeler is the true victim here."

"WHAT?" My sisters, CC, and I all cried simultaneously.

"That is so beyond ludicrous it doesn't even deserve a response!" CC shouted. "Did you hear any version of the actual truth? Or did he just feed you a bunch of lies too?"

Chief Seager opened the notepad in his hand. "Ludicrous, you say? Okay, let's run through it then. First of all, your children broke his window, which I believe Mr. Wheeler never received damages for."

"Did he tell you he then attacked my daughter in retaliation?" CC fumed.

"Don't interrupt me!" Chief Seager ordered. "I was just getting there. Now about that. Here's the thing, Mr. Munch. I don't believe any such attack actually occurred. I think Mr. Wheeler briefly grabbed your daughter Becky's wrist in a moment of anger, completely justified if you ask me because of his broken window, then let go. The children decided together to lie about the injury. And what's my evidence for thinking this? Well, it's simply because you, Mr. Munch, have none. No evidence. No medical records, photos, police reports, nothing. In fact, and here's what's most damning of all, you claim after seeing Becky's wrist just minutes after this supposed attack happened, the wound had already faded away. Frankly, Mr. Munch, I'd be embarrassed to even try to claim an attack was made. I'm also surprised you didn't realize your children had obviously made it up. How naive are you? Either your children are liars or you are."

CC stood in silence, seething with rage. He glowered at Big Boss with a knowing, accusatory stare. "When did Mr. Wheeler come to see you about this? This is the first time we've contacted the police," CC said between clenched teeth.

"He had a feeling you'd go to the police because you threatened to call them when he last spoke to you," Chief Seager replied. "He wanted to clear with me if he had committed any crime. But the only crime here is what your children are doing to this man."

"Chief Seager, I am really trying my best to contain my temper right now," CC growled. "So before I explode, you better explain to me how my children are at fault for their own harassment."

"Yes, I will do that, Mr. Munch," Chief Seager affirmed. "And I'd watch your tone and show me some respect! Mr. Wheeler has shown nothing but neighborly kindness to your children. In every instance, he tried to engage them in polite conversation but was always met with open hostility. They made up vicious lies about him and are now trying to have him charged with crimes he didn't commit. They have repeatedly victimized him."

CC burst into acrimonious laughter. "Wow, that is a great story! That is a complete distortion of the facts! You know what? I'm going to let my daughters respond to that!" CC turned to us and held his hand out towards Chief Seager in an open invitation. "Go ahead, kids! Tell Chief Seager here just how much 'neighborly kindness' Big Boss has shown you," he snickered.

We pounced on CC's invitation.

"He's insulted us and spoken to us in an intimidating way just about every time we've seen him," Breezy stated.

"He keeps calling us brats!" Allie cried. "I've told him to stop repeatedly but he keeps doing it!"

"He knows information about us we never gave him, then throws out that information in conversation as I think another attempt to intimidate us," Ashley said.

"And then when we ask him how he knows this stuff, he just smiles in this creepy way," Allie added. "Either that or he gives these vague answers like he's the Riddler or something, like 'I do my homework' or 'That's my little secret.'"

Breezy told Chief Seager about Big Boss trapping us against the wall and Hazy revealed how he made fun of her voice.

"And Mr. Seager? Or Chief Seager, sorry," Breezy stumbled. "I almost hate to bring this back up again, but I'm sorry, this needs to be said. It's important because it shows what kind of person Big Boss is. When Big Boss grabbed Becky, it *was* an attack. He squeezed her wrist so hard Becky screamed in pain. We all shouted at him to stop, but he kept squeezing her wrist. When he finally let go, Becky was crying, and the wound he left on her wrist was really bad. There was a square-shaped cut where Big Boss pressed his ring. We think before he even grabbed her, he turned his ring around so it would press into her skin and hurt her even more. That shows it was premeditated. It was not a weak moment of anger. It was a cruel and malicious act."

Chief Seager rubbed his chin. "Mr. Munch, I have to say, your children make a pretty compelling case. If I was a more gullible person, I would buy it all, hook, line, and sinker. But you don't get to the position I'm in by being naive. I don't know how much of what your daughters said is true, but I wonder how much is made up."

"Made up? You think my kids are lying, but you're willing to accept everything *he* tells you as true?" CC seethed, pointing at Big Boss. "Since you pride yourself on not being naïve, what makes you think he's not giving you lies and half-truths? Because he is. He's playing you for a fool."

"That's enough, Mr. Munch!" Chief Seager shouted. "I'm no fool! To be frank with you, I don't trust your children. They look sweet and innocent, but I know there's more to them than what meets the eye. And maybe you should be less trusting of them too. You weren't present in any of the instances between your children and Mr. Wheeler, so how do you know what they say is the truth?"

"Darn," Allie said dryly. "I guess the jig is up, guys. It's true. We've been secretly terrorizing Big Boss the whole time. Our mission is to follow him and make his life as difficult as possible. We're running a whole underground ring and set up core operations in our basement. Making CC believe us was the essential part of our plan, and now you've foiled it. Looks like it's back to the drawing board, guys. I'm sure there's another neighbor we can hit for our next target."

Ashley, Hazy, Breezy, and I broke into cathartic laughter. After hearing Chief Seager imply we lied to CC, I wanted to punch Chief Seager in his big fat nose. What Allie did was so much better. CC chuckled, shaking his head knowingly at Allie's sharp humor.

Chief Seager turned to Big Boss and pointed at Allie. "That's her?"

"Yep, that's her," Big Boss said with a simmering smile.

Chief Seager stomped up to us and aimed his finger at Allie. "You're Allie, right? I might have guessed. I heard a lot about you. You've got a smart little mouth on you. You're the one mainly giving Mr. Wheeler so much trouble."

"I'll wear that as a badge of honor," Allie said.

"Oh, you think you're really funny, don't you, kid?" Chief Seager hissed. "Mr. Wheeler was right, you are a cocky little brat. You need to learn some respect for your elders."

"Respect isn't something that's just given, it has to be earned," Allie shot back.

"My, are you an impudent child!" Chief Seager scolded. "Do you know who you're talking to like that?"

"No, I don't, because you still haven't told us who you are and who you work for!" Allie cried. "All you said is you're Chief Donald Seager. Chief of what? Chief of police? Fire chief? Chief of an indigenous tribe? Chief is the nickname you had as a kid? We don't know. For all we know, you may not be a chief at all! Because even though you flashed what looked like ID at those two officers and scared them straight, you haven't shown us anything! I bet you don't even work for the police. You should've never been allowed to take our case! I don't know why we're still here, since you're convinced we're a bunch of liars and aspiring criminals, and Big Boss is a shining example of the model citizen, and we're not going to persuade you otherwise. So no, I don't know who I'm talking to!"

Chief Seager studied Allie carefully, looking her up and down. "You audacious brat!" he fired. "If you did know who you were talking to, you'd think twice before shooting your mouth off like that! If you were my kid, I'd beat the brazenness right out of you! You need a real lesson in obedience. I have half a mind to do it myself. Someone ought to, you sassy little brat!"

"Hey! Hey!" CC roared. He stormed towards us and shielded Allie behind him, getting right in Chief Seager's face. "I don't know who you are or who the hell you think you are, and frankly, I don't care! You DO NOT speak to my daughter like that!"

"You need to back off, Mr. Munch," Chief Seager snarled. "How dare you talk to me like that! I see where your brazen little daughter gets it from. She needs to learn some respect!"

"Everything she just said is true!" CC shouted. "Who are you really? You've never shown us any ID!"

"Do you think those two officers would've left if I didn't have any authority here, Mr. Munch?" Chief Seager answered. "You need proof? Fine." He shoved his hand in his pocket and pulled out his wallet, flashing a card in CC's face. I glanced at it and saw the title "Chief of Police" in bold letters.

"There, you happy?" Chief Seager growled, stuffing the ID back in his pocket. "Not that I should have to prove myself to you. Now back to the matter at hand. If you attempt to file a report on Mr. Wheeler, I'll toss it in the garbage. Do not call the police on this man ever again. You hear me back there, Allie? Don't call the police again. If you insist on continuing this charade, I will arrest you for filing false charges. Is that clear?"

CC stared Chief Seager down, breathing heavily through his nose. "This is ridiculous. You can't forbid us from getting help. You didn't come to investigate our case. You came to intimidate us. I'm not going to let you continue to bully and bluster me and my children." He turned to us and tried to smile. "We're leaving."

"Well then it looks like our business here is closed," Chief Seager announced. "Just remember what I said, Mr. Munch. Don't contact the police again. This case is officially closed."

CC had to hold back from hitting Chief Seager. Big Boss looked at us and finally spoke. "I just want to say before we go, I'm really sorry about the way this all turned out. I was just trying to be friendly, but I guess I overstepped my boundaries. It was never my intention to frighten any of you."

"Big Boss?" Breezy said softly. "Big Boss, I know you're lying. I don't mean I think you're lying. I mean I *know* you're lying. I can see it as clearly as if the word 'liar' were branded on your forehead. You can't lie to me, Big Boss. So save your breath."

CC beamed with fatherly pride at Breezy. "I have something to say to you as well, Robert," CC called out. "I don't care what he says," he said, pointing his thumb at Chief Seager, "and I don't care what the police say. If you ever pull anything like what you did today on my children again, you'll regret it. And that's not a threat. That's a promise."

CC signaled us to go. The ball of fear inside me had blown into a giant-sized boulder, threatening to crush me. All I could think about was what just happened, and worst of all, the repercussions. I stood frozen in a state of petrification. That's when I heard Big Boss and Chief Seager whispering together. I saw them quickly glance at the minivan where CC and my sisters were, then Chief Seager leaned in close to speak to Big Boss.

"Allie's going to be a problem," Chief Seager whispered.

"Oh yes. She already is," Big Boss returned.

"You were right. She *is* really smart," Chief Seager breathed.

"Yep. Extremely smart and acutely perceptive," Big Boss whispered.

"You weren't kidding," Chief Seager replied.

"Let me walk with you to your car," Big Boss said in a louder tone.

I felt like I'd just been whammed in the head. I couldn't believe what I had just overheard. At the minivan, CC and my sisters finally realized I wasn't there and were motioning me to join them. I stood staring blankly into space. Breezy ran over to comfort me and lead me to the minivan. CC hugged me. At the Jaguar, Big Boss and Chief Seager said goodbye. Big Boss turned and walked back down the sidewalk, not giving us a second glance. To think we were laughing earlier about what could possibly happen on a simple trip to the store, completely oblivious to the danger we were about to literally run into. I'll never tempt fate like that again.

CC's face was a mask of dismay, his jaw clenched tight, his face long and pallid. Allie was shaking, her face deathly ashen, and her eyes filled with dread. She moved like a zombie to CC's side, staring at the street through vacant eyes. She spoke in a voice I've never heard her use: low and trembly, strained, and sounding like it was coming from miles away. She struggled to get out each separate word.

"What…just….happened…CC?"

CC wrapped his arm around Allie and pulled her close, kissing her gently on top of her head. Shivering from the cold, he gazed into the approaching nightfall and the possible terrors hidden in the shadows, clutching Allie tightly to his side.

Chapter 24

CC warmed some soy milk on the stove and made us hot cocoa to calm our nerves. My sisters and I sat next to each other at the dining room table, still shell-shocked by what happened. CC put a plate of sugar cookies in front of us, told us it would be okay, and sat scrolling on his phone, searching for Chief Donald Seager. Even though Chief Seager's ID stated he was Chief of Police, CC couldn't find anything on *where* he was chief. He couldn't find any information about him at all.

"If he is really Chief of Police somewhere, wouldn't he have a public profile?" CC questioned aloud. He sprang from his chair with his phone and moved to the kitchen to call the police.

We sat in silence, tense as drawn bowstrings, listening to CC on the phone in the next room.

"Yes, I need to file a police report. I need to talk to somebody in charge."

Breezy and Hazy took turns sipping their cocoa in an absent-minded manner. Ashley stared straight ahead, every so often blinking as if in surprise.

"Casey Munch... What do you mean that file has been closed?"

Allie nervously ate cookie after cookie. I don't think she

was fully cognizant of what she was doing.

"I didn't sign off on anything! If there's a signature, it's been forged!... Well then reopen the file!"

The few cookies I ate were sitting heavily at the bottom of my stomach. I sat with my fingertips fixed on the table, like a cat ready to pounce.

"What do you mean the case was transferred to another department? What department?... I don't want to talk to Chief Seager!"

Allie gnawed on a cookie, then suddenly pulled it from her mouth. "I figured it out! When Big Boss left before, while we were talking to the police, he must have called Chief Seager. That's how Chief Seager knew where we were. Then Big Boss came back because he knew Chief Seager was coming!"

Breezy nodded. "Yes, but the real question is how does Big Boss know Chief Seager?"

That made me remember the conversation between Big Boss and Chief Seager I overheard earlier. "Um, that reminds me," I muttered, wincing a little. "I need to tell you what I heard Chief Seager say to Big Boss. I really don't want to upset you guys even more, but...well, try not to freak out."

I told them exactly what I heard. Breezy, Hazy, and Ashley gaped at me. Allie froze and her eyes went wide with terror. She whipped around in her seat and shouted out towards the kitchen in a frightened voice. "CC! CC! Cap needs to tell you something really important!"

CC appeared in the doorway with the phone to his ear, and held up his index finger at Allie, signaling her to wait. "Hold on, sweetheart," he whispered. CC disappeared back into the kitchen to continue his losing argument with the police. "Look, Chief Seager's ID said he was Chief of Police, but there's no information online about him. How can that be?... What higher department is he chief of?... How do you not have the clearance to tell me?"

"What does Chief Seager mean I'm going to be a problem?" Allie blurted out. "A problem for what? Big Boss said I'm going to be his biggest challenge. A challenge to what? What are they going to do?"

"I'm scared, Breezy," Hazy whimpered, looking at her twin with her brown eyes filled with fear.

"I know," Breezy said gently, putting her hand on Hazy's shoulder. "We all are."

CC moved closer to the doorway again. "No, this is a complete conflict of interest! Why does Chief Seager have to handle it?... That doesn't make any sense!... You know we're talking about the wellbeing of children here, right? Do you even care?... Fine! Thanks for nothing then! I'm glad the police care *so much* about the safety of their citizens!" CC hung up, so enraged he almost threw his phone against the wall.

Fuming with anger, CC told us the police said Chief Seager has higher authority from another department, but they don't have the clearance to tell him which department. He decided to go to the station to try to talk to them in person. CC left us alone in the house sometimes when he needed to run errands, but he made sure he was never gone very long. "Do me a favor," CC said as he was preparing to leave. "Go around and tell everyone I need to talk to them tonight." He let out a frustrated sigh. "It looks like we're going to have an impromptu family meeting."

"CC? What about Thanksgiving?" Hazy asked.

In everything that happened within the last few hours, I had completely forgotten about Thanksgiving. CC looked up at the ceiling and heaved another long sigh. "I'll figure something out."

"CC?" Hazy murmured, her voice cracking into a sob. "I'm sorry we didn't get to the store. You were counting on us to get groceries." She broke into tears.

CC hurried to Hazy's side. "Oh…no, no…hey, hey, Hazy," CC consoled Hazy, hugging her. "It's okay. Don't worry about it, honey. It wasn't your fault."

Breezy wrapped her arm around Hazy. "She's scared about what happened, CC."

"I know. It's going to be okay," CC lovingly reassured us, smiling at all five of our frightened faces. "Remember, I won't let Big Boss hurt you."

We said goodbye to CC and sat in silence. Allie slapped her hands down on the table with a loud thunk. "Well, I'm officially terrified, how about you guys?"

Ryan, Kevin, and Chase entered the dining room, laughing. They stopped in surprise when they saw us.

"Hey!" Kevin exclaimed. "What happened to you guys? You look like you just got back from battle or something!"

"Yeah," Ryan laughed. "Is that what was so important when you called before?" he asked Allie. "You needed backup for battle? What happened?"

We didn't say a word. Ryan took a closer look at our blank faces and his expression immediately changed. "Okay, you guys are actually scaring me now. Seriously, what happened?"

Breezy exhaled loudly. "I'll tell you everything, but you better sit down. It's a really long story and….well, just trust me, you'll want to be sitting down."

Ryan, Chase, and Kevin sat across from us at the table and Breezy told them the whole story. Our brothers listened in agape amazement. Breezy finished, and they sat staring into space, at a complete loss for words.

"That's crazy!" Kevin cried at last. "Is this even legal?"

"It sounds like Chief Seager is hiding his real identity. I don't think he's really Chief of Police. I bet that ID he showed you is fake," Ryan said.

Kevin scrunched his face. "So if he's not Chief of Police who is he? And what higher department does he work for? And wait, does this mean if we call the police on Big Boss again, they won't help us?"

Allie looked up. "Yep."

"Okay...um...so, that's not good," Kevin said fretfully.

Allie gave Kevin a sad smile. "No. Definitely not good, Kev."

"What should we do then if we need to call the police on Big Boss?" Ryan asked.

Allie raised her hand in a helpless gesture. "I guess we're on our own. What I'm worried about is what Big Boss is going to do the next time we run into him, knowing he can't get in trouble with the police," Allie revealed, her eyes a little panicked.

Fear clouded over Kevin's face. "Um, yeah...I never even thought of that... "

Chase shrugged. "We'll just blast him with our magic then. We don't need the police. If he tries anything again, we just hit him. No sweat."

"No!" Allie cried. We all jumped in our seats, startled by the force in her tone. "Don't do that! Don't just assume you'll be able to use magic! I tried to tell you this before, Chase. Don't underestimate him! Big Boss is a psychopath. After today, I'm sure of that. You should have seen the way he lied so easily to the police! How he was able to put on a big show for them like he was neighbor of the year!" She shuddered a little at the memory. "We are dealing with a genuine psychopath here. We live...next door...to a psychopath," she stressed, karate chopping the table at the same time. "Just let that sink in a moment. Don't blow off not being able to contact the police! I don't think you've realized it yet, but we are in serious trouble! And don't think we'll just be able to use magic! We couldn't today because there was a risk of someone seeing us. How do you know that won't happen again? And now the police won't even come to help us!"

Chase scanned the room in open-mouthed dismay as he took in everything Allie just said. "Um...I'm sorry. I didn't mean to downplay everything. Of course this is bad. I'm so dumb. I'm really sorry," he mumbled, looking down at the table.

Allie put her elbow on the table and rested her hand on her cheek, giving Chase a slightly reproving look. "Chase, stop calling yourself dumb. You're not dumb. You know, you should really work on your self-esteem issues. It's okay. I know you don't always see how serious things are."

"So what do we do now?" Ryan sighed.

"Well, CC wants to talk to us all tonight about this," Breezy said.

"You know what that means?" Allie said with a small smile. "Family meeting time."

Our brothers emitted a collective groan. Breezy announced we have to tell everyone about the meeting. Ashley said she'd tell Kitty, and Ryan said he'd tell Justin.

Allie looked up in sudden realization of who was left and hurriedly spoke in rapid-fire succession. "Last-one-to-call-not-it-has-to-tell-Twisty-Carlie-and-Becky-1-2-3-NOT IT!"

"NOT IT!" Kevin, Chase, Ryan, Ashley, and I shouted over Allie at the same time.

Breezy sighed. "I'll tell them."

Chapter 25

Family meetings are usually very loud, boisterous affairs, but this one was eerily quiet. Before the meeting even started, everyone had already heard what happened. CC arrived home and walked dejectedly into the living room to find thirteen pairs of eyes looking up at him questioningly. CC slumped into a chair, heaving a terrible sigh. Things at the police station didn't go well. The officers repeated the same non-answers they gave on the phone. They became increasingly irritated with CC and his insistent demands and finally threatened to have him arrested if he didn't leave. My siblings seemed more than a little shaken up after we gave them the full story, especially after I told everybody about the conversation I overheard between Chief Seager and Big Boss. All at once my siblings frantically threw out questions.

"Does that mean Chief Seager is working with Big Boss?"

"Why are the police going along with it then?"

"Are the police in on this too?"

"In on what? What are they doing? What's the plan here?"

CC broke in, raising his hands in a quelling manner. "Okay, everyone, calm down. We have to try not to get all upset."

CC said we'll take extra precautions so Big Boss can't run into us again. Until further notice, we were not to go anywhere without him, including to and from school. We were to travel together in the white passenger van, CC's other van that was big enough to seat all of us. My siblings emitted a mighty groan at this news, not happy CC had to chaperone us wherever we went. I, however, couldn't have felt more relieved with this plan, terrified of meeting Big Boss again. I noticed Breezy, Hazy, Allie, and Ashley weren't protesting either.

"If we're taking the van, I call shotgun!" Becky exclaimed.

"Nooooooo!" We all cried in a resounding chorus.

"You can't have shotgun! It's not your turn!" Chase objected.

"Yeah! I'm next on the list!" Ryan cried.

"Stop!" CC shouted. "We're not fighting over shotgun again. This is the very last thing I want to deal with right now. I'm picking the seats. I don't want any arguments."

"Well, I'm not sitting next to Kevin or Allie!" Twisty cried.

"Me neither!" Carlie echoed.

CC dropped his head in his hands as if he suddenly had a migraine headache.

"Oh, don't worry, I'm not sitting anywhere near either of you!" Kevin shot back.

"And I'm not sitting next to Allie either!" Becky declared.

"I don't want to sit near *any* of Allie's friends!" Twisty yelled. "Except Breezy. Breezy I'm cool with. But the rest of you, if you're friends with Allie, you're no friend of mine!"

Allie glowered at Twisty. "CC, if you want to put me next to Twisty, fine. But fair warning: I may try to throw her out of the van," she said through grit teeth.

Twisty's eyes flared. "I'll throw you out of the van, Allie!"

CC snapped his head upright and stood up, vigorously

waving his hands at us all to stop. "Whoa! Whoa! Enough! What is this? Are you all fighting? What's going on here?"

Allie blurted out Twisty, Carlie, and Becky all hate her.

CC turned to the three. "Is that how you feel? You hate her?"

"I don't hate her. I just don't like her," Becky said flatly.

CC handed Becky a harsh glare, indicating he didn't like that response.

Becky shrank back a little. "I don't have to like everyone," she justified weakly.

CC cast his eyes down at Carlie. "And what about you, Carlie?"

"I don't like Allie either," she stated.

"Why?" CC challenged.

"I just don't," she said.

"That's not an answer," CC responded. "Can I guess why? Is it because Twisty doesn't like her?"

Carlie looked stubbornly at the wall. "That's not the only reason," she mumbled.

"You know, Carlie, you don't have to act and think the same way Twisty does," CC lectured. "You have a mind of your own. Use it."

CC stepped in front of Twisty, and she quickly looked away, trying to avoid CC's hard glare. CC crossed his arms and lifted his eyes towards her in an interrogative manner. "So let me get this straight," he said to Twisty gruffly. "Not only are you holding a grudge against Allie, but also all of Allie's friends?"

Twisty dropped her eyes to the floor. "Not Breezy."

"You better come up with a better answer than that," CC warned sharply. "It sounds like you're just being petty. I'm not going to seat you next to Allie. Believe me, I know better than that. But you better drop this hostility you're holding against three-quarters of your family this instant!"

Okay," Twisty squeaked.

"And at some point, you need to end this war with Allie too," CC continued sternly. "This has been going on for far too long."

CC gave us another short lecture about needing to get along better and how there should never be any talk of us hating each other. Before dismissing the meeting, CC reminded us we're not allowed to leave the house without him.

"Why don't you just chain us up inside?" Carlie cried out.

We all turned towards Carlie in surprise. She was wearing an angry scowl on her small face, her eyes upturned towards CC.

"Carlie, don't talk to me like that!" CC snapped. "I don't like this any more than you do."

"You're keeping us prisoner inside our own house!" Carlie shouted. "This is all because of Allie! If Allie didn't get smart with Big Boss again, he would've left them alone today. None of this would've happened!"

"That's not true!" Ashley cried. "It wasn't Allie's fault! He wasn't letting us pass and we couldn't use magic! What were we supposed to do? Just stand there and let him bully us? You weren't there, Carlie! So stop talking because you have no idea what you're talking about!"

Allie flashed Ashley a huge smile of gratitude.

"Carlie, sometimes I really can't believe you," CC reprimanded. "Ashley's right. Allie's not responsible for Big Boss terrorizing them."

"Big Boss even said himself he trapped them against the wall to teach Allie a lesson!" Carlie argued.

"And you believe him?" CC scolded. "Over you own

sisters? I don't care what Allie said. No adult in their right mind would respond in that manner."

Twisty broke in to back up Carlie's argument. "It does seem Allie made the situation worse. I bet if Allie wasn't there, it wouldn't have gone as badly."

Carlie smiled at Twisty. "Yeah, that's all I'm saying."

CC shook his head at the two of them. "And I'm saying it doesn't matter. An adult should know better. Allie didn't cause this. Honestly, what is with you two?"

"Are you actually defending Big Boss?" Kevin said.

Before Twisty or Carlie could respond, Allie burst out with something no one expected her to say.

"Of course they're defending him," Allie said. She turned to face CC. "CC, there's something you should know. We saw Twisty and Carlie talking privately with Big Boss."

Chapter 26

It was as if Allie just tossed a live grenade into the middle of the living room. For a moment, everyone, including CC, just stopped. Twisty and Carlie stood with frozen expressions in petrified horror, their eyes wide as saucers. The faces of my other siblings were as fixed as if they were figures in a wax museum.

CC looked as if he was coming out of a deep stupor, blinking like the first blinding lights were stinging his eyes. He stared at Allie as if he were looking right through her. "I'm sorry, Allie. What did you just say?" he croaked.

"Twisty and Carlie have been talking privately to Big Boss. We saw them," Allie repeated.

The initial shock had worn off, and now Twisty and Carlie were glaring at Allie with such violent hatred it honestly scared me.

CC was still trying to get over the blow. "When?"

"Couple weeks ago," Allie answered.

"And you're just telling me now?" CC rebuked.

"We didn't all see it," Ashley said quickly. "Just the Four Musketeers. They saw them talking."

"Talking how?" CC spoke in a crisp, staccato-like rhythm.

"They were whispering together," Allie answered. "They stopped as soon as they saw us."

"What were they saying?" CC's voice climbed higher.

"We couldn't hear them," Allie stated. "I asked Twisty and Carlie what he said, but they told me it was none of my business."

CC finally exploded. "None of your business? None of your business?" He wheeled on his heel and spun towards Twisty and Carlie cowering in the corner. "None of her business? Are you kidding me? This better not be true!"

Twisty was suddenly stricken with the inability to speak. Carlie stuck close to Twisty's side, her defiance suddenly lost.

"Is it true? Were you talking to Big Boss?" CC roared.

Twisty nodded her head, not daring to raise her eyes from the floor.

"This is just unbelievable!" CC fumed. "What could you possibly have been talking to him about?"

Carlie finally opened her mouth. "He was just making small talk."

CC turned red with anger. "Then why were you whispering with him? Are you lying to me, Carlie?"

"We weren't whispering. Allie's making that up," Carlie accused.

"I see," CC said thickly. He turned again towards Allie, Breezy, Hazy, and I. Allie shook her head vigorously, but it was me, Breezy, and Hazy CC questioned, and the three of us affirmed what Allie said.

"It wasn't just Allie who saw you," CC said to Carlie in a severe tone. "It was Capricorn, Breezy, and Hazy too, and they all say you were whispering with him. You better stop lying to me and tell the truth, Carlie!"

"They're just defending Allie!" Carlie cried. "Of course Allie's closest friends are going to back her up!"

"You're accusing Breezy of lying?" CC shouted furiously. "Breezy! You better think very carefully about what you say next!"

"I saw them too," Kitty piped up from across the room in a small voice. "Through the kitchen window when I was cooking. They were talking at the backyard fence. Last week."

We stared at Kitty in shock. CC looked angry enough to spontaneously combust. He whirled back on Twisty and Carlie. "Another time? How many times have you been talking to him? What has he been saying to you?"

Carlie kept insisting it was nothing. CC took Carlie by the shoulders and moved her away from Twisty. Then he swung back towards Twisty, demanding the truth.

Twisty lifted her trembling hands in a helpless gesture. "I-I can't really say...but...it's…nothing…"

"THERESA MUNCH!" CC thundered fiercely. "You better tell me what he's saying to you this instant!"

Twisty jumped in the air at the sound of her real name and CC's harsh tone. "Okay, okay. I'll tell you, but please don't be mad...we're talking about Allie, don't be mad please…"

"About Allie?" CC barked. "What about Allie?"

Twisty winced, reluctant to continue. "Um...just how rude and disrespectful she is, and he um...doesn't know how we uh...deal with her. And we…just agree with him."

"You agree with him?" CC shouted.

"Yes, we agree, because Allie is rude and annoying!" Carlie shouted. "Big Boss sees it as much as we do! He says someone should teach Allie a lesson!"

Twisty stared at Carlie in horror. It was clear Carlie said more than Twisty wanted to reveal. Allie's mouth dropped open. CC stood like a pent-up volcano ready to erupt.

"He said that to you?" CC shrieked. "And you went along with this? You're conspiring against your sister with Big Boss?"

"Yeah, well he's right!" Carlie shot right back at CC. "And we should be able to talk to whoever we want! Big Boss is nice to me and Twisty! He's not as bad as you think!"

"What are you talking about?" Becky screamed out. She was shaking with intense anger. "He's not bad? He's nice to you? And you don't care at all he *hurt me*, Carlie? What are you even saying?"

"Are you too stupid to see he's trying to turn you against your own sister?" Ashley shouted. "He's not being nice to you, Carlie, he's completely playing you!"

CC cursed Big Boss under his breath. He sent Twisty and Carlie to their room and dismissed the meeting.

Breezy warned Allie to be careful of Twisty and Carlie as Big Boss has their ear and they seem out for blood. An image immediately popped into my head: Twisty and Carlie glaring at Allie with enraged, hateful faces. Then, like an invading force, another image burst through my mind: Big Boss's sinister smile.

Chapter 27

CC's plan worked like a charm and we didn't see hide nor hair of Big Boss. He wasn't the only adversary we were granted a reprieve from. Carlie and Twisty were grounded in their room for their treachery with Big Boss. When they came out for meals, everyone gave them the silent treatment. Even Becky slipped them the cold shoulder.

One thing that didn't change was how often my siblings used their powers. Once CC started chauffeuring us around everywhere, everyone assumed it was safe. Confined inside our house, with CC busy working in his office most evenings, my siblings used their powers like there was no tomorrow.

It was mid-December on a Saturday evening and I had just emerged from a nap. I walked through the house and noticed CC wasn't around. In the living room, I found Chase, Kevin, Ryan, Justin, and Allie. I asked where CC was.

"He went to the store with the Bopsy twins," Allie answered. "Ashley and Kit Cat went with them too. CC asked for volunteers to help, and everyone fought for the chance to go. I won't say how badly, but let's just say blood may have been involved. Just kidding. Sort of."

Ryan laughed. "People are itching like mad to get out of the house."

"Well, things could be worse. We could be Twisty or Carlie," Kevin grinned.

Justin frowned. "I really hate being cooped up inside the house though. I think it's a bit of overkill. Sometimes I think CC is a little bit overprotective."

"A *little bit* overprotective?" Allie laughed. "Don't you mean a lot bit overprotective? Are you really just figuring this out now, Justin?"

Justin chuckled. "Yeah, I know. He means well though."

Allie jerked her head at Justin. "Hey, Just! I've been meaning to ask you, what's going on with your DIY soup kitchen? Are you still doing it?"

Justin gave Allie a puzzled look, then recognition dawned on him. "Oh, you mean the sandwiches. No, I had to stop because of not being allowed to leave the house. I feel terrible because they came to depend on me and now I'm letting them down. It's one of the main reasons I'm hating this whole no-leaving-the-house thing."

"Justin, I'm going to start calling you Justice," Allie teased, but with great admiration. "Okay, Justice, how about this? Why don't you get someone to help you? And by the way, why didn't you ever ask any of us to help?"

Ryan, Chase, and Kevin gave them questioning looks.

Allie grinned. "Justin has been busy feeding the hungry, healing the sick, and making plans to turn Earth into a peace-filled utopia."

"She's waaay exaggerating," Justin said. "All I've been doing is making sandwiches, using magic to replicate them, and leaving them at the park for people to eat. That's all."

"That's all. He's way too modest," Allie replied. "He's

using magic to feed hungry families. And he's got big plans for how we can solve ninety percent of the world's problems single-handedly using magic."

"Again, Allie is exaggerating," Justin stated. "I haven't done anything but give people sandwiches. And if you mean what I told Capricorn," he said, turning to Allie, "that was just some stuff I was bouncing around in my head. Making it happen would be impossible. I mean, look! CC isn't even letting us leave the house right now!"

"True, but it's a dream worth fighting for," Allie said. "CC could change his mind. Don't give up on it, Justice."

Kevin asked what the dream was. Before Justin could respond, sudden quiet footsteps and scuffling sounded from the hallway. We all turned to find Carlie standing in the entranceway of the living room. She had a look of outright malice and fierce determination on her small face that frightened me.

"Hey!" Kevin yelled, pointing at Carlie. "You're supposed to be in your room!"

Carlie stared at Kevin with heated anger in her eyes. Before anyone even had a chance to think, she stepped into the living room and threw her arm out directly at Kevin. Bolts of electricity came shooting out from the tips of all five of her fingers, and each one struck painfully in different places all over Kevin's body. Kevin gave out a horrible scream as the electricity instantly seared his skin, and he fell to the ground, thrashing in pain.

"CARLIE!" We all screamed out at once.

"Oh my God, Carlie! What did you just do?" Allie shouted, rushing to Kevin's side.

My brothers were too dumbstruck to react, but I sped over to join Allie. I covered my mouth in horror at the sight of Kevin.

His entire body was covered in electrical burns that had seared through his clothes and cut through his skin. I tried my best to fight back tears. Ryan, Justin, and Chase finally came out of their stupor and stood leaning over us to look at Kevin, turning their heads away in revulsion when they saw his burns.

Allie took charge and turned to my three brothers. "Do any of you have any power left?"

With the most mortified and shamefaced expressions imaginable, all three of them shook their heads no. Allie shot them a reprimanding look and turned back to me. "Cap, I need your help," she pleaded, tears in her eyes. "I can heal him, but I can't do it alone. These burns are too severe for one person. You and I are probably the only people in the house right now with energy left to heal him! God, where are Breezy and Hazy when you need them?" Allie delicately rested her hands on Kevin's body. She closed her eyes and breathed a silent prayer as the warm healing light came shooting from her fingertips. She gently moved her hands up and down the length of Kevin's body, coating his burns with the healing glow of her hands. Kevin's blistered skin gradually became smoother as some of the burns lifted away. I watched the magical process unfold with hopeful eyes, and for a minute I thought maybe Allie would be able to heal Kevin without my help. Then, as if the thought itself jinxed her, the light emanating from her hands sputtered, and at once it was gone. Kevin, who previously was so badly burnt he was barely cognizant, emitted pain-racked whimpers like a wounded puppy.

"Shh, just hold on," Allie whispered to our brother soothingly.

Allie nodded at me and I began phase two of the healing course. I laid my hands on Kevin and scanned his body, watching the wounds miraculously melt away. I smiled as my light faded, knowing Allie and I succeeded in doing what just moments ago seemed impossible. There Kevin laid on the floor, but nothing more serious than a sunburn was present now. Kevin slowly sat up, smiling weakly at Allie and me. He whispered thank you as he regained his senses.

"What's wrong with Carlie?" Chase exclaimed. "I can't believe she did that!"

In all the panic, I had forgotten about Carlie. I swerved around and found Carlie still standing there near the doorway of the living room, staring down at Kevin with vengeful eyes, but now she was no longer alone. Twisty was standing next to her with that same murderous look on her face, but her ire was directed not at Kevin, but Allie. I suddenly had the same feeling wash over me as when Becky went up to Big Boss to retrieve our ball at the fence, and in a flash of horror, I realized what was going to happen. I managed to shout out a cry of warning just as Twisty raised her hand. "Allie! Look out!"

Allie looked up at Twisty and her mouth formed an oval of surprise. A yellow sphere of light appeared in Twisty's hand that formed into a fireball, which Twisty abruptly hurled at Allie. Drained of all magic, Allie was unable to counterattack, but she didn't even have time to move. The fireball plowed with sickening force straight into Allie's stomach, and a bloodcurdling scream burst from her lips. Allie was knocked to the ground with a violent thud, and I ran to her, screaming her name. Allie laid motionless on the floor, her shirt burnt into shards of fabric. Her exposed stomach was covered by a grotesque open wound of charred flesh, where the fire had seared right through her skin. I whirled on Twisty in a state of revulsion and terror. Twisty stood there in a self-satisfied victory stance, and her lips curled into a triumphant smile.

"Now we're even," she gloated.

Chapter 28

"TWISTYYY!!!"

In a blind rage, I barreled towards Twisty, intending to tear her to pieces. Twisty lost her smug smile and became visibly frightened. Something from behind caught me and stopped me mid-charge. I whirled around and came face to face with Ryan, who had a strong grip on my shirt, and was pulling me back from attacking Twisty.

"Let go, Ryan!" I screamed. "I'm going to rip her apart!"

"Capricorn, stop!" Ryan screamed back. "Forget her! Allie needs our help! She's hurt really bad! We need to act fast!"

My rage was immediately replaced with profound terror for Allie. I darted towards her and found Chase and Justin kneeling over her, trying to shake her awake and calling out her name. They looked up at me with huge tears streaming down their faces.

"I think she's unconscious!" Justin cried. "I don't think she's breathing!"

Panic gripped me like a vice as I bent down and tried to feel for Allie's breath and felt nothing. I grabbed her wrist and prayed like mad I could feel a pulse. I thought I sensed a very light beat, but in my distraught state, it was hard to tell. The fire had burned right through her flesh, and horrible images came to my mind of Allie's ruptured lungs. I was suddenly unable to breathe.

"We need someone with magic!" Chase cried. "Find someone who can heal her!"

Just as I thought my terror couldn't possibly be worse, a realization occurred to me that seized me by the throat: None of us had any energy left to heal her. Out of all my siblings, the only ones who hadn't spent their magic were me, Allie, Breezy, and Hazy, and Breezy and Hazy were currently gone with CC, not to mention Ashley and Kitty, who probably wouldn't have any power available anyway. Magic was already in short supply with the attack on Kevin. Allie just said it herself minutes earlier: *You and I are probably the only people in the house right now with energy left to heal him.* And Allie and I had used all our magic on Kevin. Which meant...

"Oh, God!" I squeaked. "I used all my power on Kevin! None of you have any power! Kevin, please God, tell me you have some magic available!"

Kevin looked like a deer in headlights. He still seemed a bit disoriented from the earlier attack. Sickened, he shook his head. "I'm sorry..." he heaved with a sob. "I don't."

"Why don't you just get Breezy or Hazy to heal her?" Twisty asked in a maddeningly indifferent tone. "You know they got magic."

"They're not here, you idiot!" I shrieked at her. "They went to the store with CC!"

"They're not here?" Twisty repeated stupidly.

"You stupid little twit!" I screamed with rage. "If Allie dies because of you, I'll kill you, Twisty!"

"We need to do something now or Allie's going to die!" Ryan wailed.

"Call 911!" Chase screeched. "For God's sake, call 911 RIGHT NOW!"

Then all at once, there was a great thundering sound as someone came pounding down the stairs. Becky suddenly flew into the living room and sprinted towards Allie on the ground. She cradled Allie against her, placing her hands over the horrible wound on her stomach. Then the panic released its hold on me, and I began to breathe again. Tears of relief came to my eyes as I saw the familiar yellow glow radiating from Becky's hands.

Chapter 29

As if some gift from heaven, Allie began breathing again. The only remnant of the gruesome damage was a large red scar. Allie opened her eyes and gradually the life came back into her. We openly rejoiced and brushed away our tears, painfully aware of the frightful close call we just had. Allie blinked and looked up at Becky uncomprehendingly. Her face took on a mask of mixed fear and bafflement, uncertain how she ended up on the floor staring up into Becky's face. With the crisis averted, Becky turned on Twisty, filled with hot anger.

"What the hell is wrong with you, Twisty?" Becky shouted. "You could have killed her! Do you realize that? You could have seriously killed her! What the hell were you thinking?"

Twisty looked a little taken aback at the degree of Becky's outrage, and honestly, I was extremely surprised too. I had to remind myself that it was Becky of all people who just saved Allie's life.

"I wasn't trying to kill her!" Twisty cried. "Just get back at her and teach her a lesson."

"A lesson?" Becky fired back. "You were teaching her a lesson by killing her?"

"I said I wasn't trying to kill her!" Twisty shouted defensively.

"You could have fooled me!" Ryan cut in. "You shot a fireball at her stomach! What did you think was going to happen?"

"She deserved it after everything she did!" Twisty cried.

"She deserves to die?" Becky yelled. "You almost killed your own sister!"

"Thank God you were here, Becky," Justin said. "Or she *would* have killed her."

"And did you deliberately attack her right after Carlie attacked Kevin to make sure I wouldn't be able to heal her?" I shouted, asking a question that was in my head since I first realized I wouldn't be able to save Allie.

Twisty and Carlie shared a conspiratorial glance. "I didn't want her to be healed right away," Twisty replied. "So Carlie zapped Kevin first, and anyway we wanted to get back at him too! For zapping me! Remember he attacked me first!"

I stared at Twisty with wrathful ire. "You didn't want her to be healed right away? So in other words you wanted her to suffer?"

"She deserved to suffer a little after everything she did to us!" Twisty cried. "And anyway, Allie said I got what I deserved when Kevin attacked me. What's the difference?"

"She could have died, you stupid dolt!" Kevin suddenly screamed out. He seemed to have mostly recovered from Carlie's attack. "Don't you get that? She could have died! What's the *difference*? What's the *difference*? When I attacked you, you got some small burns on your arm. Carlie shot enough volts through me to electrocute me! You burned up my whole body, Carlie!" he railed, whirling on Carlie. "I could've died! Do you even care? And Twisty, you stupid pea-brained imbecile! Before you hatched up this insane plan, did you stop to think for just one second that shooting a fireball at Allie's stomach might just kill her? Did you ever stop to *think* for just one freaking second?"

I continued, inspired by Kevin's rage. "And you knew nearly everyone in the house was overusing their powers, which *you two* encouraged them to do. If no one could heal her, Twisty, what did you think would happen? She would have been rushed to the hospital, and by the time she got there it might have been...too late." My voice started to crack, imagining the worst possibility. "We…might have lost her."

"We knew Breezy and Hazy would have power. We thought one of them would heal her," Twisty said in a nonchalant manner that made me want to punch her.

"They're not home!" I screamed at her again.

"Well, how were we supposed to know that?" Twisty asked, and I had to stop myself from clawing her face.

"Don't you think that's something you should have checked first?" Ryan cried. "Made sure Breezy and Hazy were here so they could heal her? So you don't, you know, 'accidentally' kill your sister?"

"They're usually here! How were we supposed to know this would be the one time they're not? No one tells us anything! We're just locked up in our room all day and left to rot! You all just forget we exist! Well now you *know* we exist, don't you?" Twisty vented with fire in her eyes.

"Don't you DARE make this about you!" I shrieked.

Allie was still on the ground regaining her strength, but she had been following along with everything since she awakened and fully pieced together what happened. She raised her head in Twisty's direction. "You must have known CC wasn't home. Otherwise, you would never have *dared* to do what you did," she said weakly.

Becky nodded. "They did know. I told them CC went to the store."

Twisty gave Becky a resentful look. "Yes, you said CC went to the store. You didn't say Breezy and Hazy went with him."

"I'm sorry, I didn't realize you were planning on attacking our brother and sister and that was necessary information. I'll make sure you know exactly who went with CC the next time you plan to potentially kill one of our siblings," Becky said sarcastically.

Allie burst into laughter and then immediately cringed in pain.

"Wait till CC comes home and finds out what you did!" Chase said to Twisty and Carlie. "You're going to be locked in your room for the rest of eternity!"

"No, we won't!" Twisty cried. "That's not going to happen!"

"Yeah, you're right, because when we tell CC what you did he's going to kill you," Allie said.

Twisty shot Allie a look of pure contempt. "You are *not* going to tell on us!"

Kevin and Allie looked at each other and cracked up laughing. Allie held her stomach, wincing while she laughed, and got up from the floor, walking towards Kevin.

"She *actually* thinks we're not going to tell CC about this, Kev," Allie hooted.

"That's the funniest thing I ever heard!" Kevin chortled. "*Of course* we're going to tell CC! I might even run outside and tell him as he's parking the car!"

"Yeah, me too!" Allie giggled. "Hi, CC! Guess what? Twisty and Carlie tried to kill us while you were gone. So what did you get at the store?"

Everyone, except Twisty and Carlie, broke into hysterical

laughter. I laughed in great relief to hear Allie's witty jokes again after we came so close to losing her for good.

Twisty stared at us, her eyes flaring. "If you tell on us, Kevin, we'll tell CC that you've been wasting magic."

Kevin and Allie exchanged another look and laughed even harder.

"I don't care!" Kevin cried. "Do you really think that's going to stop me from telling CC? Tell him whatever you want! Carlie tried to *electrocute me* and you *shot a fireball* into *Allie's stomach*!"

"Yeah, what do you think CC's going to say?" Allie laughed. "Trying to kill your brother and sister, that's one thing, Twisty and Carlie. But misusing your powers, now that's really serious, Kevin."

This sent up another round of uproarious laughter.

"There is nothing you can say or do to stop us from telling CC!" Kevin said. "We're going to tell him!"

That was when Carlie spoke up for the first time since she arrived and started this whole thing by attacking Kevin. What she said changed the mood in the room immediately and all remaining laughter was abruptly cut off.

"No you won't," Carlie said. "I have a message from Big Boss. He said to tell you if you tell CC what we did, he'll make you pay. He'll make you all pay."

Chapter 30

My siblings and I stared at Carlie with eyes so wide I thought they'd pop right out of our skulls. A deafening silence overtook the room that made even the sound of Ryan breathing next to me sound like a thunderclap.

Kevin was the first to find his voice. "You have…a message…from Big Boss?" he uttered tightly, forcing air into his lungs to speak.

Becky was more succinct. "What the hell do you mean you have a message from Big Boss, Carlie?"

"Just what I said. He said that if you tell CC on us, he'll make you all pay," Carlie repeated.

"Wait! You're working with Big Boss against your own family? Just whose side are you on here anyway?" Ryan asked.

"I think they've made it abundantly clear it's not our side," Allie said.

"Don't pretend like we're on the same side!" Carlie shouted with sudden fervor. "You've all *made it abundantly clear* you want nothing to do with us! It's just like Twisty said, you pretend we don't exist! We're tired of being treated like the family's shameful little secret! Locked away and allowed only to come down to eat, and even then no one talks to us or looks us in the eye! We're done with it and all of you! So hear me loud and clear! Big Boss has an ultimatum for you! If you tell CC what we did, he'll make you pay. BUT if you don't say anything to CC, he said he'll never bother any of you ever again. He'll go away and leave you alone. And you can all go back to playing outside and not have CC chaperone you wherever you go. The choice is yours."

Allie gave a quizzical look and shook her head. "That doesn't make any sense. Why would Big Boss care if you get in trouble with CC?"

"Maybe it's because he knows the way we're being treated isn't right. He wants to help us even the score," Carlie said.

Becky's face grew livid. "How can you make friends with him after everything he did? What about him attacking me? I guess you don't care about that at all?"

"He apologized several times for that and you still haven't let it go," Carlie stated.

"Let it go?" Becky screamed. "His apology is worth spit! If you believe that was sincere, you're just stupid! He lied to the police about what happened! You were there when he attacked me and saw it with your own eyes, and he lied through his teeth about it!"

"I'm not stupid!" Carlie shouted back. "Say what you want about Big Boss, but he's never called me stupid! Only my so-called family does that! He had reasons for lying to the police. He couldn't say anything about you getting healed, so he had to keep the story simple."

Becky laughed bitterly. "Is that what he told you? So you don't care at all how much he hurt my wrist? That's what he lied about! He never admitted how much he deliberately hurt me! I can't believe you're saying this, Carlie! How can you make excuses for him like that?"

"Not to mention he's been harassing us all for months, and she doesn't seem to care about that at all either," Ryan pointed out.

"Plus, you know, there's this whole little thing of keeping us from filing a police report against him and not letting us call the police for help, but that's not a big deal," Allie said derisively.

"That wasn't Big Boss, that was Chief Seager," Carlie said.

"He's working with Chief Seager!" Allie replied. "And did he put you up to attack me and Kevin? Was this his idea?"

"He wanted to help us get even. He told us how to get back at you and Kevin at the same time," Carlie revealed.

"So how is he going to make us pay if we tell CC?" Ryan asked.

"He just said if you tell CC, someone will get hurt," Carlie said.

"And you're okay with that?" Becky shouted. "You're fine with us getting hurt?"

"It's pretty clear they're more than fine with it. They just hurt me and Kevin," Allie reminded Becky.

"We don't want anyone else to get hurt, despite how badly you've treated us," Twisty said. "We want to call it even with Allie and Kevin and that's it. We'll move on."

"Even. That's an interesting word for nearly burning us to death. I got you grounded, so you burn up my stomach in return. That's fair. Now we're even. Of course," Allie said glibly.

Twisty delivered Allie another hateful look. "You did more to me and Carlie than get us grounded, Allie," she growled.

"I did nothing to you that warrants nearly killing me over!" Allie shouted. "Kevin didn't either! You're nuts, Twisty! Completely nuts! You and Carlie both!"

Carlie stared at Allie coldly. "Whatever. What's your decision?"

"Well if Big Boss is going to leave and not bother us again, maybe it's worth it," Justin suggested. "And I'm very worried about what he means by 'he'll make us pay.' Maybe it's best not to tell CC."

"Um no," Allie countered immediately. "Sorry, but no, Justin." She pointed at Twisty and Carlie. "I'm not going to go on living under the same roof as them pretending like they didn't just try to kill me and Kevin. I'm not keeping something this important from CC. How do we know they won't try to attack us again? Or anybody else?"

"We won't," Twisty said. "I promise. If you don't tell CC, in exchange we'll call a truce and all the fighting will end. Even with you, Allie. I give you my word."

Allie laughed. "Your word means nothing to me, Twisty. You just tried to kill me!"

Twisty's face hardened. "I said I wasn't trying to kill you, just hurt you. If you do tell CC though, I guarantee this war will get a lot worse."

"I can't believe Big Boss would be willing to leave just so you two don't get in trouble!" Kevin exclaimed.

"That's what doesn't make any sense about this," Allie said. "Big Boss is going to drop everything and leave, just to prevent you two from getting punished again? There's obviously more to this than he's letting on. Big Boss doesn't care about you."

Twisty and Carlie twisted their faces up in rage. "How do you know he doesn't care about us, Allie?" Carlie shouted. "Just because he hates you, doesn't mean he hates us!"

Allie looked Twisty and Carlie straight in the eyes. "*Big Boss doesn't care about you,*" she repeated with emphasis. "He doesn't care about anyone but himself. There's something in this for him. It's not that he doesn't want you to get in trouble with CC. It's more that, for some reason, Big Boss really doesn't want CC to know you attacked us," she deduced shrewdly.

Kevin nodded. "That makes much more sense. But why doesn't he want CC to know?"

"I don't know," Allie replied. "That's the part that really scares me. He's willing to leave to stop us from telling CC. And he's threatening to hurt us if we do tell him. It says he's planning something that relies on CC not knowing about the attack. It also says not telling CC is dangerous."

Twisty and Carlie scrunched their faces again. "You better *not* tell CC or you'll be sorry!" Twisty threatened. "We'll make you pay and so will Big Boss! And next time Becky might not be around to save you!"

My jaw dropped open. I balled up my fists and aimed to pounce on Twisty like a tiger. "I'm going to kill you, Twisty!" I screamed.

Again something caught me before I could surge ahead, and this time it was Allie holding me back. "Whoa, Cap," she said. "Take it easy. No more than two attempted murders in one day. Deep breath now."

I chuckled, grateful for Allie's ability to keep her sense of humor.

Allie turned to Twisty. "This is about more than the feud between you and me, Twisty. This affects our whole family if you still care. Don't you get it? I'm not the only one who's going to get hurt here! You're playing a dangerous game with Big Boss. He's using you and Carlie, turning you against your own family for some hidden purpose, and once he achieves it, he'll turn on you too. The safest thing to do is go to CC together and tell him everything Big Boss said to you and how he convinced you to attack us. CC will see Big Boss is manipulating you and he's the one to blame."

"He's not manipulating us, Allie!" Twisty hissed. "He just wants to make sure we get a fair deal for once!"

"Stop and think for just one second!" Allie shouted. "He obviously has ulterior motives here! He's using you! Playing divide and conquer! Don't be stupid! Wake up!"

"He's not using us!" Carlie cried. "He's not as bad as you all think! There's good in him!"

Allie lifted her head towards the ceiling and threw up her hands. "He is a psychopath!" she shouted back. "Psy-cho-path! There's no good in him. He's evil to the core! And up till you started talking with him, you thought so too. Come on, Carlie, in your heart of hearts you know what I'm saying is true! You would easily see it if you just put your hatred of me aside for one second! Which, by the way, Carlie, I know we were never exactly best friends, but you never hated me until Big Boss came into the picture. Twisty didn't either. This is what I'm talking about! Big Boss has completely brainwashed you!"

Carlie's face appeared momentarily gripped in confusion, then she shook it off. "I changed my mind about him," she said in a detached tone. "We both did. Now are you going to tell CC on us or not? Because if you are, all I can say is don't say I didn't warn you."

"We won't tell CC," Justin said. "We don't want anyone else getting hurt."

"No, Justin! That's a mistake! I'm telling you!" Allie cried. "We need to tell CC! It's too risky not to!"

"Allie, it's probably even riskier *to* tell him," Justin replied.

"Yeah, Allie, don't hate me, but I think Justin's right," Kevin said a little hesitantly. "I want to tell CC so bad, but I don't trust those two psychos for a minute! I don't want to spend every second looking over my shoulder! I'd rather just not tell CC and hope this whole mess ends. Maybe we'll get lucky enough for Big Boss to actually keep his word and go away."

Allie looked at Kevin, then sighed. She turned back to

Twisty and Carlie. "Fine, because you're not giving us much choice, we'll hold off on telling CC for now. But you better keep your end of the bargain. I'm reserving the right to tell CC if I see any immediate danger."

"Good, it's settled then," Carlie said. "You won't tell CC what happened."

"If by settled you mean forcing us to make that choice by literally threatening everyone in our family, sure," Allie said.

Twisty and Carlie left the room and my other siblings came up to check on Allie and Kevin. I ran upstairs to get Allie a new shirt and came back. As my siblings filtered out, Allie stopped Becky.

"I never thought I'd say this, but you saved my life today," Allie said to Becky. "I would probably be dead right now if it wasn't for you. Thank you! A million times! I'm eternally in your debt."

Becky appeared a little embarrassed at Allie's sudden outpouring of affection, which she definitely wasn't used to. "Well, uh…you're welcome," she muttered awkwardly. "God, Allie, I mean…" She stumbled to find the right words. "I know you and I never got along well, but God, I wasn't going to just let you die! I don't know what the hell is wrong with Twisty and Carlie! It's like they're completely different people!"

I told Becky I was shocked she had enough magic left to heal Allie. I assumed she had spent it up like everyone else. I asked her what changed.

"I *was* using magic however I wanted, until the day you all had that run-in with Big Boss and that Chief Seager guy," Becky explained. "I got really freaked out because Big Boss and Chief Seager were keeping us from the police. I realized if we can't rely on the police's help, we better be ready to defend ourselves. And then Twisty and Carlie admitted they were talking with

Big Boss, and I knew they couldn't be trusted. I became scared of them. I didn't know who to watch out for more: Big Boss or the two of them."

Allie let out a low whistle. "It's a good thing you trusted your intuition! I'm alive because of it! It turns out you were exactly right about them!"

"Yeah, and I'm *not* rooming with them anymore!" Becky cried. "As of tonight, I'm petitioning CC to change rooms. I don't care if I have to sleep in the hall closet! Even the bathroom is better than with them! I'm not going to be alone to fend off against those two nutcases!"

Allie invited Becky to stay in our room. Becky seemed both touched and taken aback by the offer.

"You could take my bunk," Allie said. "I can sleep on the floor in the meantime."

"Oh no, Allie, I'm not going to take your bed!" Becky exclaimed. "I'll sleep on the floor."

"You saved my life!" Allie cried. "You can sleep wherever you want! Seriously! It's the least I could do!"

I looked at the clock and questioned where CC was. He was very late. I asked if he went to the store down the street.

"No, he went downtown," Allie said. "He said he was making a bigger trip since Ashley, Kit-Cat, and the Bopsy twins went with him." She glanced nervously at the clock. "Still, you're right. He's taking an awfully long time."

As if on cue, a loud blaring ring pierced the air, and the three of us nearly jumped out of our skin. The sound kept ringing out, and we froze and stared uncomprehendingly at each other. Finally, we realized the sound was the ringing of our landline telephone. We dashed towards the phone down the hall, and I was the first to grab it.

"Hello?" I said breathlessly.

"Capricorn? Thank God! It's CC. Is everyone all right?"

CC sounded really distressed. Allie and Becky leaned in towards me to hear him.

"CC! Um...yeah, we're fine," I said, hoping he believed me.

"Oh good! That's a relief! I'm so sorry, you're all probably wondering where we are! You wouldn't believe what happened! First, the store was packed, so it took us a while just to get our groceries and check out. Then, we finally get back to our car and some low-life jerk slashed all four of our tires!"

I momentarily stopped breathing. We exchanged frozen expressions.

"Breezy and Hazy said they could fix them with their powers, and I was going to let them because we needed to get back, but the parking lot was so full of people, it was impossible to do without anyone seeing them. Finally, I decided it would be faster to call a tow truck, but the guy took forever to get there! I was so mad! He didn't even apologize, just said he got backed up! I knew you were all going to worry because we weren't home yet, and I've been calling and calling to let you know we were okay, but the phone kept going straight to voicemail! I was worried sick something happened! I must have left a hundred frenzied voicemails! Did you get any of them? Did you hear the phone ringing?"

I looked at my sisters in bewilderment and their faces mirrored my confusion. They shook their heads numbly in silent response.

"Um...no, CC," I said. "This is the first time we heard the phone ring all night."

"That's strange. Was the phone dead? The phone will go straight to voicemail if the battery is dead."

My sisters stared at me with mouths agape and I instantly knew what happened.

"Um...that must have been what happened CC," I said, my voice a little shaky. "I'm sorry we worried you so much. The phone is back on the charger now."

"Okay. Well, we're finally on our way home. We'll be there soon. Are you sure everything's okay, Capricorn? You sound a little jumpy."

"Yeah...yeah, CC, we're fine."

"Well tell everybody what happened, and we'll be home soon. I'm just glad everyone's okay."

I hung up the phone in a daze, then looked at my sisters. We shared knowing expressions, and I opened my mouth to speak, but Allie beat me there first.

"Twisty and Carlie took the battery out of the phone."

Chapter 31

CC walked into the house carrying two large reusable grocery totes, looking very frazzled. "Oh man, what a night," he groaned.

Kitty, Ashley, Breezy, and Hazy came in behind CC, also holding bags in their hands.

"You just wouldn't believe the night we had," Ashley announced.

"Oh, I bet we may have you beat," I said a little cryptically. Ashley shot me a puzzled look, but I took off before she could respond.

Breezy and Hazy smiled at me as they walked through the living room with the groceries. Breezy suddenly slowed down, and a troubled expression clouded over her face. She came to a brief standstill and scanned the room, then started walking again, heading toward the kitchen. I followed after them and Breezy put her bags down on the marble countertop, looking up at me.

"Hi, Cap," she said softly. "I heard you on the phone before. We were really starting to worry when no one answered. Can you believe what happened? Isn't it crazy?"

Before I could answer, Allie came shooting into the kitchen, bouncing around so excitably she nearly knocked the bags out of Hazy's hands.

"Hi! What's up?" Allie exclaimed with a big grin in an overly chipper tone. She leaned in close to Breezy's face and spoke in an urgent whisper. *"I need to talk to you two. I need to talk to you right now."*

Breezy gave Allie a deeply inquisitive look. "Okay…hi, Al," she half-laughed. "That was...an interesting welcome."

"Yeah, Allie, you almost made me drop the groceries!" Hazy laughed.

Breezy grabbed some vegetables from the bag and I took some items to put away as well. I could hear CC telling everyone about the tires and tow truck from the living room.

"I just can't believe someone would be mean enough to slash all our tires," Breezy said, picking up on the overheard conversation.

"Yeah, well, uh the thing is...I kind of have some insight for you on that," Allie replied.

"Insight?" Breezy questioned with another intrigued expression. "What kind of insight?"

"Well, I can't say right now but *Cap and I need to talk to you immediately*," Allie said intensely.

Breezy slowly closed the cupboard door where she just stored some pasta and turned around to face Allie, her curiosity now at peak level. "What's this about?" she whispered, matching the energy of her voice to Allie's.

"I can't really tell you, but I need to talk to you privately," Allie said in a hushed tone, moving within inches of Breezy's face. *"Now. I need to talk to you. I have to talk to you right now."* Allie spoke with a fierce and pressing insistency.

"Allie, what's so important she needs to drop everything

and talk to you this minute?" CC asked, walking into the kitchen just in time to hear Allie's whispered words of urgency.

Allie immediately backed away from Breezy. "Oh, hi CC!" she said cheerily, flashing her freckly grin at him. "Oh, it's uh...nothing. Hey Hazy, let me help you with the rest of those groceries!" she exclaimed, quickly changing the subject to avoid CC's suspicious look.

Allie snatched things from the grocery bag like she was racing to beat a timer. She zipped around the kitchen, putting things away so fast Hazy started giggling. CC stood in the kitchen watching her with a half-bemused expression. "Allie? There's no prize for finishing first," he said.

"Huh?" Allie said as she threw carrots in the refrigerator.

CC walked over to her as she slid across the kitchen floor and put his hands on her shoulders to stop her. "*Slow down.*"

Kevin came into the kitchen and approached Allie. "Hey," he whispered in her ear. "Did you tell them yet?"

"No, they just got home. I haven't been able to tell them anything. I'm putting away groceries," Allie said quickly under her breath in a sing-song tone.

"Okay, well let me know when you tell them. I'll be in my room," he whispered back.

Allie nodded and Kevin headed out, waving at CC as he walked by.

"Kevin?" CC said, making a beckoning gesture. "Come here a second."

Allie whirled around and stood with her back against the counter, sharing a panicked look with Kevin. Kevin walked hesitantly over to CC.

CC stood in front of Kevin and examined him closely. "Your skin is all red. Really red. Did something happen?"

"Oh, uh...it's just sunburn," Kevin responded weakly.

I saw Allie widen her eyes and slightly shake her head at Kevin.

CC folded his arms and gave Kevin an incredulous stare. "It's December."

"Oh, I know. I mean, not sunburn, but light burn. I fell asleep under a bright lamp. It burned me," Kevin lied.

CC gave Kevin another look-over. "That must have been some lamp. Be more careful."

"Okay, I will," Kevin said, scurrying out of the kitchen.

Allie tried to hurry with the groceries before CC asked more questions. I helped her, and Hazy jumped in the middle, pulling multiple cans of corn from the bag. Allie, getting anxious with CC in the room, started rambling nervously.

"Wow, how much corn did you get? That's a lot of corn. I guess dinner is going to be really corny. Are we making something with this much corn? Like corn soup or something? Is that a thing, corn soup? Or corn chowder?"

Hazy giggled at Allie's babbling and walked with her to the pantry closet. "I think we're going to need a whole other shelf for all this corn," Allie continued. "We could turn the kitchen into a corn store. The slogan could be 'We got you covered with corn.' Seriously, why is there this much corn?"

Hazy laughed her head off and CC eyed Allie quizzically. "Allie, you are even more hyper than usual. What's going on?"

Before Allie could answer, Kevin came back in and walked over to us. "Hey, Allie," he whispered. "I can finish putting away those groceries for you so you can, you know, talk now."

"Really?" Allie said. "Okay! Thanks, Kev!"

"After what you and Capricorn did for me, don't even mention it," Kevin said.

"What did they do?" Hazy asked interestedly.

Allie grabbed Hazy's hand and led her to Breezy. She

looked at me and jerked her head, signaling me to follow them. She pulled Breezy and Hazy out of the kitchen, with me tagging behind them before CC had a chance to say anything else to us.

Chapter 32

"Something really big happened while you were gone," Allie said, once we were secure in our room with the door closed. "And by 'big' I mean hugely monumental."

Hazy's expression contained puzzlement, but Breezy nodded knowingly. "Does this have anything to do with what happened in the living room?" Breezy asked.

Allie and I looked at her in surprise.

"I could tell as soon as I walked in something bad happened in the living room," Breezy explained. "There was a tense and panicked energy I felt immediately."

"So that's why you stopped and looked around when you came in the house," I noted.

"God, Breeze, I have to say it is really eerie when you do that," Allie said.

"So what happened?" Hazy asked eagerly.

"Okay, I'm not sure where to start, but…let me show you something first," Allie replied. She lifted her shirt and exposed her scarred, lobster-red stomach.

Breezy and Hazy simultaneously drew in their breath. "Oh my God, Allie!" Breezy shouted.

"Shh! I don't want CC to hear you," Allie whispered.

"Oh my God!" Hazy cried, staring at Allie's stomach. When Hazy said God, it sounded more like "goad," which made me want to hug her like she was a plush toy. "Allie! What happened to your stomach?"

"Before I tell you, promise me you won't freak out and scream," Allie requested.

"It's that bad? What happened?" Breezy asked, her piercing blue eyes bright with concern.

"Okay, well, Twisty shot a fireball at my stomach," Allie revealed.

"WHAT?" Hazy and Breezy shouted together.

Allie clasped her hands over each of their mouths. "Shh! CC!" she reminded them.

Breezy pulled Allie's hand away and lowered her voice a little. "Twisty shot a *fireball* at you? Why would she do something like that?"

"Well, let us tell you what happened," Allie said.

Breezy and Hazy sat on Breezy's bottom bunk listening to us in horrified silence. Breezy, her deep eyes wide with shock, held her hand over her mouth, sick with disgust and dismay. Hazy cuddled her stuffed pig close to her chest, repeatedly squeezing its soft, squishy belly. Her gentle brown eyes watered with tears as she listened, her tiny lip quivering. When we finished, they both stared at us, struck with the sudden inability to speak.

"I can't believe Twisty did that!" Hazy finally cried out. The tears that had pooled in her eyes began falling lightly down her cheeks. "Allie, you could have died! Oh my God, we would have come home, and you would have been gone! Dead!"

Breezy gave up holding back her own tears after seeing Hazy's. "We could have lost you forever!" she sobbed. "Kevin too! Thank God you and Cap were there! And Becky!" She whirled towards the door and balled her fists tight. "I could seriously *hurt* Twisty and Carlie right now!" she expressed in a rare moment of vengeful anger.

Allie gave Breezy and Hazy affectionate hugs. "It's okay," she comforted them. "I'm still here."

"I just can't believe they would do this!" Breezy sniffed, wiping her tears. "I knew they were upset with you, Allie, but I never thought they'd go this far!"

"What happened to them?" Hazy questioned in dismay.

"I'll give you two words what happened to them," Allie replied. "Big Boss."

Breezy frowned and nodded. "He's completely brainwashed them. Allie, let me heal your stomach for you. That must hurt."

Allie lifted her shirt and Breezy went to work on healing her injuries. "Thanks, Breeze," Allie said "I'm glad you didn't use your magic fixing the flat tires."

Breezy's mouth snapped open. "Allie, wait a minute! You said you had insight for us about that. You think...you think Big Boss is the one who slashed our tires, don't you?"

"There's no doubt," Allie answered. "Twisty and Carlie are in cahoots with Big Boss. They obviously planned this whole thing together. They've probably been sneaking out of their room and meeting him at the fence while CC worked in his office. I think they even met with him earlier today, otherwise, how did he know CC was at the store? They must have told him before they attacked us. Then Big Boss's job was to slow CC down, stop him from arriving home too early. Which is why he slashed the tires on CC's car. And I have to wonder if even the tow truck driver was in on it."

Breezy's eyes filled with icy dread. "Oh my God, Allie! You're right! And Twisty and Carlie could have even talked to Big Boss over the phone if he gave them his number."

"Phone!" Allie cried. "Yes! They probably called him and after hanging up, they removed the battery from the phone to stop CC from getting in touch."

"They removed the battery from the phone?" Breezy and Hazy said at the same time.

Allie nodded. "CC said the phone would go to voicemail if the battery's dead. That's when we realized Twisty and Carlie took the battery out. They wanted to make sure CC couldn't contact us before they got us to agree not to tell CC what happened. And when they finally browbeat us into agreeing and left, they put the battery back in."

"Allie, if this is true, this is really serious," Breezy said gravely. "Twisty and Carlie are working with Big Boss to plot against us. And I don't even want to know what they're planning next. Allie, I'm scared. This is really bad. We need to go to CC immediately."

Just then there was a knock on our door. "Hey, it's Kevin," came the voice from the other side. "Can I come in?"

I went to the door and welcomed Kevin in. Allie crossed her arms at a half-tilt and raised an eyebrow at him. "Sunburn?" she said with a wry smile.

"Yeah, yeah, I know, but I had to think of something fast," Kevin replied.

"And sunburn in the middle of December was the fastest thing you could come up with?" Allie teased. "Yeah, CC, it's sunburn...from four months ago."

"Well, I panicked," Kevin defended. "But I recovered fast, right? I came up with that light burn thing. Falling asleep under a lamp, that was good, right?"

"Yeah, that was good…" Allie said slowly, leaving the sentence hang. "If the lamp was actually a tanning bed," she finished.

Kevin playfully smacked her arm. "Well, we can't all be wordsmiths like you, Allie."

Hazy offered to heal Kevin and gestured him to sit on the bed next to her. Hazy laid her hands on his bare skin carefully and concentrated. Within seconds the yellow light emanated from her hands, and Hazy moved them up and down Kevin until his scarlet-red skin gently faded back to its normal golden beige color. Kevin stood up and smiled. "Wow, that feels much better! Thank you, Hazy!"

Breezy said we need to talk about the agreement we made with Twisty and Carlie and repeated how vital it is to tell CC what happened. "Our safety may be at stake," she stressed.

Kevin winced. "But Breezy, I can't live in constant fear of an attack by Twisty or Carlie or Big Boss."

Allie nodded. "Yeah, Breeze, of course I agree with you, but they are practically holding a gun against our head here."

"If we go to CC, he can make sure we're all protected," Breezy responded. "He would make sure we're safe, but he can only do that if he knows what's happening. If CC doesn't know, Big Boss is free to plot against us even more. We *need* to tell CC." Breezy's voice took on a tone of pleading.

"But Breezy, what if CC can't protect us?" Kevin asked. "He couldn't today."

"That's because he was at the store," Breezy replied. "That's why you need to tell him. No way will CC leave you alone in the house with Twisty and Carlie if he knows what happened. But honestly, I'm more worried about Big Boss." Breezy filled Kevin in on Big Boss slashing CC's tires and Twisty and Carlie removing the phone battery.

"We *cannot* play around with this," Breezy stressed again. "Who knows what Big Boss is going to do next? Please, let's tell CC before it's too late!"

"I have an idea," Allie announced. "I told Twisty and Carlie I would hold off telling CC *for now*. Let's wait a few days and see what happens. If things get worse, then we go to CC. But if things get better, like if by some miracle Big Boss really leaves or Twisty and Carlie stop doing their hired killers act, then we won't tell CC."

Breezy thought about this and reluctantly agreed. "Can we all revisit this though in a few days?"

Allie agreed to that and looked at Hazy, Kevin, and me for our vote. We all nodded in agreement. "Okay, so it's official. We'll wait a few days and reconvene. This meeting is now adjourned. Where's my gavel?"

There was another knock at the door, and Allie answered it. Becky was standing on the other side with a blanket and pillow in her hands. "Hey, so, uh, is it still okay if I sleep on your floor tonight?"

"Of course, but I'm the one sleeping on the floor, remember? Come in," Allie said.

Becky walked awkwardly into the room, seeming really out of place. Allie asked Breezy and Hazy if Becky could sleep in our room for a while.

"Of course she can," Breezy said, smiling at Becky. Hazy nodded and gave Becky a shy smile.

"Okay, thanks," Becky said. "I'm going to talk to CC and see if I can get another permanent place to sleep. I'm just going to sleep on the floor, you won't even know I'm here."

"Okay, but if you don't take my bunk like I offered, I'm going to auction it off to the highest bidder," Allie joked. "And that could be anybody. Like a small baby who cries every hour. Or someone with insomnia who stays up listening to loud music. Or a surgeon who gets late-night emergency calls, so she rushes to the hospital in the middle of the night. I don't think you'd want to room with any of them, so to be on the safe side I'd take the bunk."

Hazy went into another spell of belly giggles and Breezy, Kevin, and I laughed. Becky, however, scrunched up her face in bewilderment. "Huh?" she uttered.

"She's joking," Breezy explained. "She's saying she wants you to take her bunk."

"Well, that was a very convoluted way of telling me that," Becky declared.

Breezy raised her hands in a shrug and laughed. "That's Allie."

"I really don't mind sleeping on the floor, Allie," Becky said.

"Yes, but I do mind if the person who saved my life sleeps on the floor," Allie asserted. "So take the bunk. Unless you want another bed, like with golden mattresses or a plushy waterbed with a fancy headboard, or how about one of those swan beds you see in those lavish weekend getaway places? Ooh how about a canopy bed or maybe just a nice hammock?"

Becky looked at us with another slightly baffled face. "Does she always do this?"

"Pretty much all the time," Hazy giggled.

"Oh come on, Becky, how long have you known Allie?" Kevin said.

"Well, yeah, I know, she makes jokes, but... we never spent much time together," Becky said, seeming a little embarrassed.

Breezy smiled. "Don't worry, you'll get used to it." Breezy and Hazy thanked Becky emphatically for saving Allie's life. We filled Becky in on waiting on the decision to tell CC. Becky asked if she could be made part of the decision as well.

"Sure, you're part of the team now, like it or not," Allie smiled.

Chapter 33

Kitty made breakfast in the kitchen. I slipped some warm, fluffy waffles on a plate and doused them with maple syrup and coconut butter, then sat between my fellow Musketeers.

Our dining room table sat six on one side, seven on the other, with CC at the head of the table. Becky looked at her usual seat next to Twisty and Carlie, made a face, and quickly grabbed a seat on the other side of the table next to Allie. This little change did not go unnoticed by CC, already at his seat, and he raised a curious eyebrow at Becky as she sat down. Kitty took her usual seat, eyeing Becky next to her in surprise, as that seat was usually Ashley's. That left all six seats on our side of the table filled. Kevin, Ryan, Chase, and Justin had already taken their seats on the opposite side of the table, down away from where Twisty and Carlie always sat at the first two seats. Ashley walked in, noticed Becky sitting in her spot, and realized she was going to be stuck sitting next to Twisty and Carlie. She seemed less than thrilled about this. She must have heard what happened yesterday while she was at the store.

Ashley walked by Ryan, who was sitting in the fourth seat

next to the empty chair, and bent down to whisper in his ear. "You know, if I wanted to be mean, I could sit in the first seat, which would force *you* to sit next to them too."

"You wouldn't dare," Ryan whispered, looking nervously at the empty seat next to him.

"Lucky for you, Ryan, I'm not that mean." She plopped down loudly in the seat next to him, clanging her plate on the table. She leaned over and spoke to Becky across from her. "Thanks a lot for stealing my seat," she said gruffly.

Becky just shrugged at her.

Twisty and Carlie were the last to sit down, taking their first and second seats at the table. As soon as Carlie sat down in the chair between Twisty and Ashley, Ashley scooted her chair as far away from Carlie as possible, practically running into Ryan. This prompted Ryan to move his chair down and started a chain reaction down the whole table to Kevin at the end. At the same time, everyone on our side of the table moved their chairs back and away from Twisty and Carlie.

CC watched us all carefully, his fork hung in midair. He glanced at Twisty and Carlie, then used his fork to point at us, making a circular motion in the air. "What's with all the musical chairs?"

We exchanged looks, then Becky spoke on behalf of us all. "We just don't want to sit anywhere near Twisty and Carlie, CC."

"Why?" CC questioned. "And why don't *you* want to sit by them? You always do. Did they do something to you?"

"No, I just..." Becky struggled to find the right words. "I was thinking about it and I'm really not okay with what they did. Conspiring with Big Boss, I mean. I just don't want to have anything to do with them right now."

CC nodded and said he understood.

"Hey Allie, give me that syrup bottle," Becky commanded.

Normally Allie would needle Becky for her rudeness, but this time she smiled and handed the bottle to Becky.

Becky squirted some syrup on her waffles and handed the bottle back to Allie. "Thanks."

"Sure thing," Allie replied.

I caught Twisty and Carlie rolling their eyes at each other. CC eyed Becky and Allie with piqued curiosity.

"Don't get me wrong, I love that you two are getting along so well all of a sudden, but I have to ask, why the sudden change?" CC pried. "Normally I have to stop you from fighting."

Becky shrugged and said she and Allie called a truce.

Allie nodded. "Also CC, is it okay if Becky sleeps in our room for a while?"

CC nearly choked on his waffle. Coughing hard, he grabbed his coffee and took a swig. "Allie," he said hoarsely, "Did you just ask me if *Becky* could sleep in *your* room?"

Becky cut in. "Yeah, CC, I slept in their room last night. I was wondering if I could stay there a few days."

"Let me get this straight," CC said, still getting over the shock. "You want to sleep in the same room as *Allie*?"

Twisty and Carlie snickered nastily.

Becky said she didn't want to stay with Twisty and Carlie anymore and asked if she could switch rooms.

"Switch rooms?" CC exclaimed. "I can't just switch your room. Where am I supposed to put you, Becky?"

Becky said she doesn't know but Allie invited her to sleep in her bed in the meantime.

"She was kind to me, CC, so I'm repaying the favor," Allie explained in response to CC's astonished face.

"That must have been some favor," CC said. "Becky,

didn't you tell me a few weeks ago you didn't like Allie?"

"Well, what can I say? She's not as bad as I thought," Becky replied.

Allie smirked at Becky. "Gee, thanks."

CC sighed. "Like I said, it's wonderful you two are finally getting to be friends. But I need to think about this whole room swapping thing. Becky, do you find what Twisty and Carlie did to be so objectionable you can't see yourself ever wanting to share a room with them again?"

Becky didn't hesitate for a second before responding. "Absolutely."

Twisty and Carlie looked up and gave Becky an evil look. CC turned to them. "Did you know she wanted to leave?"

"We don't want her," Carlie stated coldly.

"Let her leave. We don't care," Twisty added in an equally harsh manner.

CC flinched at their icy tone. "Becky is one of your closest friends, so you should care. And it concerns me greatly that you genuinely appear not to care. What is going on with you two?"

"That's what I mean, CC," Becky interjected. "They've changed. They're not the same people anymore. They're mean, nasty, and hateful."

Carlie laughed scornfully. She whispered something to Twisty and they both cackled wickedly, shooting vicious glances at Becky. "Have fun sleeping in Allie's bed," Carlie sniggered snidely.

Hazy suddenly locked eyes with Carlie, glaring at her with pure hateful contempt. It was a look I never thought Hazy in all her innocence was capable of making. Carlie, frightened by Hazy's sudden ferocity, shrank back and returned to snickering with Twisty. They cast disdainful looks at Hazy and broke into hooting laughter. CC scowled at them.

"If you two keep laughing like that, making catty remarks about your sisters, you can leave this table, go back to your room, and forget about eating again until dinner!" CC scolded.

Twisty and Carlie cut their laughter and returned to eating in silence.

CC told Becky he'll figure something out, but in the meantime, she can stay in our room. He looked over the table at all of us. "Did something happen yesterday while I was out?"

I was a little taken aback by the sudden question, as were my siblings. "What do you mean, CC?" I asked a little nervously.

CC gave me a look that said he's not easily fooled. "I come home, Kevin looks as red as a beet, claiming he got sunburn in December, or light burn, which frankly, Kevin, makes as much sense as sunburn, Allie is running around the kitchen, whispering to Breezy and Hazy she needs to talk to them, now I find out Becky slept in your room last night, no one wants to sit anywhere near Twisty and Carlie, and Becky is suddenly making friends with Allie," CC listed off. "So either something happened yesterday, or there's a lot of strange changes occurring suddenly."

I looked at my siblings, searching their faces for a clue on how to respond, but they appeared just as panicked as I felt. I was about to give up and tell CC everything, but then Twisty spoke up.

"Something did happen, CC," Twisty said. "Carlie and I left our room yesterday. We fooled around with our powers, and Becky and Allie caught us. We threatened them not to tell you, and they told everyone, so now everybody's mad at us." Twisty told CC before anyone tells on them, she decided to come clean and tell him herself.

I stared at Twisty and wondered if she had spontaneously

created that story or if she had already concocted it for a situation just like this. Allie dropped her fork with a tinny clank and glowered at Twisty with deep disgust radiating from her eyes.

"What were you doing with your powers?" CC asked.

"We played a joke on Kevin," Twisty replied. "We turned his skin red. It was a dumb joke, but we were bored and going crazy in our room."

Way down the table, Kevin gave Twisty a stony look filled with detestation.

CC said using their powers like that was unacceptable, but he gave Twisty credit for being honest with him. I almost laughed at CC's unknowingly ironic statement.

The next day, as CC pulled up in our driveway after picking us up from school, we noticed a moving van parked on the street. We climbed out of the passenger van and eyed it curiously. Some movers came out of the truck and went into Big Boss's house. Big Boss stood on his porch, puffing a cigarette.

CC was the last to get out of the van. He slammed the driver's side door, looked at the moving van, and walked up towards Big Boss, jerking his head at him. "What's all this?" CC asked him gruffly.

Big Boss turned towards CC and took his cigarette out his mouth. "Well, Casey, I'm sure you'll be happy to hear I'm moving out. You won't be seeing me around much longer."

My siblings' mouths hit the ground.

"This sounds too good to be true," CC said.

Big Boss scoffed. "Believe it, Casey. I'm really leaving."

"Why now?" CC asked.

Big Boss eyed CC and took another drag from his cigarette. "Well, Casey, if you must know, it's because of you." He looked disdainfully over us staring at him in astonishment. "You and your darling children, of course. Chief Seager told me to avoid any legal trouble, I need to stay at least 40 feet away from your children. He advised me to move away from you if I can. I don't want to be charged with some crime I didn't commit, so I'm moving. So there you go. I'm sure I've made you and your kids very happy."

In my head, I was jumping up and down ecstatic at this news, but I was also a little leery.

CC seemed just as suspicious. "Chief Seager told you that? Like I said, this seems too good to be true."

Big Boss took one last whiff of his cigarette and crushed it out with his foot. "Believe whatever you want, Casey. Frankly, I don't care anymore. I'll be gone by tomorrow morning. You can stop hiding your kids from me now. You've won. Goodbye, Casey. I wish you and your children all the best." Big Boss gave us one final nod and disappeared inside his house.

Chapter 34

"I can't believe it! He's LEAVING!" Kevin cheered as soon as we stepped in the house, jumping with his fist in the air. My siblings burst into cries of elation.

Allie bounced up and down like a spring. "If I didn't see the moving truck myself, I wouldn't believe it! I'm throwing a party! A big party! Christmas will have nothing on this party! Sorry, Christmas, but move over!" Allie grabbed Hazy's hands and the two leaped into the air, alternating like a seesaw. They spun wildly in circles around the room, bumping into furniture, dizzy with laughter.

CC held up his hands. "Allie! Hazy! I know you're excited but try to tone it down a bit. You're going to break something."

"But I don't get it," Justin said. "After all this time, why is he leaving now? Is it really because Chief Seager told him to? After hearing what he was like, I find that hard to believe."

"I do as well," CC said. "Chief Seager made it clear he would do nothing to help. It's hard to believe he'd direct Big Boss to do anything in our interest." He looked over our faces and smiled. "If he is leaving, this is a gift from the universe. But knowing him, he'll pull something at the last minute and decide to stay. Just be prepared. I'd hate for you all to get your hopes up, only to face crushing disappointment."

CC was voicing some of my own reservations. When the exhilaration finally died down, I stayed in the living room with my fellow Musketeers.

"I'm sorry," Breezy expressed. "I want to be as happy as you guys are, but I'm sensing something isn't right here. I have this strong feeling we haven't seen the last of Big Boss."

Hazy's face tightened. "What do you mean, Breezy? He's moving out. We saw it ourselves."

Breezy nodded. "I know. But that doesn't mean we won't see him again."

"Why would you say that?" Allie moaned. "Everything was perfect, and then you say *that.*"

"I'm sorry, Allie," Breezy said. "But it's this feeling I have I just can't ignore. I think it would be wise not to let our guard down just yet."

"Killjoy," Allie muttered in a half-teasing manner. She glanced around the room to make sure CC was out of earshot and asked if we think this has anything to do with the agreement we made with Twisty and Carlie.

Breezy answered it might, but that makes her even more concerned because it meant Big Boss has a highly vested interest in keeping us from talking to CC.

Allie shot Breezy a sour look. "Will you stop doing that! God, Breeze! You bring a whole new meaning to the phrase 'rain on your parade.'" She turned to Hazy with her wry smile, determined to cheer her back up. "Watch out, Haze! She's a gray raincloud! Stay back, raincloud!" she ordered, backing away from Breezy with Hazy in tow. "I'll ward you off with Hazy, my ray of sunshine!" She held Hazy out in front of her as if she were a shield. She belted out a familiar children's tune.

"Sunny day, sweeping the...breeze away, on my way to where the air is hazy, can you tell me how to stop, how to stop Breezy from driving me crazy?"

I cracked up. Hazy laughed so hard she almost fell over.

"Stop it, Al," Breezy giggled. She repeated she just wants us to be cautious in case this is some sort of trick.

"You sound more and more like CC every day, Breeze," Allie ribbed. "One day, we'll wake up in the morning, and you'll have completely morphed into him."

Breezy gave Allie a tiny smile. "You know, Al, at some point I have to wonder if I should take all this teasing personally."

"Oh, come on, Breeze, you know I love you," Allie said with her winsome grin. "Sorry, you're right. We shouldn't let our guard down. So let's see if Big Boss is really gone by morning. If he is, then first, we meet with Kevin and Becky and decide on telling CC, and second, we throw a party. If this isn't a reason to celebrate, I don't know what is. We'll call it the Ding, Dong, the Psychopath is Gone Party!"

The next day, as if we had cast some spell with our powers, Big Boss had moved out and was nowhere in sight. And just like that, he was gone.

As the days turned to weeks and Big Boss was nowhere to be found, we finally let go of our fear of him returning. My fellow Musketeers and I reconvened with Kevin and Becky.

Allie attempted to bring the whole matter to a speedy conclusion. "By some miracle, Big Boss is gone. I don't know why he left, but if it's because of our deal with Twisty and Carlie, there's no way I'm messing that up. I want him to stay far away. If that means never telling CC, so be it."

Becky, Kevin, Hazy, and I emphatically agreed. "We've somehow hit the universal jackpot! Telling CC now would be like giving the money back!" I cried.

"So, so far it's unanimous," Allie chirped. She turned towards Breezy. "So far," she emphasized, looking at Breezy expectantly. "Okay, Breeze. I'm ready. Hit us with all your reasons why you still think it's a bad idea."

Breezy smirked at Allie. "Actually Al, I agree with the rest of you. I never expected Big Boss to really leave. I don't want to take the chance of bringing him back either, so let's not rock the boat."

Allie dropped her mouth open. "Wait, what? Wow, I think we've somehow stepped into a parallel universe. One where Big Boss is out of the picture and Breezy doesn't endlessly debate you until you resign to her point to keep from falling over in exhaustion. Well, we have full consensus! Now we can all get back to our normal lives. As normal as our lives get anyway."

"Does this mean we resume being adversaries, Allie?" Becky asked.

"Only if you want to be," Allie said. "But I'd much prefer we stay friends. And you saved my life, so no matter what I'm indebted to you. I know this is all a little weird, but come on, whose company do you really prefer? We're a little quirky, but we've got to be better than the Demented Duo."

Becky laughed. "Yeah, anyone's better than Twisty and Carlie. And I can't believe I'm saying this, but I'm beginning to actually enjoy your witty jokes, Allie."

"Be careful, that's how it starts," Allie teased. "Soon we'll completely indoctrinate you and you'll be officially received into our cult."

Very slowly, things started returning to normal. It took a while before CC trusted things were safe enough to stop chaperoning us around. But by the time February started, CC finally allowed us to walk to and from school by ourselves again.

By April, we ran errands for CC and went to the park ourselves. Before we knew it, it was May, and a whole year had passed since we first met Big Boss. He was fading away like a distant memory, and I could almost dismiss him as some long-ago nightmare. Except there were a few things that had fundamentally changed.

First, our relationship with Twisty and Carlie. No one forgot what they did, so no one trusted them anymore. CC roomed Becky with Ashley and Kitty and switched their room with Twisty and Carlie's.

Second, our siblings' use of magic. Right after Big Boss left, no one dared to use magic at all, completely scared off after what happened with Kevin and Allie. But as things returned to normal, my siblings returned to their previous level of haphazardly using magic. When I called them on it, they would give me the same excuse they learned from Big Boss, Twisty, and Carlie: "It's our magic, we can do what we want with it." "Also," they'd remind me, "Big Boss is gone, so what are you worried about?" Without a reasonable rebuttal, my warnings appeared like attempts to control them, and they began to tune me out. Still, I persisted in badgering everyone, afraid of a repeat scenario like what occurred before.

"Hey, Cap?" Allie called me over, after witnessing me trying in vain to convince Kitty to stop using her powers. "Let them go," she said gently. "The harder you push them, the more they'll pull away from you. Let them make their own mistakes. It's the only way they'll learn."

"But you almost died before because of them squandering magic, Allie! Are we really going to risk that happening again?" I cried.

Allie laid her hand on my shoulder. "Cap," she whispered. "Big Boss has been gone for months. He's not coming back.

You don't have to be scared anymore."

I smiled at Allie and finally let go. My siblings continued using their powers according to their own whims and wishes, and no one, including me, said or did anything to stop them.

And that was a dreadful mistake.

Chapter 35

Do you know that expression "The calm before the storm?" That expression perfectly describes the time leading up to *that day*. The day I would come to call The Day That Changed Everything. May 30th. Last year.

The day started innocently enough, except for CC making a major revelation to us at breakfast. We were gathered around the table, eating French toast Kitty made from scratch, when CC asked us what we planned to do this summer. He suggested this year we try summer camp. "It would be good for you all to get outside and interact with other kids. Make some new friends outside this family."

"We have enough friends here," Ashley said. "We don't need anybody else."

CC frowned. "I'm afraid you kids are becoming a little too...insular. There's a whole world outside this house, and you haven't even begun to explore it. That was supposed to be the whole point of sending you to school, and even there you keep to yourselves. For God's sake, get outside and meet some new kids. Normal kids."

"But we aren't like other kids, CC," Chase replied. "We

don't get along with normal kids."

"You could get along if you would make the effort," CC answered harshly. "You could try to act normal at least. But you don't even try."

We shrunk back, stung by CC's rebuke.

CC shook his head roughly. "Fine. You don't have to go to summer camp. But I'll tell you this right now: You're *not* spending the summer running around the house, foolishly using your powers to make and do whatever you want, that's for sure," he scolded us severely.

I almost spit out my orange juice in surprise. My siblings froze and gaped at CC.

"You...you know about that?" Ryan uttered with shamefaced astonishment.

CC gave us a stern look. "Of course I know about that," he snapped. "Do you really think I don't know what goes on in my own house? You kids are not as clever as you seem to think. Your rooms are full of items I didn't buy. You have snacks around I never bought. You'd think you'd at least be a little more careful hiding your evidence."

My siblings were speechless. I laughed to myself that CC knew this whole time.

"But...if you knew, then why…uh didn't you say anything?" Ryan stammered.

CC fixed Ryan with a hard stare. "What would be the point, Ryan? It's not like you listen to me anyway. I have warned you kids time and time again about those powers, and you still break all the rules and use them however you want. I'm tired of talking to you about this. I can't make you stop and I can't very well ground you every day either. So I give up. Do what you want with the powers. Maybe in time, you'll learn to be smarter with them, but I'm done with the whole thing."

I resisted the urge to jump up and declare that we, the Four Musketeers, didn't waste any of our magic. My siblings looked hurt by CC's words.

"CC," Ashley spoke up, "We're sorry...but we think we should be able to do what we want with our own powers. We should have that right."

"You want rights without responsibilities, Ashley," CC argued. "You still have no idea how to use those powers responsibly. Not that that's all your fault, you're just kids after all. If I had any control over it, I would never allow such power to be in the hands of children. I honestly think those powers cause more problems than they're worth sometimes." He sighed and sat back in his chair. "I need to run some errands today. Go to the park and play. It's a beautiful day. I'll be back in a few hours."

I thought after CC's big guilt trip, my siblings would be too humbled to use their powers, but they started almost as soon as CC was out the door. They whipped up snacks, candy, and cookies to take to the park with us. We found a place to play at the park where there weren't many people, and my siblings and I (except Carlie and Twisty) engaged in a game of hide-and-seek. I crouched behind a bush and for several minutes all was silent. I was about to peep out to see what was happening when I heard Allie scream. I dashed out from behind the bush and everyone came running from all directions.

"Come here! Quick!" Allie cried out to us from a nearby tree.

We rushed over. The grisly sight that greeted us at the tree made me stop short and draw my breath in. There, laying on the ground underneath the pine tree, were four baby bunnies. Their bellies were slit open, and they writhed on the ground, emitting the most pitiful and agonized squeals. Laying in a quickly expanding puddle of blood, the poor animals were bleeding to death.

Chapter 36

I had one of those moments of sheer shock that leads to a momentary out-of-body experience. I heard the voices of my siblings as if they were coming from a distance.

"Oh my God! Oh my God!" Breezy whimpered.

"We have to help them!" Hazy cried, tears running from her eyes.

"Who did this?" Ashley shouted. "Who would do such a thing?"

"I bet it was Twisty and Carlie!" Kevin cried. "They're the only ones not here!" He spotted Twisty and Carlie on the other side of the park and screamed out to them. "Come here! Did you do this? Get over here and look!"

Twisty and Carlie ran over. Carlie gasped when she saw the rabbits, and Twisty stared at them in horror.

"Did you do this?" Kevin shouted at them. Carlie staggered back, almost looking through Kevin, her face pale.

"No!" Twisty cried. "You think we would do something like this? What kind of monsters do you think we are? I hate you guys! I swear!" Twisty screamed.

"It doesn't matter!" Allie roared out. "We need to help

these rabbits before they die!"

"Allie's right," Becky said. "We need to save them with our powers."

Ryan looked around the park nervously. "We better make sure no one is watching us."

Of course, my fellow Musketeers and I were the only ones with enough power to save them. Allie bent down and carefully slid her hands under one of the babies, scooping her up, and nestling the bunny close to her stomach. Allie's T-shirt was immediately spotted with blood. Breezy and Hazy each picked up another rabbit, and I took the last one. Justin directed us to a place behind the bushes. The struggling movements of the rabbit in Allie's arms became more and more feeble, and then suddenly her small body went frightfully limp. Allie ran behind the bushes, while the rest of us stood in front and kept a lookout. The yellow light radiated from the bushes as if the leaves were glowing. Allie emerged with a smile of relief on her face. In her arms was the same bunny, who now appeared wide-eyed and alert, with a fully mended stomach. Allie bent towards the ground and let the bunny loose, and the baby scampered away.

Breezy and Hazy stepped behind the same bushes with the rabbits in their hands and performed the same little miracle. The two came out with skittish but completely healthy bunnies and released them immediately.

I took the last bunny behind the bushes. Breathing heavily, the blood from the rabbit's tiny body seeping through my shirt, I brought the energy flow quickly to my hands. I ran the light down the rabbit's stomach, closing the hemorrhaging wound, and watched the little being instantly come back to life in front of me. I brought him out of the bushes and let him go free to run deep into the park.

Justin exhaled in relief. "You guys did it. The rabbits will all live now thanks to you."

I suddenly felt a self-righteous vindication, now that the rabbits were safe. "This is exactly what I've tried to tell all of you," I reprimanded. "This is why you can't waste your powers on things like candy and toys. Those rabbits could have easily bled to death. It's a good thing Allie, Breezy, Hazy, and I were here and we haven't been squandering our magic, or they would have!"

Carlie and Twisty rolled their eyes at each other. "Capricorn is way too good for us. She thinks she's so superior to the rest of us who use our magic to treat ourselves as anyone in their right mind would. But not Saint Capricorn!" Twisty mocked me.

"Cap, thank you so much for not being in your right mind and being so superior to the rest of us lowly folk," Allie quipped back in my defense. "You must be so much better than everyone else, we should anoint you in holy oil," she said smirkingly in ridicule of Twisty.

Twisty glared at Allie hatefully. "You aren't funny! Nobody thinks you're funny!"

"I think she's pretty funny," Becky defended. "Just about everybody thinks so except for you."

"Shut up, Becky!" Twisty yelled. "You're suddenly best friends with Allie!" she cried, spitting Allie's name as if it were poison. "You're stupid then! She looks down on you just like everyone else!"

Becky scoffed. "Speaking of being better than you, let's get back to Kevin's question about who did that to the rabbits. Because I'm also betting it was the two of you! You are the only ones here capable of doing something like that."

Twisty narrowed her eyes at Becky, immense with rage.

"Screw you, Becky! We're not capable of doing that! How dare you!"

"Whoa!" Ryan exclaimed. "Strong words for the girl who once tried to kill her brother and sister. You could see, given that, why people would think you're capable of it."

"Shut up, Ryan!" Twisty screamed. "I hate you! All of you! And I've told you before we weren't trying to kill Allie and Kevin, and it doesn't matter to you because you're convinced we're just plain evil! As soon as we're able to, we're moving out and getting away from this whole stupid family!"

"Good luck with that," Kevin laughed. "And please don't let the door hit you on the way out."

"Stop it, please," Justin pleaded. "Twisty, nobody wants you to leave. Despite everything you've done, you're still part of our family. And the rest of you need to stop. If Twisty says they didn't do it, I believe her."

Just then Ashley looked around frantically. "Where's Kitty?"

We looked at Ashley questioningly, then with growing realization, we looked between the group of us, scanning for Kitty's face. When we didn't find it, we started counting each other off, first in our heads, and as the increasing panic set in, out loud. Each time we counted, the number came out the same: twelve. With sudden alarm, we turned and looked around the park in all directions, searching to no avail.

It was true. Kitty was gone.

Chapter 37

My heart thundered in my chest, as I felt a darkened sense of deja vu, re-experiencing the same emotions as when we found the rabbits.

"Kittyyyyyy!" My siblings whirled wildly in circles, calling out Kitty's name. "Kittyyyyyyy!"

"Okay, let's not panic," Breezy said. "She's got to be around the park somewhere."

"Yeah, she probably never came out of her hiding place when we were playing hide-and-seek," Hazy reasoned, trying to smile reassuringly. But I could see the trepidation in her eyes.

"Let's split up and look for her," Ashley suggested. "Maybe she found a hiding spot deep in the park where she can't hear us."

We all ran off, looking for Kitty. I looked behind numerous trees, bushes, in the playground, and in the bathrooms. No Kitty. The butterflies inside me took on a powerful, frenzied flutter. Something was wrong. Things were starting to feel a bit too coincidental. First the rabbits, now Kitty goes missing? I felt a chill run through me, as I headed back to meet up with my siblings, knowing our search for Kitty was a failure.

"Any luck?" Ryan asked as I approached. I shook my head, suppressing the fear I felt.

Justin gave voice to the thoughts replaying in my head. "Um...do you guys think Kitty disappearing and the rabbits being hurt are connected?"

"I don't know," Allie said, her voice shaking. "But she's not here. We searched this park from top to bottom and called her name out a zillion times."

"Okay, let's take this one step at a time," Breezy said, trying to quell the deepening panic. "Let's all go home and see if she's there. We might be getting all worked up for nothing."

I knew the chances Kitty was home were zero to none. I asked the obvious question. "What if she isn't there? What do we do then?"

Breezy took a deep breath. "Then we'll have to call CC."

Just as I predicted, Kitty wasn't home when we arrived back. I knew it even before we desperately searched every room upstairs; the house had that quiet feel of vacancy. We heard a sudden ringing cutting through our noise of searching. It was our landline telephone downstairs.

"Maybe it's Kitty!" Breezy exclaimed. We all ran downstairs at breakneck speed. Ashley, being the fastest, reached the phone first.

"Hello?" Ashley answered.

Ashley listened silently for a minute, and her face fell. Her eyes took on a glassy stare. "What?" she said into the phone. "Is...is this a joke? If it is, it isn't funny." My heart pounded so hard I was afraid I'd keel over. Ashley's voice was high-pitched with terror.

"What's wrong, Ashley?" Breezy whispered, taking on Ashley's fear in her eyes. "Who is it?"

"Hold...hold on," Ashley said to the person on the phone.

As if in a trance, she slowly put the phone down at her side. She looked at us with blank eyes and spoke in a trembling voice that seemed not to belong to her. “It’s Big Boss,” she said woodenly. “He wants me to put him on speakerphone. He wants to talk to all of us.”

Breezy’s face contorted in anger. “Tell him no. We don’t want to talk to him.”

Ashley didn’t move and kept staring ahead in transfixed horror. “He says he has Kitty.”

Chapter 38

Breezy's eyes widened with dread, and without stopping to think, she rushed to take the phone from Ashley and pressed a button to move to the speaker.

"Big Boss!" Breezy said, her voice coming out in a strident squeak. "You have Kitty?"

There was a mad flurry as Breezy put the phone on the table and we charged towards it to listen. Within seconds I heard that awful sound I tried so hard for months to forget: The icy, smooth tone of Big Boss's voice.

"Why hello, Breezy! How are you doing? It's been a while since we've talked," Big Boss said, his voice penetrating the room like a knife.

"You have Kitty?" Breezy repeated.

"Is everyone there?" Big Boss asked. "All thirteen, oops sorry, I mean all twelve of you?"

All at once, everyone shouted into the phone. "Where's Kitty? What did you do with her?"

Big Boss slashed through the cacophony of our shouting with his sudden cold laughter. "I guess that answers my question. Hi, brats! How's it going?"

"Do you have Kitty, yes or no?" Breezy asked again in an interrogative manner.

"Well, I was hoping we'd take the chance to catch up first, but okay, let's get down to business," Big Boss said. "Listen very carefully, brats. Yes, I have Kitty, and if you ever want to see her alive again, you need to follow my exact instructions. All of you, and I mean all twelve of you, need to come over here right now. Don't call your father or the police. If you come here, I'll give you Kitty back. If you don't, or you do something stupid like call CC, I promise you you'll never see Kitty again. I'll make her disappear forever. So don't be stupid. Have we got a deal?"

We stared at each other in wide-eyed horror.

"Come over where? Where are you?" Ryan asked.

"Ah, yes, I forgot to say, sorry," Big Boss said. "Come over next door. At my old house. You remember it well, I'm sure."

"No, hold on!" Allie shouted. "You're threatening Kitty's life, saying we can't call CC or the police, and we're supposed to just go over next door and do what you say? Absolutely not!"

"Then you'll never see Kitty again. The choice is yours," Big Boss replied.

"How do we even know for sure you have Kitty?" Becky asked.

Big Boss laughed. "She's missing, isn't she? Who else do you think has her?"

"Can we talk to her?" Breezy implored. "Just to make sure she's okay?"

"I'm afraid that's not possible," Big Boss answered. "But rest assured she's safe. For now."

"And we're supposed to just trust you?" Ashley said tightly. "How do we know you didn't already hurt her?"

"You don't, but I give you my word I haven't," Big Boss said.

"Your word means nothing, Big Boss!" Becky shouted into the speaker.

"Why do you want us to come over there? What do you want?" Allie inquired.

"I want to talk to you," Big Boss answered.

"We're talking now! Say what you want to say!" Allie demanded.

"No, I want to talk to you in person," Big Boss insisted.

Allie snickered. "Sure you do. We're not coming over there until you tell us what you want."

"What's more important is what you want," Big Boss countered. "And I'm guessing what you want is your sister back. And you'll get her back when you come over here. Simple as that."

"Why do we need to come over there to get her back?" Allie shouted again.

"You'll find out when you get here," Big Boss answered cryptically.

"Oh no, we're not playing this game!" Allie cried. "How stupid do you think we are? You think we're just going to waltz over there and walk into your little trap or whatever you got planned? We're not idiots, Big Boss! We're not falling for this!"

"Falling for what? I just want to talk to you," Big Boss contended.

"Right, you just want to talk to us," Allie said. "Sure, okay. How about we come over for a little visit right now? We can sit, talk, have tea and crumpets, and laugh merrily about how you kidnapped our sister, then we'll bid each other a fine farewell and all join hands to sing Kumbaya!"

Despite my state of stark terror, I stifled a chuckle at Allie's sardonic wit.

There was a pause before Big Boss answered. "I knew that

was you, Allie. I'd know the sound of your sarcastic, cocky little voice anywhere."

"Tell us what you want!" Allie cried.

"I want you to come over here," Big Boss toyed.

"Why? And why can't we call CC? It can only be so we can't get help! What are you planning to do?" Allie questioned.

"I don't want CC or anyone else involved. This is between me and all of you. Of course, you don't have to comply. But then you lose your precious Kit-Cat, Allie, and you're down one member of your family," Big Boss taunted viciously.

Allie pounded her fist on the table next to the phone. "If you hurt Kitty, Big Boss, you'll pay for it!" she screamed. "We'll make you pay! So will CC! And you hurt those rabbits too, didn't you? It was you! You did it, you sick psychopath!"

"Rabbits?" Big Boss questioned. "I don't know what you're talking about, Allie."

"You know exactly what I'm talking about!" Allie said. "Admit it! You hurt those baby rabbits at the park! And then you took Kitty! You hurt them to distract us from noticing Kitty was missing!"

"You brats are trying my patience," Big Boss replied. "Enough questions. Are you coming over and getting your sister back or not?"

"You're not really leaving us much choice, Big Boss," Breezy trembled.

"The choice is all yours," Big Boss crooned. "It all depends on how much you really love your sister, doesn't it?" he laughed wickedly. "Tick tock, brats. What's it going to be?"

"I guess we don't have much choice but to come over," Chase said.

"No!" Allie cried.

"Can we have a few minutes to talk this over?" Breezy pleaded.

There was a momentary pause. "Sure," Big Boss slithered. "Put me on hold and I'll wait for your decision. But don't wait too long, brats."

Breezy hit the hold button and nodded it was safe to talk. Allie plowed in immediately.

"Okay, please tell me you guys can see as well as I can that this is obviously a huge trap!" Allie cried. "We can't go over there! Who knows what he's got planned! Let's wait for CC to get home and handle this. I'm sure he'll be back soon anyway! He can get Kit-Cat back!"

"But Allie, we can't wait!" Breezy returned helplessly. "Kitty could be…could be…" She winced, extremely reluctant to finish the rest. "Dead by then."

Allie blinked back tears. "But if we go over there, all we're doing is putting ourselves in danger too! How does that help Kit-Cat? Please, let's wait for CC!"

"What if he kills her?" Ashley said, her voice unnaturally high.

Allie swallowed hard. "What if he kills us?"

"What do you two have to say about this?" Kevin said, pointing at Twisty and Carlie. "He's supposedly your friend. Or at least he led you to believe he was. What do you think now?"

Twisty and Carlie had been deathly quiet up to now. Twisty had an uncomprehending expression on her face, and Carlie looked genuinely frightened. "I...I don't know," Twisty answered feebly. "This has to be some kind of joke. He really wouldn't kill Kitty."

"He wouldn't?" Becky said incredulously. "Of course he would! He's evil! Just plain evil! And you two have refused to see that, just allowed yourselves to be played by him! Well what now, Twisty? Your so-called friend just kidnapped your sister!

Maybe you should go to him and nicely ask for our sister back!"

"Stop it!" Twisty shouted. "I don't know why he's doing this, but there's got to be some reason!"

"The reason is he's a psychopath, as I've been saying all along!" Allie cried. "And we'd be crazy to go next door and ring the psychopath's doorbell, hoping he'll just hand Kit-Cat back and say goodbye. We need to get CC! He can save her! We can't! None of us even have any power left to defend ourselves! How can we help if we're in danger too?"

"But what's CC going to do?" Kevin asked. "What can he do that we can't?"

"This is a kidnapping case, Kevin," Allie pointed out. "How about call the police? There's a whole procedure they follow for kidnapping."

Ryan frowned. "But Allie, I thought CC wasn't allowed to call the police on Big Boss. Isn't that what that Chief Seager guy said?"

The floor dropped out from under me. In my head, I heard the clicking of pieces starting to fit together. I did *not* want to see the finished puzzle.

Allie bit her lip and a pained expression came over her face. "But…this is completely different. He *can't* mean for kidnapping, he just can't…." she stammered desperately.

"I think we should assume CC won't be able to get help from the police," Justin said. "Which means it's up to us to save Kitty. If we don't go, and he does something to Kitty, it will be too late for CC to save her. We need to act *now*."

Allie looked tortured, like she was being torn in pieces by two different parts of her mind. "But we can't! I'm telling you this is a trap! Why else do you think he wants *all* of us to go? He doesn't want any of us left! But….Oh God, Kit-Cat!" she said with an anguished cry, breaking into tears.

"Um, hey guys, I don't think Big Boss is going to wait much longer," Chase said.

"If we had any powers left, we wouldn't even be worrying about this!" Kevin cried. "We'd just go over and demand Kitty back or we'll use magic against him. Why isn't Big Boss afraid of that anyway? He knows we can defend ourselves."

"Let's go and pretend we have enough energy left to attack him," Chase suggested. "We threaten to use magic on him unless he gives us Kitty back."

Something flickered in my head, a thought like a persistent, buzzing fly I couldn't catch. There was something important here we were all missing.

"We need to get back on the phone before he hangs up," Breezy said. "We're taking too long. We're going over, right? I think we all agree we have to."

Allie looked at the ground and her breathing became very shallow. "Fine, we'll go, but I'm leaving CC a note," she half-sobbed. "I want CC to know what happened and where we are in case...." Allie trailed off, choking back another sob. "In case we don't come back," she whispered with a shiver.

Breezy fought back her tears and pressed the talk button on the phone receiver. "We're back, Big Boss," she said in a wobbly voice.

"You brats sure do take your time to make a decision," Big Boss hissed. "You're lucky. I was about to hang up. What did you decide?"

"You're not giving us much choice, so we're coming over there," Breezy stated. "But you better give us Kitty back."

"Sure, sure," Big Boss said in a maddeningly indifferent manner. "Just come over and she'll be here."

"And if you don't give her back to us or you try to do anything to us, we'll make you pay for it, Big Boss!" Kevin threatened. "We'll attack you! We'll use our powers on you!"

There was a pause on the other line, then Big Boss burst into loud, malevolent laughter. We looked at each other, paralyzed with fear. Allie grabbed my hand tightly, and I flinched at the touch; it was cold as ice. "Go ahead, give it your best shot, brats," Big Boss chuckled. "I'm not too worried about it."

"What does that mean?" Kevin asked, his voice shaking. "Why are you laughing?"

"If you brats really intend on coming over here, you better get a move on," Big Boss said. "And oh, yes, one more thing. Don't try to do anything stupid to get around not contacting CC by leaving a note for him or anything. Or else Kitty is going to suffer from a horrible accident."

Allie let go of my hand and squeezed her eyes shut, covering them in defeated despair. From beneath her hand fat tears rolled down her cheeks.

"We get the point, Big Boss!" Breezy cried, trying hard not to let herself be overwhelmed by Allie's tears. "We won't call CC, leave him a note, or anything else. We'll do what you say! But you need to keep your end of the bargain too! If we do this, you've got to let Kitty go!"

"Of course, Breezy," Big Boss said smoothly. "That is the deal. So come on over. See you soon, brats."

With that, the line went dead. Dead, I thought morbidly, as we're all about to be.

Chapter 39

We walked out of the house together slowly, feeling like we were marching off to our execution in front of a firing squad. My heart pounded in tune with our heavy footsteps on the ground. I took extra physical effort to force myself to keep lifting my feet. What are we doing? I thought. Allie's right! This is crazy!

"This is a really bad idea, this is such a bad idea, Oh God, this is a *really really really* bad idea," Allie said repeatedly.

"Allie, stop!" Ashley cried. "You're making me more freaked out than I already am!"

"Allie, don't worry, he's not going to do anything to us," Chase reassured. "He knows we can attack him with magic. He won't take that chance."

"But we don't have any power left," Ashley pointed out.

"Shh, don't say that too loud, Ashley!" Becky whispered. "He might hear you!"

"Yeah, we have to make him think we have magic left," Kevin said quietly. He pointed to Allie, Hazy, Breezy, and me. "You know, normally you four would have enough to attack him, but because of the rabbits, you don't now. Just our luck, right?"

And then, after Kevin inadvertently laid it out so clearly, I knew what that fly in my head was warning me about. Oh my God! How did I not see it before? Allie said the rabbits were a distraction, but she was only half right. The rabbits were actually... I opened my mouth to warn everyone, but Kevin just made Allie come to the same realization. She stopped dead, all color instantly drained from her face.

"Oh God," Allie trembled. "The magic...there were four rabbits...he...he set us up! We...we have to turn back now!"

"Allie, we can't go back! We've got to save Kitty," Breezy said.

"No, listen! There were four rabbits! Four!" Allie yelled, grabbing Breezy by the shoulders to face her. "Not three! Not five! Four! Don't you see what I'm saying?"

Everyone stopped walking and stared at Allie uncomprehendingly. Except for me. I knew exactly what she was saying.

"The rabbits were for us!" Allie explained to everyone, pointing to herself, me, Breezy, and Hazy. "To use up our magic! So we wouldn't have anything left! Don't you see? Kevin just said it! He said normally the four of us would have enough power to attack him, but we don't because of the rabbits. That was deliberate! That's why he hurt those rabbits! Because he knew we'd heal them!"

My siblings stood agape in horrified realization of what Allie said. Then we heard Big Boss's voice behind us: "Wow, Allie, you really are one smart cookie, aren't you? I knew you were going to be my biggest challenge."

With great dread, we all turned to face Big Boss's house and found him standing on his porch in front of the door, holding it slightly ajar, smiling malevolently at us. "Hi, brats. It's nice to see you again."

We stood like statues, so petrified we could barely breathe.

"You admit it then! You did hurt those rabbits!" Allie cried.

"Yes, well I had to get the four little Musketeers to use their powers up somehow," he said, his voice dripping with mocking scorn. "And I knew you little bleeding-heart animal lovers wouldn't be able to resist saving those poor little bunnies' lives," he laughed cruelly.

We stared back at him in aghast disgust.

"Aww, don't look at me like that," Big Boss said. "I'm not a monster. But I had to take measures to ensure you couldn't attack me, so I'm afraid the little cottontails had to suffer. But I knew you'd save them. I was just defending myself, that's all."

Allie exploded with rage. "Anyone who would do something like that *is* a monster! *Defending* yourself? Defending yourself from what? Kidnapping our sister? You're not trying to defend yourself! You're making sure *we can't defend ourselves*!"

Big Boss shrugged. "Same difference, Allie. The point is I had to make sure you couldn't use your powers on me. With your other siblings here, they pretty much did the work for me. But you four are not so easy. I knew you wouldn't use your powers unless it was for an important reason, and you would consider saving a few stupid little animals a very important reason. So I got four rabbits, one for each of you. And now none of you have any power left, do you?"

We gaped at him, gripped by sheer terror, still glued to the spot. Breezy looked at him like she was staring into the face of the devil, and somehow found the courage to speak. "Where's Kitty, Big Boss?" she asked shakily, trying to ignore the boastful confession he just made. "We're here. We did what you said. Now, where's Kitty?"

"She's inside," Big Boss said. "Come on in and get her."

"No!" Allie shouted. "No, no! We're not going in there!

That wasn't part of the deal! You bring her out to us!"

"No offense, Allie, but you're not exactly the one calling the shots here. You need to come in and get her or you won't get her back at all," Big Boss replied with a cold grin.

"Big Boss, you told us if we all come here, you'll give us Kitty back. We kept to our end of the bargain, so you keep to yours. Please bring Kitty out," Breezy pleaded.

"You need to *come inside the house and get her*, Breezy," Big Boss directed. "If you don't, then sorry, no Kitty Cat for you. You want her back, or don't you?"

"We don't have much choice but to go in," Justin whimpered.

"We can't go in there! It's a death trap! We'd be idiots to walk in there! He just admitted to making us use up our magic so we can't defend ourselves! If we go in there, he'll attack us!" Allie cried in a high-pitched voice.

"Come on, brats, I don't have all day," Big Boss complained. "Are you coming in or what?"

"Come on, let's go. We've got to get Kitty. Just stick together," Ashley said.

"I'm not going in there!" Allie shouted. "I'll wait right here!"

"The deal is you all need to come in, or Kitty doesn't come out with you," Big Boss declared. "So if Allie doesn't come in, no Kitty."

"You're already breaking the deal!" Allie screamed at Big Boss. "You told us to come to your house, not that we had to go inside!"

"Like I said, you are in no position to call the shots here, Allie," Big Boss sneered.

"We're not going in your house where nobody can see us where you can easily murder us!" Allie screeched, her eyes welling with tears.

"Murder you? Oh, Allie, you're so overdramatic," Big Boss chided. "I'm not going to kill you. Why would you ever think that?"

"Oh, I don't know, maybe it's a crazy hunch, or maybe it's because you're threatening to kill our sister!" Allie cried.

Big Boss laughed. "I don't want to kill Kitty or any of you."

"*Then what do you want*?" Allie screamed so loudly it made us jump.

"Keep your voice down, Allie," Big Boss ordered. "You don't want to scare the whole neighborhood."

"No! I'm done with this! If you don't bring Kitty outside right now, I swear to God, Big Boss, I'll scream at the top of my lungs so everyone within a ten-mile radius will come running!" Allie threatened.

"Do it and Kitty dies," Big Boss abruptly said in a low icy manner.

"Allie," Breezy finally cut in, grabbing Allie's wrist. "Please don't antagonize him. We don't want to push him into hurting Kitty," she whispered.

Allie turned away, her face wet with tears. "Right, because he doesn't want to kill Kitty or any of us!" she shouted bitingly in Big Boss's direction, repeating his words back.

"I'm going to count to three, brats," Big Boss said coldly. "If you aren't in this house by the time I get to three, I'll slam the door and your chance to get Kitty back is over. You'll never see her again. One…"

"Okay, Big Boss, we're going, we're going," Breezy said imploringly. She gestured for us all to follow her, practically dragging Allie by the arm. Somehow we all found the strength to move towards Big Boss's house, and before I knew it we were on his porch and walking through the front door Big Boss held open for us. We entered a barren room with nothing in it, not even the slightest piece of furniture.

"This way," Big Boss said, leading us further inside the house. We walked through several nearly identical rooms that were just as empty and stopped at a closed door. "She's in here," Big Boss said, opening the door and ushering us in. We all filed into the room and heard a child sobbing as soon as we entered. The room was dark but we could just make out the shape of a small girl sitting in the corner. Kitty!

"Kit-Cat, Kit-Cat! Thank God!" Allie squealed, running over to Kitty.

"Kitty! Are you all right?" Ashley cried, throwing her arms around Kitty.

Kitty stared at us in disbelief. "What are you all d-d-doing here?"

"We're here to save you!" I cried.

And then, there was the distinct sound of the door closing behind us, plunging us into near darkness. We gasped, and when my eyes adjusted to the dark, I saw Allie skidding across the room towards the door, and I ran to follow her.

"No, no, no, no, no!" Allie cried, willing the door to open again. She closed her fingers around the doorknob and turned it futilely, then frantically twisted it back and forth to no avail. "No!' she shouted, hammering the door with her fist. "He locked us in here!" she cried with choked breath. "We can't get out!" She looked at me, her breathing becoming very heavy. "He locked us in, Cap!"

I grabbed the doorknob and pulled as hard as I could. The rest of my siblings gathered behind us. Even though it was dark, I could see the panicked looks on their faces. I beat the door with such force I nearly broke my knuckles. "Open the door, Big Boss! Let us out of here!" I shouted. Allie and I banged on the door screaming. "Let us out! Let us out of here!"

Breezy put her hand between us to quiet the pounding. "It's no use. Save your strength. He's not going to open the door," she said in a grim whisper.

"Yeah, there's no point hurting yourselves," Justin added sadly.

"Why-why don't you use magic to open the door?" Kitty whispered.

Allie collapsed against the door. The soft sound of her sobs echoed throughout the empty room.

"We can't, Kitty!" I answered. "None of us have any magic left!"

"He...he made us use...use it all...the rabbits," Allie gasped between sobs.

"Rabbits?" Kitty asked quizzically.

"Wait, do...do you guys smell that?" Kevin asked, his voice high with trepidation.

We looked at Kevin and that's when I noticed the putrid stench of gas quickly filling the room. I started coughing immediately.

"Gas!" Breezy shouted. "It's gas! Everyone cover your mouth and nose! Don't breathe it in!"

We quickly obeyed Breezy, but it was already too late. We started coughing terribly, and my vision rapidly became blurred. My head felt woozy, and the last thing I remembered was seeing the forms of my siblings dropping to the ground. Then everything went black and I fell into deep oblivion.

Chapter 40

I opened my eyes and my lungs were on fire. I sat up abruptly and started coughing so hard I thought one of my lungs would fall from my mouth. My throat burned and every breath I drew was painful. My siblings laid on the floor next to me, and one by one they regained consciousness, jerking upright, and coughing vigorously. I immediately noticed there was now more light in the room because I could clearly see my siblings' faces.

"Wh-what happened?" Ryan croaked.

"Oh God, it feels like someone's banging a drum inside my brain," Allie said in a throaty whisper, her fingers on her temples.

"It hurts to breathe! I've never had a worse headache in my life!" Chase wailed with his head buried in his hands.

"It's not a headache, Chase. Big Boss knocked us out," Justin said, launching into a coughing fit. "He…he gassed us," he uttered.

"How long do you think we were out?" Ryan asked.

"It was 12:30 when we left to come here. I have a watch on," Ashley said, checking the time on her wrist. "Holy crap! It's 7:10!"

"What? 7:10!" Allie cried, snapping her head up and immediately regretting it. "Owww!" she roared, massaging her head. "We've been gone for nearly seven hours? CC will be worried sick!"

"Well the good news is that means he'll be looking for us," Breezy said hoarsely.

Allie shook her head very slowly. "He won't think of coming here. He'll probably check the whole park first."

"Hey wait, Allie!" Ryan cried. "If it's been that long, that means you have enough energy to use magic again! Open the door and let's get out of here!"

Allie smiled and pointed her hand at the door, concentrating on unlocking it. The light didn't appear, however, not even a spark or fizzle. After a few minutes, Allie lowered her hand in defeat. "I guess I don't have the energy to do it yet," she said dolefully.

"You should, though," Breezy said, scrunching her face in puzzlement. "Healing power, which is the last thing you did with the rabbit, takes a few hours to recover from at the most. Those baby rabbits were so small, it shouldn't take nearly as long to recharge."

"Breezy, I know that, but I'm telling you, I've got nothing," Allie said. "You try it."

Breezy raised her hand towards the door, tensing her face so hard I was afraid she'd have a brain hemorrhage, but not even the slightest flicker of light appeared. Finally, like Allie, she dropped her hand and gave up.

"See, what did I tell you?" Allie said, feeling a little self-satisfied.

"Maybe the gas weakened us so much we can't use our powers right now," Justin offered.

Breezy turned her deep blue eyes towards me. "Something's

wrong," she said in a breathy whisper. "We should have at least some energy by now." A look of great distress clouded over her face. "When I was trying just now, Cap, it was like..." she paused, trying to come up with the right words. "Like it wasn't there at all," she finished, her bottom lip trembling.

Suddenly there was a click and the door swung open. We looked up in alarm as Big Boss strolled into the room, shutting and locking the door behind him. He carried a cardboard box that he set on the floor. We scrambled upright as he stopped in front of us with a smug smirk on his face. "Hi, brats! I see you're awake. How're your heads?"

"What did you do to us?" Ryan shouted.

"You gassed us! You knocked us out! Why?" Ashley cried.

"When CC finds out about this, you're dead meat, Big Boss!" Kevin raged.

Big Boss regarded us with an amused smile as we continued shouting at him. He waved his hand dismissively. "I'll answer your questions, brats. But first, I want you to do something. See that box I brought in over there? I want you to levitate it using your powers. Since I know many of you can't do that because of the time it takes to recharge, I'll ask the four little rabbit-saving Musketeers to do it."

We stared at him in utter perplexity. Levitate a box?

"Why?" I asked Big Boss. "What's the point?"

"I want to see what you can do with your powers," Big Boss simpered. "Want to do it, Capricorn?"

"Let me get this straight," Allie piped up. "You kidnapped Kit-Cat, forced us to come here by threatening to kill her, locked us in, gassed us, and knocked us out for hours, just so you could have a demonstration of our powers? You're insane."

"How about you, Allie? Want to give it a try?" Big Boss returned.

"No, I don't want to *give it a try,* Big Boss," Allie answered, mocking Big Boss's peppy tone. "I want to go home. I already tried to use magic to unlock the door, which is a better use of energy than your stupid box, and it didn't work. You gassing us completely wiped us out. You do realize this is thirteen separate counts of kidnapping, right, Big Boss?"

Big Boss laughed. "You sure do have some moxie, Allie. It's up to you then, Capricorn."

"Fine, I'll do it," I grumbled. I put my hand out and focused on the box. Levitating an object, especially as light as a cardboard box, is one of the easiest things we can do with our powers. That's why I knew instantly when I was unable to lift the box that something was horribly wrong. "I can't do it," I gasped.

Breezy sat in the corner with Hazy was by her side, and I could tell from their troubled expressions they were having another serious conversation with each other inside their minds. Hazy shook her head. "It can't be true," she whimpered. She lifted her hand and moved to levitate the box herself, but when nothing happened, she lowered her hand and crumbled her forehead to her knees. Big Boss walked over to Breezy and Hazy, and Breezy immediately draped her arm defensively around Hazy, pulling her close.

"Looks like you're the only one left, Breezy," Big Boss sneered.

Breezy turned her head up to Big Boss and looked him dead in the eye. "You know I can't do it, Big Boss."

Big Boss gave Breezy a knowing smile, and Breezy turned her head away. "Wow, all four of you can't move the box?" Big Boss said. "Enough time has passed since you healed the rabbits. I gave you a good number of hours. Are you sure you can't do it? Okay, here. Why don't you let me try?"

And then, to our absolute horror, Big Boss waved his hand at the box, created a small beam of light, and made the box float gracefully in the air and back down on the ground. He turned back to us with a victorious smile.

Instinctively, some of my siblings scattered back towards the wall, moving as far away from Big Boss as humanly possible in the cramped room. The rest of my siblings were too terror-stricken to breathe, let alone move.

Breezy looked up at Big Boss, struggling not to cry. "You stole our magic, didn't you, Big Boss? You somehow stole all our magic when you kn-knocked us out."

Big Boss shot Breezy another vicious grin. "Now, brats," he said, looking over our frozen faces. "Let's talk. You want to know how this is possible, right? Want to know how I did it? Well, it was easy. Easier still once I realized how incredibly naive you are. Well, most of you anyway. Allie always gave me a real run for my money." He nodded at Breezy. "You as well, Breezy, due to those impressive psychic skills you have. That's okay, though. I enjoyed the challenge. If it wasn't for the two of you it would have been too easy. I'll tell you one thing, though: It would have been a lot harder if I hadn't enlisted my two little unknowing accomplices." He stopped in front of Twisty and Carlie, who stared at him in abject disbelief. "Twisty, Carlie, thank you so much for all your help! I owe so much to you! You helped me convince your siblings to overuse their powers so they could eventually be rendered defenseless and wrangled over here, and all I had to do was promise a little consequence-free revenge."

In my head, all the puzzle pieces were coming out at once and slamming together to reveal the brutal truth.

"I saw the strong animosity between the two of you and Allie," Big Boss continued, "and knew I could play it up. That led to the whole fight where Kevin attacked Twisty, and that was too good of an opportunity to miss." He looked up to address the rest of us. "So I told them I know a way you can get revenge on Allie *and* Kevin. Get all your siblings to overuse their powers. Then you'll be able to attack and no one will be able to counterattack. And lo and behold, they actually convinced the majority of you to waste your powers on trivial things like snack foods!" Big Boss threw his head back and laughed maliciously. "You stupid foolish little brats gave up the ability to easily protect yourselves for things like chips and candy! I just couldn't believe it!" He turned and fixed his sinister smile on Allie, Breezy, Hazy, and me. "And I asked my accomplices how the plan was going, and they told me the Four Musketeers were not overusing their powers. They asked how to get Allie to use up her power so they could attack her. I said attack Kevin first with Allie there. Allie will use all her power to heal Kevin, then you can attack her. It worked like a charm, didn't it?"

Some of my terror was boiling into seething hatred, as I listened to Big Boss rub his victory over us in our faces. He seemed to be really enjoying this and I'm sure he was looking forward to it for a long time.

"Now I needed some inside eyes and ears to keep me abreast of how you were using your powers. My little accomplices were more than happy to provide me that information, in exchange for my services in helping them get away scot-free with their revenge against Allie and Kevin. I told them to attack when CC's away from the house, and I'll even slow CC down for you. On the day of the attack they called and told me where CC was. I went to the store parking lot, found his car, sliced his tires, and slipped the tow truck driver a hundred bucks to wait. I told my accomplices CC will call you when he sees his tires, so take the battery from the phone. They followed my orders to the T."

Twisty and Carlie looked absolutely miserable, finally realizing they've been duped. I can't say a part of me didn't take some pleasure in that.

"So why did you *really* not want CC to know about the attack, Big Boss?" Breezy questioned, her face showing she was also deeply disgusted with this braggart display.

"Isn't it obvious, Breezy?" Big Boss chuckled. "So CC wouldn't bring you on all his trips outside the house. So he wouldn't have to cart Twisty and Carlie along every time he left. So there would be another time when all thirteen of you were alone without CC. That's the only way my plan would work. I needed *all thirteen* of you. So thanks for all coming over here."

Breezy squeezed her eyes shut, and Hazy burst into tears.

"I didn't mind going away to keep CC from finding out, anyway," Big Boss said. "I knew if CC was ever going to let you play outside by yourselves again, I'd have to be out of the picture. But I kept a watch on you. I waited for months for a day like today, where CC was gone and you were all alone in the park, completely defenseless. But I knew the Four Musketeers weren't careless with their powers like the rest of you. I realized I could use the same strategy Twisty and Carlie used to attack Allie: Get them to use up all their power on saving someone's life. And that's where the little cottontails came into play. After leaving them at the tree for you to find, I found Kitty hiding in the park during your game of hide-and-seek, and, knowing she had no powers left, easily snatched her. Kitty served as great bait for luring the rest of you over here."

I felt like screaming. Big Boss's plan was as diabolical as they come, and it was clear he had the whole thing thought out far in advance.

Twisty and Carlie looked like they were going to be

physically sick. "You...you used...us," Twisty sputtered to Big Boss. "You used us to trap us all...to get our magic..."

"Ding ding ding ding ding!" Big Boss rang scathingly. "Nothing gets by you, Twisty!"

Carlie started to cry. "But I thought you were our...fr-fr-friend."

"You are my friends, Carlie!" Big Boss exclaimed. "Like I said, I couldn't have done it without you! I needed you brats completely powerless, so I had to get you wasting your powers on things that quickly drain your energy. I first put the idea in your heads, true, but Carlie, you and Twisty were the ones who really got the whole thing moving! All to get revenge on Allie and Kevin! Wasn't it worth it? All it cost you were your powers!"

"You're a horrible person!" Carlie sobbed.

"Now Carlie, I know you're upset, but let's remember all the good times we've had," Big Boss laughed. "I really do appreciate all your help. While I do enjoy a challenge, I *really* love the gullible ones the most."

Allie had about enough of Big Boss's pompous showboating. "My God," she said, her voice dripping with disgust. "Do you *ever* get tired of listening to yourself talk, Big Boss?"

Big Boss flashed Allie a hateful grin. "I could ask you the same question, Allie. Keep talking, Allie. I've got plans for you, Allie. Big plans."

"What is that supposed to mean?" Allie screeched. She became completely undone by this statement. "You've got plans for me? What plans? You can't say that and not explain what you mean! You can't do that!" she screamed. She exploded into uncontrollable sobs.

Breezy rushed to Allie's side and hugged her close. She rocked her gently, doing her best to console her. "Are you done now, Big Boss?" Breezy asked Big Boss accusingly. "Or are you going to hold us here just to keep *terrorizing us*?"

Allie's weeping was heart-wrenching. "I just want to go home!" she wailed. "I don't care about the magic! I just want to go home!"

I wanted to hurt Big Boss. I wanted to hurt him badly for making Allie cry like that.

"Don't worry, Allie, you'll get to go home," Big Boss said. "Now that I've got your powers, I have no more use for you."

"Are you *ever* going to tell us how you stole our powers?" Ashley shouted. "Since you want to stand here and gloat about everything else, how about telling us that!"

"It was easy, Ashley," Big Boss replied. "The powers are in your bloodstream. When I knocked you out, I drained blood from each of you. I collected the blood in blood bags and injected it into my own veins. Presto-changeo, I have your powers in my blood now."

Wait!" Kevin exclaimed. "You took our blood? Are you serious?"

"Yes," Big Boss answered. "Take a look at your wrists."

We gasped to find our wrists wrapped in bandages. I couldn't believe none of us realized that before, but attributed it to the weak, gas-induced, and terror-stricken state we were all in.

"Wait, but...How did you know that?" Ashley asked. "How did you know our powers are in our blood? And that you could get the powers by taking our blood? And injecting it into your veins? Because *we* didn't even know that! So if *we* didn't know that, how the hell did *you* know that?"

"You know what, Ashley? That's a really damn good question!" Becky cried. "How *did* you know that?"

"Wow, brats, I've never heard you swear before," Big Boss

remarked amusedly. "Does CC know you talk like that?"

"Answer the question!" Kevin demanded. "How did you know that?"

Big Boss laughed wickedly and went to the door, unlocking it with the key in his hand. He opened the door wide and looked at us with a scornful smile. "Run, Munch brats," he said. "Run. Run and go tell *Daddy.*"

We shot out of the room together like a speeding train, not daring even once to look back.

Chapter 41

We bolted into our house in a frantic state of terror. We hurriedly made sure everyone was inside, then slammed the door, racing to lock it behind us. Trembling like mad, I turned the lock on the knob and latched the bolt into place with frenzied fingers.

"Does that matter?" Kevin asked me with a shiver, indicating the door. "He has our magic now. If he wants to get in, can't he just use magic to unlock it?"

Kevin's question seized me and sent me wheeling into a whole new plane of panic. "CC!" I wailed, running into the house like a bat out of hell. The rest of my siblings followed right behind me, screaming CC's name.

CC came out from the kitchen when he heard us, appearing both simultaneously relieved and angry. "Where have you been? I've been looking all over for you! Do you know how worried I was? You were supposed to be home hours-" CC stopped short when he saw us, his words stuck in his throat. He took one look at our tear-stained, distraught faces, and rabbits' blood-stained shirts. "Oh my God," he gasped. "What happened?"

Allie tore across the room and threw herself into CC, burying her face in his chest, bawling her eyes out. CC froze in shock, then he put his hands on Allie's back. "Hey... no, no, shhh...Allie sweetheart...shhh...Allie honey....shh...you're okay, sweetheart," he whispered gently, caressing Allie's hair. Allie kept on crying, completely inconsolable.

Fear appeared on CC's face, never seeing Allie in this kind of state before. He picked Allie up and held her in his arms, closing his eyes and rubbing her back, still trying to alleviate her tears. "Shh...sweetheart...Allie…hey, come on…" CC opened his eyes and looked at the rest of us, waiting for one of us to talk.

Breezy spoke first. "CC, something terrible happened."

CC nodded somberly. "I guessed that. Is everyone here? Is everyone safe?" He scanned us over and did a quick mental headcount.

"Yeah...for now," Ryan muttered.

CC frowned. "What do you mean 'for now?'"

"CC...we...we lost our magic!" Hazy cried, tears coming down her cheeks.

"No, we didn't lose it! It was stolen!" Kevin corrected.

"What are you talking about?" CC said, furrowing his brow. "How could you lose your magic?"

"CC, we were just kidnapped!" Kevin announced.

"What?" CC exclaimed.

I wanted to explain, but I was so shaken I could only utter a series of words that came out as incoherent babble. "The rabbits...Kitty...kidnapped...Big Boss..."

CC tightened his face. "Big Boss! How did I guess this involved him? I thought he was gone!" CC exhaled deeply to steel himself for what was coming. Allie's heavy sobs had finally receded into muffled sniffles. CC directed us into the living room. He sat on the couch, still holding Allie against him. "Okay. Now everyone take a deep breath," CC instructed. "Then start from the beginning and tell me exactly what happened."

We did just that. When we got to the point where we found Kitty and Big Boss locked us in the room, CC interrupted the story and looked up at Kitty with great concern. "Kitty, honey, are you all right? Did Big Boss hurt you?"

Kitty spoke in a barely audible tremble. "No, but he…he had the knife that now I know he used on those rabbits, it still had blood…he told me when he grabbed me if I screamed or made a sound he would plunge the knife in my thr-throat and made me go with him. I...I thought he was going to kill me," she stammered, bursting into tears.

CC took one of his hands off Allie's back and held it out towards Kitty, beckoning her to come to him. Kitty sat next to him on the couch and he put his arm around her, kissing the top of her head. "Thank God you're safe," he breathed. "I'm so sorry."

We continued our story to the end. CC wore an expression that contained simultaneous anguish for us and rage towards Big Boss.

"I understand why you went over there, I know you were thinking of saving Kitty, but I really wish you would have listened to Allie and waited for me," CC said finally. "I can't blame you though. You were scared and worried about your sister. You felt like you didn't have any choice. It's just...Oh God, kids! What did you think you'd be able to do? Especially without any powers…"

"I'm sorry," Kitty sobbed. "This is my fault. If I didn't get kidnapped, nobody would have come over and got trapped. We'd still have our magic!"

"Kitty, my God! This isn't your fault!" CC exclaimed. "You're the victim here, sweetheart! You can't blame yourself for being kidnapped!" He looked up at all of us. "But kids, I think you've learned the hard way what I meant by being responsible with those powers. I was always afraid of something like this happening. I don't think I need to tell you this wouldn't have happened if you followed my rules for using those powers." CC said he's sorry the most to us, the Four Musketeers, who *were* responsible, and that we suffered the consequences for our siblings' mistakes. He let out a long sigh. "What am I saying? You're just kids. You just did what I'm sure every kid would do who had those powers. I'm sorry. The last thing you need right now is a lecture."

My siblings looked down in shame, wiping away tears.

"Capricorn," Ryan said to me. "We should have listened to you."

"Yeah," Ashley agreed. "I'm sorry I called you the magic police. You were right about everything."

CC said he was taking Allie and Kitty to bed and we should rest too. "Twisty and Carlie," CC called. "Stay here a few minutes. I want to talk to you two. I want to know more about this attack on Kevin and Allie nobody ever told me about. And what in God's name would ever possess you to work with Big Boss against your own family!"

Twisty started sobbing heavily. "I'm sorry, CC! I'm so so sorry! I'm stupid! I'm such a stupid stupid idiot!"

CC put his hand up in a calming gesture. "You're not stupid, Twisty. A little naive, yes, but not stupid. I know you're sorry. You're going to be okay, stop."

"CC, I'm sorry too! Please don't send us away!" Carlie wailed. "We'll be better! I promise we'll be better! Don't get rid of us!"

CC got up from the couch holding Allie, who had fallen asleep in his arms, worn out from crying and pure mental exhaustion. He walked over to Carlie and put his hand on her tiny shoulder. "Carlie, I am very upset and disappointed with you and Twisty, but I want you to know I would never get rid of you. You're my daughters. I love you. I would never get rid of you."

Carlie, overcome with relief, grief, and shame, collapsed against CC and hugged him.

"CC," I asked as we were walking up the staircase, "Are you calling the police?"

"Yes," CC answered. "As soon as I'm done talking to Twisty and Carlie. Then I might just go next door and rip Big Boss's throat out."

I laid wide awake on my bed, trying to process everything that just happened. Allie was above me on her top bunk where CC had tucked her in, fast asleep. Breezy and Hazy fell asleep together on Breezy's bed, Breezy's arm locked around Hazy. I kept trying to rest myself, but my body was pumping with so much adrenaline, sleep was impossible. Finally, I gave up and quietly left the room so I wouldn't disturb my sisters.

The house was very quiet. I figured most of my siblings were sleeping, and I wondered in amazement how they could do that. I tiptoed downstairs and found CC sitting at the dining room table with his palm on his chin, appearing deep in thought. He rose to his feet when he saw me.

"What's wrong, Capricorn? You can't sleep?" CC asked me.

I shook my head no. "I'm too shook up to sleep, CC."

CC pushed my hair back behind my ear in a loving gesture. "Are you hungry, Capricorn?"

"Yes, I'm actually starving!" I answered. I just realized the last thing we ate was Kitty's French toast this morning, which seemed like a lifetime ago.

"Well go into the living room with your brothers and I'll fix you something to eat," CC said. "The police are on their way over."

I found Ryan, Chase, and Kevin sitting on the couch together in the living room, still appearing a little shell-shocked.

"Hey, Capricorn," Ryan greeted me. "You can't sleep either, huh?"

"Nope," I said, plopping in the chair next to them. "I don't know how anybody could."

"Me neither," Chase agreed. He sat with a numb expression, staring straight ahead. I thought about how before all this Chase saw taking on Big Boss as a fun thrill ride at a carnival. One look at his face told me he now understood the immense danger that was there all along. Twisty and Carlie weren't the only ones who were naive. Things were becoming very real for my brothers and sisters very fast.

The doorbell suddenly sounded and scared me out of my wits. I let out a scream and sprung about three feet in the air from my seat.

CC came into the living room and put a steady hand on my shoulder to calm me. "Easy, Capricorn, honey. It's the police," he reassured me.

I nodded, feeling a little foolish, and CC went to answer the door. I looked at my brothers, expecting to get teased for my overreaction, but they didn't say a word, seeming to judge it somewhat appropriate. I suddenly wanted to hear what the police had to say. I got up and ran to the front door, just in time to see CC swinging it open. My mouth dropped and I felt like screaming again, only this time louder. On our front stoop, writing pad in hand, stood Chief Donald Seager.

"No!" CC shouted. "No way! Absolutely not! I'm not talking to you! They told me on the phone they were sending some officers over! Get out of here and send some real cops! I have nothing to say to you!"

Chief Seager seemed unperturbed by CC's hostile welcome. "Mr. Munch, nice to see you again," he said coolly, pushing himself inside. "As I've explained to you before, Mr. Munch, any business regarding your children and Robert Wheeler is to be directly handled by me. Now I've just received a complaint you called in about your children being kidnapped by Mr. Wheeler. What's this about?"

"Are you dense?" CC yelled in Chief Seager's face. "I said I'm not talking to you! I want to talk to a real police officer, not Big Boss's chief co-conspirator! And I did *not* invite you into my house!"

"That's fine with me, Mr. Munch, but nobody else is coming over," Chief Seager replied. "I have complete jurisdiction over any matters involving your family and Mr. Wheeler. So you either talk to me or nobody at all. I'll assume you're declining to file charges then?"

CC growled under his breath. "I don't know why I should even bother, because it's not like you're going to treat this seriously, but fine! Yes, I want to press charges! Get this straight! Mr. Wheeler, your fine upstanding citizen, just kidnapped my daughter at knifepoint, held her hostage, and threatened to kill her to force the rest of my children over to his house! Then, he locked them in a room and knocked them out with some kind of gas! While they were unconscious, he drew blood from them, God knows how much, then when they finally came to, he terrorized them for a good while longer, then finally released them! They came back here extremely distraught and terrified out of their minds! Now are you going to go over there and arrest that sadistic monster or am I going to have to do it myself?"

"Slow down, Mr. Munch, slow down," Chief Seager said condescendingly. "Let me come in and take a full statement from you," he said, brashly walking further into the house. CC ran after him, but he plowed forward, barely acknowledging me standing there. "You have a beautiful home, Mr. Munch," Chief Seager said, looking around. He reached the living room and nodded at Chase, Kevin, and Ryan on the couch, who looked up at him in astonishment. "Hello boys," he greeted heartily, making himself a seat like he owned the place, sitting on the chair I was just on. "What are your names?"

CC stormed into the room in a heated rage, marching up to the chair Chief Seager sat on. "What do you think you're doing? I didn't invite you in here or offer you a seat! Get off my chair! And don't talk to my kids! I don't want you talking to any of my kids!"

"If you want me to take your statement so you can file charges against Mr. Wheeler, Mr. Munch, I'm going to have to question your kids about what happened," Chief Seager scoffed. "Where are they all anyway?"

"The rest of my children are upstairs resting because they've been completely traumatized by what Mr. Wheeler did to them today!" CC shouted. "*And I'll be damned* if I let you talk to them and upset them even further!"

"Who am I supposed to talk to then, Mr. Munch?" Chief Seager asked.

"You can talk to *me*, I'm their father," CC asserted. "They're minors. I can file charges on their behalf!"

"But you weren't there today, Mr. Munch, your children were," Chief Seager argued. "I need to talk to someone who was there to get the story straight. Unless you want me to solely go by Mr. Wheeler's version of the story?"

Kevin's face lit up in sudden realization. "Hey! You're that Chief Seager guy, aren't you?"

From where I was watching all this unfold in the back of the room, I locked eyes with my brothers and nodded.

Ryan leaped to his feet. "CC, what's this guy doing here? He's working with Big Boss! He shouldn't be here!"

"Yeah!" Chase jumped in. "Maybe he already knows everything! Maybe they planned the whole thing together!"

"I see you've biased your children against me, Mr. Munch," Chief Seager said. "It's fine, Mr. Munch. I'll take a statement from Mr. Wheeler. It's just from what little you told me, some things in your story already don't add up."

"What things?" Kevin cried indignantly.

"Kevin, honey, let me handle this," CC said.

Chief Seager ignored CC and replied to Kevin. "Well, for one thing, son, can you tell me why anyone would bother going through the trouble of kidnapping a whole family of children, just to take their blood? Why would Mr. Wheeler want to steal your blood?"

"Because he's psychotic," CC answered for Kevin. "He's a full-blown, cold-blooded psychopath. Are you really going to question the motives of a psycho like that? And I told you not to talk to my kids!"

"Okay, Mr. Munch," Chief Seager said. "We obviously have very different opinions of Mr. Wheeler, but if that's what you're going with, fine. But tell me this: Where exactly did Mr. Wheeler hold your children? What house did they go to?"

"The one next door," Kevin said. "The one he lived in."

"Kevin, don't talk to him," CC directed.

"Son, Mr. Wheeler hasn't lived there in months," Chief Seager said to Kevin. "He moved out last December."

CC moved in front of Kevin and set his eyes fiercely on Chief Seager. "First of all, he's not your son, he's mine, so stop calling him that. Second, we are well aware Mr. Wheeler hasn't lived there in months. My children were overjoyed when he moved out. But he was in that house today, and that's where my children were held captive for hours."

"Well then where's Mr. Wheeler now, Mr. Munch?" Chief Seager questioned. "I went next door and the house is deserted. There's no sign of Mr. Wheeler anywhere."

"Not surprising," CC said. "He's guilty as sin and fled the scene of the crime."

"Yeah, about that, Mr. Munch," Chief Seager continued. "I investigated the house and got a team of detectives in there to comb the place for any signs of a kidnapping. We looked specifically for all you've described on the phone: gas, needles, tubes, bandages, blood, fingerprints, or any other sign your children were there. You know what we found? Nothing. Absolutely nothing. If your children were really held in that house, there's got to be some evidence. So maybe they should come clean and tell me the real story here."

"That is the real story!" Kevin shouted before CC could respond. "Are you saying it didn't happen?" He threw out his arm and exposed his bandaged wrist. "How about this? Is this enough evidence for you?"

CC put up his hand up to calm Kevin then turned to Chief Seager with fiery ire. "Did it ever occur to you Mr. Wheeler made sure to get rid of all evidence before he left? I'm sure a bonafide psychopath like him knows exactly how to do that! You want evidence? Look at my children's traumatized faces! They have just been through hell, and you're going to sit there *in my house* and call them liars? I won't let you do that to them! So why don't you do your freaking job and find Mr. Wheeler, make him confess, and arrest him?"

"I can't do that, Mr. Munch, without probable cause," Chief Seager said. "And there's no probable cause because there's no evidence." He turned back to Kevin. "And son? A bandage on your arm proves nothing. You, any of your siblings, or your father could've put that on yourselves."

"Why don't you just admit you're working with Big Boss?" Kevin exploded. "That's why you don't believe us! We know what you said! Our sister Capricorn heard you!" He pointed to me in the back of the room. "She heard you whispering with Big Boss about our sister Allie! So just admit you're working with him!"

Chief Seager shook his head. "I'm sorry, son, but I have no idea what you mean. I've never talked to Mr. Wheeler about your sister."

"That's a lie!" I squeaked, piping up at last. "Kevin's right. I heard you! I heard you plain as day!"

Chief Seager turned to CC with an amused grunt. "Wow, Mr. Munch, your children sure do love to make up stories."

CC snapped and advanced towards Chief Seager, clenching his teeth. "Get out of my house! Get out of my chair, get out of my living room, and get the hell away from my kids!" He shoved Chief Seager, forcing him up. "Get out! Now!" he raged, pushing Chief Seager out the room.

"Mr. Munch, I could have you arrested for assaulting a police officer," Chief Seager warned.

CC shoved Chief Seager hard in the back, forcing him forward, all the way to the door. "I want you out of my house and away from my family!"

"I get the point, Mr. Munch. It's not necessary to push me out the door. I can see myself out," Chief Seager said. "I'm going to assume you're not pressing charges against Mr.

Wheeler and this matter is closed."

"Just GET OUT!" CC gave Chief Seager one final push and slammed the door in his face.

Chapter 42

The next day, CC kept us all home from school to recuperate and have a family meeting. We gathered in the living room after a very quiet breakfast. I sat on the couch next to Breezy and Hazy, who sat upright and alert, their eyes wide open. Allie sat at the end of the couch, nervously chewing on her thumbnail. CC started by telling us that as of today he would resume chaperoning us wherever we go. This time no one objected.

CC spent quite some time talking to us about the loss of our powers. He said it will be difficult at first because we had become somewhat dependent on them, but in time we will learn new ways of doing things, and he will teach us some essential skills that "the normals" use, like first aid.

Everyone was most concerned about Big Boss and whether or not he'll make a reappearance. CC told everyone about what happened with Chief Seager, which didn't help ease anyone's mind.

"So Big Boss is going to get away with this?" Ashley asked in dismay.

CC cringed. "Unfortunately, yes. But it seems what he was after the whole time was your powers. Now that he has them, he will probably leave you alone. But we do need to remain super vigilant, at least until we have a better sense of whether or not he'll come back."

Allie spent the whole meeting compulsively seesawing between nibbling her thumb and closely examining it, not saying a single word during the entire meeting. As everyone got up to leave, she suddenly looked up in confusion and uttered the first words she spoke all day.

"Is....is that it?" she asked CC.

"Yes, honey," CC answered. "Unless there's something you want to say."

"But....but what about Big Boss?" Allie questioned.

"What about him, sweetie?" CC said. "We'll stay together and keep safe. We won't let him get you all alone again."

Allie found little comfort in this answer and twisted her face in anguish. "But...but he has our magic."

"Yes, I know," CC lamented. "Unfortunately, I think it's gone for good. I don't think it's possible to get it back."

Allie waved her hands impatiently. "I don't care about that, CC! I'm saying Big Boss has our magic! He could use it to do whatever he wants! What if he comes back and uses it on us? What's to stop him from coming in here and attacking us? With our magic, he could do anything!"

Allie's words were like a lightning bolt that struck fear in our hearts. Some of my siblings reflexively looked around the room, as if expecting Big Boss to pop up behind a chair.

CC shook his head. "No, honey, he can't do whatever he wants. Thank God there are limits on those powers. There's a lot he can't do. Plus, if he does use magic, he'll have to wait before using it again. Don't panic, sweetie. He's not invincible." Nobody knew it then, but just about every word CC just said was dead wrong.

Allie made another pained face. She seemed to be weighing a thought in her head, deciding whether to give voice to it. Flustered, she finally spurted it out. "CC, CC...I think we should move."

"Move?" CC said. "Allie, this is our home!"

"It's not safe here!" Allie cried, terror held in her eyes.

"Our home is as safe as anywhere else. This is our house and I'm not going to let Big Boss chase us out of it!" CC affirmed. "Plus, if we left, he could still find us."

"Then we could stay on the run!" Allie cried.

"Allie, just think about what you're saying," CC reproached. "If we went on the run, where would we go? Where am I supposed to house all fourteen of us?"

"Um...we're sitting in a house like that right now, CC," Allie said.

"Right! Exactly, Allie. Our house. Which is perfect for us. But if we left, where would we go?"

"Another house," Allie immediately answered. "That was my point, CC, there are other houses like this. You have money, you can buy another one."

"That's not the point!" CC snapped. "There's no reason why we should have to leave our own house!"

"There's every reason!" Allie returned. "What about Chief Seager? We can't even get the police to press charges! As long as we live here, we won't get any help! Let's go somewhere and start over! We'd eventually have to do that anyway!"

"Yes, but right now there's nowhere for us to go!" CC explained how extensive the moving and home buying process is.

"Well, what if we just left and took off?" Allie asked.

"Take off where? What would we have?" CC asked.

"We'd have each other!" Allie cried. "That's enough!"

"Yes, but Allie, where would we sleep? In the van?" CC said. "I'm not driving all over the country, spending day after day with a vanload of kids."

Allie started to pout. "We should still leave!"

"Allie, we're not leaving our house! I'm sorry, but no," CC stated.

Allie rose to her feet. "But CC, just listen…" she whined.

"Allie, I said we're not leaving and that's final," CC declared.

"CC…" Allie uttered, her lip starting to quiver.

"Allie, I said we're done!" CC scolded. "I don't want to hear another word about-"

"DADDY!" Allie screeched. Her voice rang out across the house, loud as a siren.

CC stopped cold, Allie's plaintive cry rendering him instantly speechless.

"Daddy…" Allie whimpered. "I'm really scared...please…"

CC stared at Allie in open-mouthed shock. "Allie, you have never called me Daddy in your life," he said in a choked tone, suddenly very emotional.

Allie looked at CC with doleful eyes where little pools of tears already formed and broke down into heavy sobs again. Her whole body shook intensely with each gasping breath. CC's demeanor instantaneously changed, as he switched back to the consoling parent role. "Allie, honey," he said tenderly. He bent down on one knee, beckoning her towards him. "Come here, baby," he whispered, holding out his arms. Allie hurled herself into CC, and he wrapped his arms around her in a great bear hug. "Sweetheart," he said softly, "It's going to be okay. I'll keep you safe. You'll be okay."

Allie cried so hard her sobs constricted her breathing. "He…he said...he said…" she heaved, breathing way too fast.

"Take a deep breath, sweetheart," CC instructed gently. "You'll have a panic attack. Hold my hand and breathe with me."

CC led Allie in inhaling deeply and letting her breath come out nice and slow. As her breathing steadied, her tears slowed, and she gave CC a weak smile. "There," CC whispered, wiping the tears away from Allie's cheeks with his thumb. "That's much better," he soothed, pushing her hair away from her eyes. "Now sweetheart, what were you trying to tell me? Take another deep breath first."

Allie did as CC directed. "He said he had big plans for me. Big Boss."

CC's face momentarily wrinkled in anger, then he took Allie by the hands, holding them out in front of him. "Look at me, sweetheart. Look at my eyes." He looked directly into Allie's blue-green eyes and spoke emphatically from the heart. "I am not going to let Big Boss get you. He will never hurt you again. None of you. I'll keep you safe." He looked up at the rest of us. "Keeping you safe is most important, so I just decided leaving here *is* an option. Let's plan to stay for now, but if we ever find it's too dangerous to remain here, we'll move. We won't stay if you're in danger."

We nodded at CC in agreement. Allie put her arms around CC in a loving hug. "Thank you, Daddy," she whispered.

Chapter 43

The terror that initially held us captive slowly gave way to an immense sense of sorrow and grief that equally enchained us. The loss of our magic was greatly felt by all of us, and a melancholy mood blanketed our whole household like a death shroud. CC assured us this grief was normal, and we'd feel better as time passed.

It was the last day of the school year, and possibly our last day of school period, as CC was already talking about having us all homeschooled starting September. I should have been in brighter spirits, but as I looked outside our dining room window at breakfast that morning, I saw grey rain clouds rapidly moving across the sky, threatening to block out the sun, and morbidly thought of it as an ominous omen. I pressed my palm against my face and stared out the window gloomily, wondering if the rain will at least wait until we get inside our school.

Kevin noticed me and nudged his head towards the window. "Nice last day, right?"

I sighed heavily. "At least we probably won't have to go back next year."

CC came in from the kitchen, looked out the window, and

frowned. "There's a bad storm coming. We should leave early and try to beat the rain. Hurry up and finish your breakfast."

My siblings' moods seemed to match my own. They sat at the table, drearily picking at their cereal without really eating it. Since her ordeal with Big Boss, Kitty hadn't been cooking, so breakfast wasn't exactly gourmet the last few weeks. My cereal had turned to mush and I couldn't tolerate the taste. I scooped up the sludge and watched it slide from my spoon with a wet plop.

CC came back in, had us clear the table, and rushed us out the door. As we stepped outside, the expanding black clouds veiled the sun in shadows and made the day appear as night. We slumped down the steps and trudged towards the van in our driveway, then came to an abrupt stop. There, standing on the other side of our driveway, obviously waiting for us, was Big Boss.

Big Boss stood with a nonchalant stance and a smug smile. He flapped his fingers at us in mocked greeting, provoking us. CC clenched his fists and lunged towards Big Boss, clearly intending a full-on assault. Big Boss raised his hand and pointed it at the oak tree at the other side of our driveway that must have been at least ten times taller than CC. With a sharp crackle, an enormous bolt of lightning burst from Big Boss's hand and struck the trunk of the oak tree, hitting it at the base. For one breathless moment, all was silence, then there was the great deafening sound of the oak tree cracking at the roots. CC was in the middle of the driveway and noticed the tree just as it started to wobble and sway, then all at once came crashing down with a thunderous boom. My siblings and I screamed and leaped back as CC jumped away from the tree just in time, seconds away from it crushing him. The tree landed right between the side of our driveway and the ground where Big Boss stood, creating a giant physical barrier between us. We gaped at Big Boss in open-mouthed horror.

Big Boss yelled across our driveway to be heard above the sudden howling wind. "You should be more careful, Casey! A thunderstorm is coming and lightning is dangerous!"

CC spun towards Big Boss and screamed back, frothing with rage. "Are you crazy? You could have killed us, you maniac!"

Big Boss laughed. "Why do you have such big trees growing around your property anyway, Casey? Don't you know that's not safe? Need a number for a tree removal service?"

"Shut up!" CC roared. "I'm going to kill you, Robert! I'll kill you for what you did to my kids!"

My siblings and I huddled close together and took cover behind CC.

"You call me a manic and then say you'll kill *me*?" Big Boss yelled. "But go ahead, Casey, get it all out! I know you're very angry with me!"

"When I get my hands on you, I'll rip you apart, Robert!" CC yelled. "How dare you hurt my kids! You won't get away with this! I know you're in cahoots with Chief Seager, but I don't care! You wait and see what I do to you!"

Big Boss chortled. "Feel better now, Casey? You might want to keep your voice down! You sound like a raving lunatic! I did nothing to your precious children to kill me over!"

I wanted to yell back but couldn't make my mouth move. I suddenly felt ice cold. I wrapped my arms across my chest protectively, shivering so hard my teeth chattered.

"You think kidnapping them, threatening to kill Kitty, gassing them, stealing their blood, and robbing them of their powers qualifies as nothing?" CC couldn't help screaming back.

I whipped my head around nervously, wondering if anyone

heard CC scream about powers.

"They're alive, aren't they, Casey?" Big Boss shouted. "I returned them to you in one piece! So lay off the vengeful father act!"

"You completely traumatized them! You did everything short of killing them!" CC yelled. "And what about the brainwashing job on Twisty and Carlie, you sociopath!"

I reflexively turned towards Twisty and Carlie. They were staring at Big Boss with transfixed eyes of terror.

"That was all them, Casey!" Big Boss volleyed. "If you've got a problem with what they did, take it up with them!"

"They're kids!" CC shouted. "You manipulated them! You toyed with the minds of two children!"

"Fine, Casey!" Big Boss replied. "I'm not coming after your children again, so you won't have to worry about me anymore!"

I didn't have to have Breezy's psychic abilities to know that was a huge lie.

CC gave out a bitter laugh. "Do you think I'm an idiot, Robert? You just tried to kill us with a freaking tree!"

"That was just to warn you what could happen if you come after me, Casey! So stay away from me and I won't bother your little Munchkin brats again!"

The sky finally opened up and the rain came down in buckets. CC turned to us, pointing to the van. "Kids, go get in the van! Now!" He pressed the unlock button on his keys.

We looked at each other and sped to the van. Ashley threw the door open and jumped inside. We tumbled over each other in a panic, clambering inside the van, crying out as the rain rapidly soaked us to the bone.

CC shouted at Big Boss above the tumbling rain. "If you go anywhere near my kids again, I'll get a gun and blow your damn head off! I'll do whatever I need to protect my kids, so consider this your last warning!"

CC ran to the van and flung the driver's side door open, slamming it closed. Big Boss kept standing in the pouring rain, making no effort to move.

"Is everyone okay?" CC asked us as soon as he was inside.

Somehow we all got ourselves seated safely. We numbly nodded at CC and asked if he was okay. "Yes," he answered. "That psycho nearly killed me, but luckily the tree missed me."

I looked out the rain-splattered window and saw Big Boss still standing there, getting soaking wet, looking at us. I shivered in fear.

Allie was watching him too, her eyes frozen with terror, and she trembled fiercely. "Daddy…Daddy…he's watching us," she whimpered.

CC turned around in his seat and squeezed Allie's shoulder reassuringly. "It's okay, sweetheart, he's not going to hurt you," he said resolutely. He took a deep breath and hit the steering wheel. "Okay, I've decided. We're leaving here today."

"You mean our house?" Ashley asked. "We're really going to leave everything behind?"

"Yes," CC said. "I'm not putting you in any more danger. It took a tree nearly falling on me to realize just how dangerous Big Boss is now with those powers. I won't take the chance of anything like that happening again. Plus, your sister is really scared," he noted, pointing to Allie. "She doesn't feel safe. It's not fair to her to stay here. While you're in school today, I'll buy fourteen plane tickets for a flight out of the country. Maybe if we lay low for a while, Big Boss will disappear, and we'll come back someday when it's safer. For right now though, we're getting far away from here." He eyed all of us. "Sometimes, it's smarter to pull back and reassess what's most important."

Allie, sitting behind CC, jumped up from her seat to hug

him from behind. "Thank you!" she cried.

Kitty cried tears of relief. Ashley put her arm around her. My siblings were solidly in favor of CC's plan. We couldn't be happier to leave Big Boss far behind.

CC explained we'll have to pack lightly and stick to the bare necessities, which meant we couldn't take most of our toys and belongings with us.

"It's okay, CC," Breezy said. "It's just stuff. At least we have each other and we're safe."

My siblings and I all nodded in steadfast agreement, even to my shock, Twisty and Carlie. The fact that none of us expressed the slightest gripe, complaint, or word of objection about leaving our home and belongings, showed how much my siblings have grown in maturity within just the last few weeks. After all, this is the same crowd who naively squandered magic away on video games, toys, and junk food less than a month ago. CC, maybe sensing the same thing, smiled at us with pride and swallowed a lump in his throat. He turned around to face the windshield, started the van, and backed out of the driveway.

I turned around in my seat, as the van moved down our street, to look out the rear windshield. Big Boss still stood there, with raindrops dripping from his wet hair to his face, watching our van drive away. Right before the view of Big Boss became too blurry to see through the rain, he lifted his hand in a wave. And I knew, I *knew*, like an intuitive punch to the gut, we would see him again very soon.

Sneak Peek!

Here's a sneak preview of the second book of The Munchkins series, *Capricorn's Journal: My Family's Fight for Survival...*

Chapter 1

I thought the school day would never end. As 3:30 dismissal approached, I kept compulsively looking up at the clock, my mind racing with thoughts.

"Hey, Cap?" Allie said, leaning over her desk. The classroom was so noisy our teacher gave up and started summer vacation early, so there was no need to whisper. "If you stare at that clock any harder, it might grow a mouth and tell you to stop looking at it," Allie said with a little smile.

I chuckled. "I know, it's just the longest day ever. I can't believe it's not 3:30 yet."

Allie sighed. "Yeah, it's taking an eternity. Are you worried about what's going to happen?"

"Yes, I can't stop thinking about it," I answered. "I have a million questions in my head. Like where are we going to go? What are we going to do?"

Allie twisted her pencil, standing it upright on her desk. "I know, I keep thinking about where we'll go too."

Breezy overheard us and gave us both a reassuring smile.

"CC will figure it out, don't worry."

"Honestly, I'm just so relieved we're leaving I don't care where we go," Allie remarked.

Hazy pointed at the clock. "Only five more minutes. Thank God."

The bell finally rang, and we made a beeline for the door with the other students. "Have a great summer," our teacher called after us in a half-hearted tone.

We ran down the hallway to meet the rest of our siblings in front of the main entrance. Most of them were already there.

"How did you get out of class so fast?" I asked them.

"Are you kidding? I was literally standing in the doorway, ready to bolt as soon as the bell went off," Chase answered me.

Ryan laughed. "Ms. Woodcheck kept saying, 'Chase, sit down,' but he just wasn't having it."

I smiled. "CC's not here yet?"

"Nope, not yet," Ryan answered.

My other siblings filed in and within minutes all thirteen of us were gathered. We watched the other kids run past us as they rushed out the door cheering. Billy Bratton, one of the kids who enjoyed picking on us, nearly mowed me over as he tore out the building. "Watch it, Munch freak," he growled at me and shot out the door before Allie had a chance to shout one of her snarky comebacks at him.

Allie looked at me and rolled her eyes. "Gee, I'm really going to miss Billy Bratton," she said in a droll tone. "What will we do without hearing him call us 'the freak family' ten times a day? We just won't cope."

I grinned. "Or telling everyone to watch out the Munch freaks don't cast a spell on you."

"Yeah, he told everyone we were witches," Kitty added quietly.

Becky lifted her eyes. "So that explains why people kept coming up to me all school year asking where my broom was! I thought they were telling me to sweep the floor!"

Allie and I sputtered with laughter.

"I wish I would have decked him," Twisty said. "I wanted one good shot at him before he left."

"Yeah, I second that," Kevin nodded.

"That wouldn't have accomplished anything except getting yourselves suspended," Justin pointed out.

"It would have been worth it," Kevin said. "I hate that kid."

Twisty actually smiled at Kevin in agreement.

"Where's CC?" Ashley asked suddenly. "He's late."

"Yeah, he's usually here by now," Ryan added.

"He is *always* here by now," Allie amended. She looked out the glass door of the building, searching the street for any sign of CC's van. "In fact, he's usually early. What's going on?"

"Maybe he got held up," Chase offered. "Or he lost track of time."

Allie shook her head. "No, CC wouldn't do that. Especially not today. If I know CC, he was doing the exact opposite. Watching the clock all day like a hawk."

"He's just running late," Breezy reassured.

Several minutes passed and most of the kids had emptied out the building, but we were still standing in front of the door. Ashley checked her watch and announced it was 4:00. CC was now a half-hour late.

Allie anxiously paced in front of the door. "He would never be this late," she stressed. "Not today. Not the day we're leaving. He just wouldn't do that."

"Allie's right, CC wouldn't do this to us," Justin affirmed. "There must have been some emergency he had to take care of."

"A bigger emergency than the one we're already in?" Allie

questioned with a raised eyebrow.

"Yeah, that's a good point," Justin nodded. "I don't know, but I'm starting to get very worried."

By the time it was 4:15, the building had cleared out and the school had the feel of a vacant ghost town. The sound of our principal's high-heeled shoes clacking on the floor came reverberating down the hallway. She rounded the corner, coming into our view, and our presence startled her.

"The Munch children! You're still here?" she gasped. "It's the last day of school! Isn't your father picking you up today?"

"He's supposed to, Ms. Walsh, but he isn't here yet," Breezy answered.

"Well it's already quarter after four," Ms. Walsh replied. "I was planning on closing the building soon. Would you like me to call him for you and see what's holding him up?"

"Yes, please," Breezy said. "Thank you."

"Why don't one of you come with me and we'll call him in my office," Ms. Walsh suggested.

"I'll go," Allie immediately volunteered, raising her hand.

Ms. Walsh gave Allie a quick nod. "Okay, Allison, follow me," she said, leading Allie down the hallway.

That heavy ball of dread began to form again in my stomach. CC should definitely be here. Given we had decided this morning to flee the country, we were in full-on emergency mode, and CC would've been anxious to pick us up and leave as soon as possible. The fact that he wasn't here yet told me there was something very *very* wrong.

Stay updated on the release of the second book and find more on The Munchkins series at **munchkinsbooks.com**

Acknowledgments

I want to thank everyone who helped make this book possible. First and foremost, to my amazing wife Dana Grande, for all her support and encouragement, help with editing, and spending countless hours listening to chapters read out loud, providing feedback, and discussing plotlines and characters.

To my editor, Fiona McLaren, for believing in the book and giving me great editorial suggestions to trim the story down and create an even better book. To my friend Tiffany Schleich, my main test reader and biggest fan of the story, who read every chapter as soon as it was written and couldn't wait to get ahold of the next one.

To Jeff Brown Graphics for the beautiful cover design that perfectly depicts the characters and brings them to life, and to Lorna Reid, for the interior design.

To my brother, Jared Zawoiski, for when I dreamed up the idea of The Munchkins all those years ago when we were kids, spent all that time with me making up Munchkins stories, acting them out, and imagining them into being.

And last but not least, to my parents, who always believed in me as a writer and never stopped encouraging me.

Printed in the USA
CPSIA information can be obtained
at www.ICGtesting.com
CBHW030833030224
3972CB00004BA/27

9 781737 233909